A DEAD MAN'S BOOTS

"If I'm out of *my* mind, then we both must be," Blake shouted. He gave Abel a stiff-armed shove. "Now give me the damned boots and shirt!" His rifle barrel came up level with Abel's chest.

"Go to hell!" Abel shouted. "I'm through with your craziness. I can't stand it anymore!" He spread his arms, the pistol hanging in his hand.

"Don't you mean *our* craziness?" yelled Blake. "Or are we one person only when it's to your liking?" He shoved his brother again. "Why is it we share everything but the craziness? Can you explain that? Why is it I'm the only one that's always wicked and crazy if we're both the *same* person? Give me the shirt, damn it to hell!"

"I'm warning you, Blake!" Abel backed away another step but then stopped and planted his feet firmly beneath him. "If you want this shirt and boots you'll have to take them!"

"Then by God I will!" said Blake. His thumb reached across the rifle hammer and pulled it back.

DEAD MAN'S CANYON

Ralph Cotton

A SIGNET BOOK

SIGNET
Published by New American Library, a division of
Penguin Group (USA) Inc., 375 Hudson Street,
New York, New York 10014, U.S.A.
Penguin Books Ltd, 80 Strand,
London WC2R 0RL, England
Penguin Books Australia Ltd, 250 Camberwell Road,
Camberwell, Victoria 3124, Australia
Penguin Books Canada Ltd, 10 Alcorn Avenue,
Toronto, Ontario, Canada M4V 3B2
Penguin Books (NZ), cnr Airborne and Rosedale Roads,
Albany, Auckland 1310, New Zealand

Penguin Books Ltd, Registered Offices:
80 Strand, London WC2R 0RL, England

First published by Signet, an imprint of New American Library,
a division of Penguin Group (USA) Inc.

First Printing, September 2004
10 9 8 7 6 5 4 3 2 1

For Mary Lynn . . . *of course.*

PART 1

Chapter 1

Arizona ranger Sam Burrack knew he had left his jurisdiction, tracking the Carly twins across the high country into New Mexico Territory, but jurisdiction didn't matter now. As a rule, once a duly sworn officer of the law found himself in hot pursuit of a felon or a gang of felons, most territories gave him all the room he needed to carry out his job. In this case "carrying out his job" would more than likely mean strapping the Carly twins facedown over their saddles and leading them back to the territory under a swarm of range flies. He didn't want it that way, but there it was. He drew his repeating rifle from his saddle boot as he sat atop his big Appaloosa at the fork in the narrow trail.

On the ground a single set of hoofprints led off to the left and up higher into the rocky hillside. The ranger noted that those hoofprints grew lighter at a point where a spill of jagged rocks covered the trail to his right. It was easy to see that the Carly twins had jumped off the horse right here and gone on foot across the rocks. He'd been expecting something like this ever since he'd passed their other horse staggering in exhaustion three miles back.

The Carlys had been hard and determined, he had to give them that much. Twice in the past week Sam had come close enough to call out to the identical twins and tell them to give themselves up. Both times the only reply he'd received had come from the barrel of Blake Carly's Spencer rifle just before they'd slipped away. One of those replies had felled his pack mule. Whether the Carly twins knew it or not, any talk on Sam's part about a peaceful surrender had stopped the minute the mule hit the ground. The way he saw it, they had made their intentions clear by shooting the pack animal. If they wanted to go back and face a just trial it would be up to them to mention it. Sam had no more to say.

Blake Carly was the one wanted for murder in Benton Wells. Abel Carly had only been there when his brother shot and killed the elderly town sheriff, Ed Tarpin, in front of the Three-Fingered Lady Saloon. Sam recalled the particulars of the incident, running it through his mind as he scanned back and forth across the rocky hillsides below him. Several witnesses had said that Abel had had no part in the broad-daylight killing. All Abel would have had to do was stand there and raise his hands—let folks see that he was just as surprised as they were at what his brother had done. Instead of standing fast, though, he'd foolishly grabbed his horse, jumped into the saddle, and followed Blake out of town. Now he was on the run with his brother.

But Abel Carly knew the consequences of his action, Sam told himself, swinging down from his saddle and giving the Appaloosa a nudge with his gloved hand. If he didn't he should have. The big stallion knew what that nudge meant and stepped away quickly and quietly even as Sam whispered his name softly, saying, "Go, Black Pot."

Eighty yards away in the cover of the rocks alongside the trail, Abel Carly turned to face his brother with a frightened look on his face. "He ain't falling for it, Blake!" he said. "Now what are we going to do?"

Blake sat calmly rolling himself a smoke, with the Spencer rifle across his lap. He cut a sidelong glance at his twin brother. "We're going to have to kill him, just like I've been telling you all along."

"More killing?" Abel's face turned pale at the thought of it. "When's the killing going to stop?" He swallowed dryly and shook his head as his brother raised slightly and walked over to him in a crouch, offering him a puff on the thin cigarette.

"Quit acting so squeamish, Brother," said Blake when Abel turned down his offer. "You knew damn well there would be more killing when you came along with me. So don't go looking so shocked about it." He took a long draw on the cigarette and let it out slowly, giving a careless grin. "What did you think I'd do, let this ranger walk up and slap a pair of handcuffs on my wrists? Do I look that weak and cowardly to you?"

Abel shook his head. "I don't know what I thought—it all happened so fast, I reckon I didn't do much thinking at all."

"Then maybe you should have," said Blake, still grinning. "Because you're in this up to your neck now." He shrugged. "Might as well get used to living on the run—killing, robbing, whatever it takes to keep the law off our tails."

"We weren't raised this way," said Abel. "Our

folks would lie moaning in their graves if they saw how low we've sunk."

Blake's gaze hardened. "Leave our folks out of this!" His fingers tightened on the cigarette. His right hand tightened on the rifle. "Nobody moans in their grave! Dead is dead! It's the same as if they'd never been born! They don't know what we do . . . we don't know what they do!"

"Take it easy, Blake," Abel said, seeing his brother start into a trembling rage. "I was just saying it to make a point."

"Here's the only point!" Blake shook the rifle. "We've got to kill this ranger and get on up north where nobody knows us."

"They'll hear about the twins on the run," said Abel. "No matter where we go, we'll be spotted and recognized as soon as somebody sees us together!"

"Do you want to see me hang for killing that old washed-up sheriff? Yes or no?" Blake demanded.

"You ought to know I don't want to see you hang," said Abel. "It would be like watching myself hang." He shook his head. "God, if only you hadn't shot that sheriff."

"Shut up about the sheriff—and get ready to help me kill this ranger."

As Blake spoke he raised his head enough to peer over the edge of a rock and catch a glimpse of the ranger moving closer, using the cover of the rocks along the trail.

"This ranger might not be so easy to kill," Abel said. "He's the one who killed Junior Lake and his gang."

"I heard all about it," said Blake, trying to sound unimpressed as he checked the Spencer rifle and gripped it, ready to rise up and fire at any second.

"I heard how he rides the big bear-paw stallion that Outrider Saze used to ride—how he tracked down the Lake gang and killed them after they killed Saze." Blake spit and took a nervous draw on the cigarette. "I've heard that whole story so much I'm sick of it. This ranger ain't nothing but a man, no different than you and me. Stick a bullet in his belly and all them stories end up in the same size hole in the ground." He drew a pistol from his belt and pitched it to his brother. "Here. Take this and see if you can do us some good."

"Those stories are all true," Abel said.

Blake didn't answer right away. Instead he stared out in the direction of the ranger as if considering something. Finally he said, "Yeah, maybe it is all true what they say about this ranger." He fell silent again for a second, drawing on his cigarette and studying Abel, who toyed idly with the pistol instead of checking it and getting ready to use it.

Seeing the strange and distant look on his twin brother's face, Abel asked warily, "What's going through your mind?"

"Why are you asking, Brother?" Blake took a deep breath and said, "We're twins. Don't you always say we can read one another's thoughts?"

"Yeah," said Abel, "and I don't like what I see you thinking right now." He scooted back a few feet, stood up slowly and dusted the seat of his trousers. "I see evil running through your mind. It always scares me. I don't understand it."

"There's no *evil* running through my mind. Maybe you better check your *own* thoughts," said Blake, leaning the rifle against a rock. He raised his hat an inch and wiped sweat from his forehead. "You're the one who always says we're one man wearing two bodies. Maybe what scared you is what you yourself was thinking."

"I wasn't thinking nothing," said Abel. But he had a troubled look on his face. "Leastwise, I wasn't thinking nothing about cutting out on you and leaving you here alone!"

Blake grinned. "Oh? Funny that the notion came up, then, because I sure as hell wasn't thinking it."

"All right," Abel said, his expression changing, becoming less suspicious. "Maybe I'm wrong. I'm sorry I brought it up."

"Aw, forget it," said Blake. "The trouble with you and me is that we've grown too different over the years. You've gone your way and I've gone mine. I've come to accept the fact that I'll likely play out my life somewhere in the dirt." He offered a thin smile. "You want to play yours out respectable-like, with your woman close beside you."

"What *woman*?" said Abel, sounding a bit resentful. "No woman is ever going look twice at me. I'm not exciting enough. I'm not the dashing outlaw that my brother Blake is." As soon as he said it, Abel's resentment seemed to go away. He shook his head and offered a slight smile.

Seeing his brother smile, Blake said jokingly, "You could be if you tried." The two managed to laugh in spite of their situation. "I was only teasing about you wanting to be respectable. Hell, there's times I wish I could play it that way."

"You could if you tried," Abel said, mimicking his brother.

But this time they didn't laugh.

"Well, maybe," said Blake. "Right now we've got more important things to worry about." He paused for a second, then said, "The more I think about it,

I really do hate to see you getting stuck in this with me."

"It's too late now," said Abel.

"Maybe not," said Blake. Nodding toward a thin footpath reaching up into the rocky hillside, he said, "There's a chance you could slip off along that trail there and catch up to that horse somewhere higher up."

"That horse is long gone by now," said Abel.

"No, as tired as he is, you'll find him standing around, catching his breath. If you walked him a half hour or so, he'd cool out. You could ride him a long ways while I hold this ranger off."

"Yeah, but after you've held him off, then what?" said Abel. "Do you think I could just walk away from here knowing you'll end up dead?"

Blake gave his twin a sad smile. "We all end up dead, Brother—just some of us sooner than others." He raised his head enough to peek over their rock cover again, catching a glimpse of the ranger's tall, pearl-gray sombrero, closer than it had been a while ago. "I put myself in this bad spot. Why should I drag you down with me?"

Abel looked suspicious again. "How can you change your mind that quick? A minute ago you sounded like a whole other person. Sometimes I believe there's something wrong with you."

"If there is, it's wrong with both of us," Blake countered. "But this ain't the time to discuss it. Get on up that path and find the horse and get out of here."

"I hate doing this," said Abel, looking as if he'd considered things and was about to make his move. "Are you sure?"

"Yeah, I'm sure," said Blake. Picking up the rifle

and taking a step closer to his brother, he said, "Only give me back the pistol. I'll be needing it worse than you."

Abel started to hand over the big pistol butt first. But before he did, Blake said matter-of-factly, "While you're at it, swap shirts with me."

Abel stopped short. "What?"

"You heard me. Give me your shirt," said Blake.

"Why?" Abel's expression said that he didn't like whatever he thought his twin had in mind for him.

"Jesus, Abel, can't you do this one little thing for me?" Blake's grip tightened on the rifle stock. "I want it because it's a darker color." He plucked at the front of his dirty white shirt. "If I last till dark and try to make a run for it, I might as well carry a lit torch as to wear this in the moonlight."

Abel looked down at his own dirty rawhide shirt, still not trusting his brother's reason for the exchange. He looked at the footpath, then at the rifle in Blake's hands. "What are you trying to pull?"

"Nothing, damn it!" said Blake. "Just give me the shirt!" He crowded closer to his twin, staring into his eyes. "And give me your boots too! Hurry up!" As he spoke he snatched the sweat-stained sugar-loaf hat from his brother's head.

Abel looked down at his boots, an old pair of heel-worn cavalry boots. Then he looked at Blake's newer, hand-tooled Mexican drover boots. Noting that they both wore the same type of tan canvas trousers, recognition came to his face. "I've seen you do some low, rotten things," he said. "But I never figured you'd stoop to doing something like this!"

"You've got me all wrong, Brother," said Blake. "I'm looking out for both of us, like always. You're letting your imagination run away with you!"

"You're out of your mind, Blake! I'm not turning my back on you," Abel said, raising his voice.

"If I'm out of *my* mind, then we both must be," Blake shouted in his face, "since we're one man wearing two bodies!" He gave Abel a stiff-armed shove. "Now give me the damned boots and shirt!" His rifle barrel came up level with Abel's chest.

"Go to hell!" Abel shouted. "I'm through with your craziness. I can't stand it anymore!" He spread his arms, the pistol hanging in his hand.

"Don't you mean *our* craziness?" yelled Blake. "Or are we one person only when it's to your liking?" He shoved his brother again. "Why is it we share everything but the craziness? Can you explain that? Why is it I'm the only one that's always wicked and crazy if we're both the *same* person? Give me the shirt, damn it to hell!"

"I'm warning you, Blake!" Abel backed away another step but then stopped and planted his feet firmly beneath him. "If you want this shirt and boots you'll have to take them!"

"Then by God I will!" said Blake. His thumb reached across the rifle hammer and pulled it back.

The ranger had just slipped from the cover of one rock to another when he heard the sound of angry voices followed by a single loud shot fifty yards in front of him. The echo rolled quickly out across the hills and the flatlands below as he instinctively pressed his back against his rock cover. Realizing that he had heard no bullet strike the rocks surrounding him, he listened closely for a moment, scanning the area from which the shot had come. The angry voices had stopped. He waited, knowing that even this could be some sort of trap. After a full five minutes had passed, he continued forward, slowly, silently, one rock at a time, until again he stopped at the sound of a voice. This time it was only one voice, low and sobbing, like that of a heartbroken child. But these men are not children, he cautioned himself.

By the time Sam crept to within ten yards of the voice, the sobbing had settled into a painful one-sided conversation, a graveside conversation, the ranger surmised, his senses keen and ready, his hand poised on his rifle. Yet he found himself unprepared for what met his gaze when he peeked around the edge of a rock. One of the twins was sobbing quietly, staring down at the other twin's body lying dead in the dirt. Easy, Sam told himself, knowing full well that this could be a trick. Rising up slowly until he had a clear aim at less than fifteen feet and seeing the pistol and the Spencer rifle in the twin's hands, Sam said in a calm tone, "Drop the guns. I've got you covered."

"It's over, Ranger. My brother Blake is dead," the Carly twin sighed, letting the two guns slide from his hands and fall to the dirt with a soft plop. But instead of standing up and facing the ranger, he only slumped forward a bit, shaking his head slowly and still staring at his brother's body.

Unsure of which twin he was addressing, Sam said, "On your feet, Carly. Put your hands in the air."

He'd realized from the start how difficult and dangerous this chase would be with two men who looked exactly alike. Before he'd even left town on their trail he had carefully questioned witnesses to make sure what each twin wore and which horse he rode. Still, he knew that what he'd learned could have changed. The body on the ground wore Blake's dirty white shirt, but Sam wasn't taking any chances. He saw the bullet hole in the dead man's forehead and the scrapings in the dirt where it looked as if a scuffle might have gone on. He noted the dust on the rawhide shirt before the remaining Carly twin turned to face him, his hands above his head. What Sam wanted to see now was this man's eyes as he explained what had gone on here.

"I—I shot him, Ranger," said the grief-stricken voice before Sam had a chance to ask. "I killed my own brother, God help me." He lowered his head for a moment as if praying for repentance. Then he looked up and said, "But he gave me no choice. He tried to take my shirt and boots and make a getaway. I couldn't allow this thing to go any farther."

Sam studied his eyes as he listened, but he wasn't reading anything there. "So that's what I heard you two arguing about? He wanted to leave you to face the law for him?"

"No, it wasn't like that, Ranger," said the remaining Carly twin. "He knew I could explain it to you, make you understand that I'm Abel and that I'm innocent." The twin shrugged. "He knew it would be different with you, an officer of the law, than it would if we'd had a lynching party on our tails."

The ranger glanced at the twin's worn cavalry boots as he listened. Those were Abel Carly's boots, all right, Sam told himself, recalling what the witnesses had said.

"Your brother was right about that," said Sam, stepping out from behind the rock. "I expect a town posse might not even have asked who was who. They might just have hanged you both to make sure they had the right man."

He continued to watch the twin's eyes as he

switched his rifle to the other hand and reached around to bring a pair of handcuffs out from behind his back. He pitched the handcuffs into the dirt a few feet away from the guns, at the twin's feet. "Pick them up and put them on. Then step over here to me."

The twin looked surprised. "Handcuff me? Why? I'm not the one you were after. I never fired at you either time when you caught up to us."

"Let's don't start this ride back to Arizona thinking either one of us is a fool, Carly," said the ranger. "I've asked you once to put those handcuffs on." His rifle barrel lowered toward the twin's right foot. "Guess what I'll do next?"

"All right, Ranger!" the twin said quickly, stepping over to the handcuffs. "I'm sorry! I wasn't thinking straight." He bent to pick the cuffs up. "I understand how this could confuse a person."

Sam watched closely, his hand poised on his rifle, to see if this man would make a move toward the guns on the ground. If this was Blake Carly, he had to know this was the best chance he'd get to kill the ranger and make his getaway. Once the cuffs went around his wrists his odds of escape would drop like a stone.

"There," said Carly, snatching the cuffs up from the ground and straightening up without so much as giving the guns a glance. "See, I'm doing everything just like you told me." He snapped the cuffs around one wrist, then the other, and snugged them down for good measure. "I'm giving you no reason to shoot me. I'm coming along peaceably." He raised his cuffed hands chest high.

"That's good to hear, Carly," said Sam, moving close enough to reach out and test the cuffs with his free hand. "We've got a long ride back through some dangerous country. If you're the twin you say you are, I think you'll face a jury and get yourself cleared of any charges." He looked at the body on the ground and added, "Especially the way things turned out here."

The twin also looked down at the body on the ground, and Sam saw genuine remorse cloud his brow. "God forgive me," he said. "I'll never get over what I did to my poor brother, Blake. To others I know he was wild, bad and dangerous, but to me he was always just my brother . . . my twin brother at that." He stared at the body in contemplation, then added, "Twins are one person in two bodies, Ranger. Did you ever hear that?"

"Yes, I expect I might've heard that somewhere or other."

The ranger studied his expression, his eyes, his whole demeanor, searching for any sign that this twin standing before him was the innocent one.

Seeing the questioning look on the ranger's face, Carly said, "I can see you've still got doubts, Ranger. But there's nothing I can say or do. You'll have to make up your own mind which one I am."

"You're wrong, Carly. I don't have to make up my mind at all," said the ranger, giving him a hard, steady gaze. "I'm not your judge or your jury, unless you force it on me." He gestured at the rifle in his hand, making sure the twin got his message. "My job is to take you back to the territory. How I do it depends on you." He looked the Carly twin up and down, saying in a low tone, "Now let's get your brother wrapped and over a saddle. We need to make some time before nightfall."

The twin looked around, then said, "Ranger, we

only have two horses, your Appaloosa and this dun. How's this going to work?" The grim look on his face told the ranger he already knew the answer. "You don't expect me to ride double with my brother's body, do you?"

"I'm sorry, Carly," said Sam, "but yes, I'm afraid that's what we're going to have to do. It's either that or you'll have to walk and lead the horse."

"I—I can't do it, Ranger," said the twin. "How can I ride with him, knowing I'm the one who killed him?"

"It's just till we get out of these high rocks," the ranger said. "Once we get to some milder ground we can make a travois frame and pull his body along behind if you want to. Till then you'll have to make do."

"How far are we from Taos?" the twin asked.

"A good ride will take us into Taos by tomorrow night," said Sam. He gave the twin a searching gaze. "How do you feel about riding into Taos?"

The twin shrugged. "I guess I don't feel one way or the other about it. Why? Do I have any say in it?"

Studying his eyes a moment longer, Sam said, "No, I suppose you don't at that." He looked away along the trail in the direction of Taos, having seen nothing telling in the man's eyes or demeanor. "We'll pick up fresh horses once we get there." He nodded toward the tired horse and said, "Come on, let's get moving."

Chapter 2

————

Dayton Clifford stepped off the sun-bleached stage-coach in Pie Caliente with a black leather travel case in his left hand. He set the case at his feet, slapped the fine brown powder from the sleeves of his long riding duster, and looked around, his teeth lightly clenching the stem of his briar pipe. His gaze centered on three men walking toward him from the direction of a small adobe cantina where a dark-skinned young woman stood in the doorway staring after them.

Without taking his eyes off the men he reached down, struck a match on his belt buckle and held the flame to the bowl of his pipe. When he shook the match out and flipped it away, a stream of gray smoke rose up around him in the still air. His hand instinctively rested near the bone-handled Colt in a holster strapped high and level across his chest.

"Hold on, Mister Clifford," said the man walking a foot ahead of the other two. His right hand raised chest high in a show of peace. "I'm Ben Mazzel. We're the men you're meeting here. You *are* Mister Clifford, I take it? The fellow Maynard Aubrey hired from Chicago?"

Clifford only gave a slight nod of acknowledgment.

"Good," said Mazzel. He thumbed toward the two men behind him. "This here is Lon Pence and Kenny Brewer." Gesturing toward a hitch rail in front of the cantina where a man wearing buckskins stood among four horses and a loaded pack mule, he added, "That's Elvy Hale over there. We all call him Rawhide."

"Indeed," said Dayton Clifford, coldly appraising all three men as they stopped ten feet away. The other two touched their fingers to their hat brims. Lon Pence stood well over six feet tall and weighed close to three hundred pounds, all of that weight being muscle that appeared to have been carved out of granite. Brewer was younger, shorter, a thin, wiry man who stood slouching on one foot, wearing a fixed grin and a pair of darkened sun visor–type spectacles riding low on the bridge of his nose. Seeing Clifford look him up and down with an expression of disdain, Brewer reached up with his middle finger and shoved the spectacles up to cover his eyes. Clifford ignored the gesture.

Mazzel extended his hand, but Clifford only puffed slowly on his pipe. Not only did he fail to extend his hand in response, but he even allowed his right hand to rest on the butt of his Colt.

"Well, then," said Mazzel, feeling the bite of the insult but letting it pass. He dropped his hand to his own gun, a big hickory-handled LeMat, in a tied-down holster riding low on his hip. "I reckon we all know why we're here." He nodded again toward the horses. "We brought you a good horse over from Rio Chama, just like Mister Aubrey told us to. It's the roan standing next to my bay. Since you're from Chicago I got you one that rides easy, in case you're not an experienced horseman." He cocked his head slightly. "Are you, though?"

"Am I what?" Clifford said bluntly.

"An experienced horseman," said Mazzel.

Clifford didn't bother answering. Instead he looked over appraisingly at the horses, then back at Mazzel. "What else did Mister Aubrey tell you to get?"

Mazzel shrugged, not liking his first impression of this big-shot gunman. "Besides the horse he said to gather some trail supplies and look for you on the stage." He glanced back at Lon Pence and Kenny Brewer as if for confirmation. The two nodded grudgingly, not liking Clifford any more than Mazzel did.

Clifford gave them a look of thinly veiled disgust and said, "What did he tell you about the job you're being paid to do?"

"Oh, the job," said Mazzel, taking on a bit of an attitude of his own. "Maynard Aubrey wired me a telegram last week, said he wanted the three of us to help you track down Blake Carly and take him back to Arizona Territory for killing a lawman. That was pretty much it. He said you'd be filling us in on any particulars when you arrived."

"There are no more particulars," said Clifford. "I'll keep it short and simple. I'm after Blake Carly." He gestured toward the pack mule at the hitch rail. "Now, break down those supplies and get rid of the mule."

"What?" said Mazzel, looking surprised.

"You heard me correctly," said Clifford. "Get rid of the pack animal. Distribute the supplies equally.

Each man will be responsible for carrying his portion of food and coffee. Each man will carry his own ammunition and water."

Mazzel looked at Pence and Brewer with a trace of a smug grin, then back to Dayton Clifford, saying, "If you don't mind me saying so, Mister Clifford, these two ole boys and me know this country where we'll be traveling better than anybody around here. Hell, that's why Aubrey hired us. We took him and two others on an elk-hunting party a couple of years ago. One of them was some high foreign muckety-muck. When I tell you we're going to need that mule, you can believe that we are *by God* going to be needing that mule."

"That's why Aubrey hired the four of you?" said Clifford, puffing on his pipe. "Because you all know this country so well?"

"Damn right that's why," said Mazzel in a defiant tone.

"Then it's reasonable that I should hold you all four responsible should you happen to get us lost," said Clifford with a sharpness to his voice.

"Get us *lost*?" said Mazzel, taking offense at such a statement. "Let me tell you something, Clifford. Me and these boys here have trekked back and forth over every rock trail and elk path from here to—"

"Get rid of the mule," Clifford said with finality, cutting Mazzel off. He picked up his black leather case, turned and walked away toward the telegraph office. "I'm going to pick up authorization from Mister Aubrey to pay you the advance."

"Oh—" Mazzel fell silent at the mention of money. He gave Pence and Brewer a pleased look, then watched in silence as Clifford walked away.

Rawhide Hale stepped over from the hitch rail fifty

feet away and asked, "What the hell was all that about?"

No one replied until Dayton Clifford was out of hearing range. Then Mazzel said in a low voice, "Beats the living shit out of me. He must've got up badly swollen this morning and ain't went down yet."

The three chuckled under their breath. Mazzel seemed to consider things for a moment and then let out a resolved breath. "Boys," he said, "looks like we got us a hard nut to crack this time."

"Worse than the Englishman that time, you think?" said Pence. He grinned.

"I don't know who he's worse than," said Mazzel. "But if he thinks he's hooked up with some newcomers here, he's got a lot to learn. We might just have to spin him around and head him back to Chicago before he knows what's hit him."

"I'll hit him," Lon Pence growled in a deep, powerful voice, crunching his big right fist into the palm of his left hand. "I'll bat his little head back and forth right now if you want me to."

"No," said Mazzel. "Just wait. Aubrey is wiring us an advance payment. We ain't doing nothing until we get *all* of that money in our hands." He smiled, looking off toward the telegraph office as Clifford stepped inside. "I don't know if we'll ever find Blake Carly or not, but this big-city gunman is about to take the ride of his life." He winked, then added, "We'll teach him to mess with us."

"What do you want us to do first?" Pence asked in his deep voice.

"Hell, boys, you both heard him, didn't yas?" said Mazzel in a feigned voice, giving Rawhide Hale a little shove. "Let's get rid of that damned mule!"

From the window of the telegraph office Dayton Clifford looked up the dusty street in time to see the four men walking over to the hitch rail. He smiled to himself as he watched them begin untying supplies from the pack frame on the mule's back. Behind him he heard the steady tapping that meant the message he'd just dictated to the telegraph clerk was being sent to Maynard Aubrey, president and owner of the bank in Benton Wells. The message had been short, telling Aubrey that he had arrived, met Mazzel and his men and was on the trail, searching for Blake Carly. While the clerk sent the message, Clifford picked up a blank message sheet from a counter, folded it and stuck it in his shirt pocket.

As soon as the tapping stopped and Clifford was certain the message had been sent, he turned and asked the clerk, "Where will I find the best map of the high country around here?"

"Most folks here seem to know where they're going before they leave home," said the young clerk. He smiled as if he'd said something witty. But at the icy glare from Dayton Clifford's eyes his smile shrank and disappeared. In a somber, no-nonsense tone he said, "That would be at the survey and title office, sir." He quickly pointed in the direction of a rough wooden building across the street. "But I'm afraid there haven't been many maps of any great detail drawn up of the high country. You might be wasting your time."

"The search for good information is never a waste of time," said Clifford. He flipped a gold coin across the handrail and turned and left.

At the hitch rail separating the supplies, Mazzel and the others looked up and saw Clifford cross the street and walk into the survey office. A grin came to Mazzel's face. "Boys, it looks like our famous gunman ain't going to be trusting enough to take our word for anything. I believe he's gone to seek himself out some *professional* advice."

"Ha," said Rawhide Hale. "He'll be lucky if that surveyor don't get him lost right there in the office!"

The four men laughed, shook their heads and turned back to their task. Ten minutes passed before Dayton Clifford came walking across the dirt street with a long rolled-up paper tucked under his left arm. His pipe left its smoke hanging in the still air behind him. By the time he reached the hitch rail, the supplies had been divided up and put away, each man taking a portion. Clifford's portion lay neatly stacked beside a big roan. "Here we are, Clifford, all done," said Mazzel, spreading his hand toward the supplies. "Of course we didn't know how you might want your portion put away—"

Clifford cut him off, asking, "Is everybody carrying the same amount of provisions?"

"Yep," said Mazzel with satisfaction. "Same amount of grub, water, coffee, and ammunition. Just like you said."

Clifford walked past the roan to Mazzel's big bay. He untied Mazzel's bedroll from behind the saddle and pitched it to the man, who caught it instinctively rather than let it fall to the dirt.

"Hey! What the hell is this?" Mazzel's eyes widened in surprise, but then his gaze narrowed and hardened, seeing Clifford lay his leather travel case up behind the saddle and start tying it down. "That's *my* horse, Clifford. I told you this roan is the one we got for you."

"I don't like the roan," Clifford said flatly, without facing Mazzel as he secured the travel case and shook it a little to test it.

Mazzel looked at the others, then said, "We got all four of these horses from the same dealer, Clifford. There's nothing wrong with this roan."

"Good," said Clifford. "Then get the supplies loaded and let's get going."

Mazzel threw his bedroll to the ground. "I've had it with you, Clifford. Nobody waltzes in here and takes my horse right out from under me!" His hand closed around the butt of his LeMat pistol and raised it slightly in its holster, his thumb going over the hammer, ready to cock it on the upswing.

But Clifford didn't even turn to face him. Instead he ignored his words, pulled the folded-up blank telegram sheet from his shirt pocket and said to the other men, "Here is the authorization from Mister Aubrey to give you men the advance you've been waiting for." He patted the lapel of his riding duster. "I have the cash right here. He asked me to distribute it tonight right after we make camp."

Holding the bogus telegram up with his left hand, he turned slowly, facing Mazzel, and saw him ease the LeMat back down in its holster, his thumb coming off the hammer and his expression softening a bit.

Clifford gave a trace of a smile around his pipe stem. Still holding the blank telegram up and waving it a bit, he said, "Let me make things clear to everybody before we leave here. This ain't no elk hunt we're on. This is a serious manhunt. Blake Carly is running and he's desperate, and he won't mind killing you if we come face-to-face with him."

"Now wait a minute. Our job is to lead you

through the high country and scout around for the man," said Mazzel. "Aubrey said nothing about any gunplay."

"Indeed he did not," said Clifford. "But if we come upon Blake Carly, what do you think he'll do, tell you boys to get out of the way so he and I can settle matters?"

"It goes without saying that if we happen to cross trails with Carly face-to-face, we'll defend ourselves," said Mazzel. "But that ain't the job we was hired for—"

"Men, listen to me, and listen closely," said Clifford, slowly putting the folded telegram back into his shirt pocket, making sure everybody saw it disappear—as if with it went the money they had been anticipating. "I need men around me that I can count on. If I can't count on you, let me know right now and drop out of this job. Don't get me out there and let me find out your heart ain't in this thing. If I find out after we leave here that you're not taking this job serious, I'm going to be angry and disappointed."

Clifford couldn't see the slight smile Mazzel gave the men behind his back. When Clifford turned around the smile vanished. "We're all good at what we do, Clifford," said Mazzel. "Aubrey didn't hire any newcomers here. Every one of us knows this country like the back of our hands."

Clifford nodded in acknowledgment. "Enough said, then. Let's get started." He looked at Mazzel. "Load your supplies and catch up to us."

Mazzel decided not to argue. Instead he said to Rawhide Hale, "Rawhide, take the lead. We're leaving up through Rocky Pass."

But as the men turned to their horses and started mounting, Clifford said, "Oh, one more thing.

There's a possibility that Carly will have some friends looking for him too. Is anybody worried about that?"

The men settled into their saddles and looked at one another. "How many *friends*?" Brewer asked, a trace of sarcasm in his voice, staring at Clifford through his darkened spectacles.

Clifford shrugged. "Not many, I'm sure. It's only something to keep in mind. A man like Blake Carly runs out of friends pretty quick once he gets on the run."

"Who are these *friends*?" Brewer asked in the same tone as the men began turning their horses away from the hitch rail.

"I have no idea," said Clifford, himself stepping up into his saddle. "Nobody worth worrying about, I'm certain." He adjusted his pipe in his mouth and turned his horse to the street, following closely behind Rawhide Hale.

Barton Creed stepped down off the boardwalk into the midmorning heat and looked around the deserted street that ran the short length of Estación del Sol. He spit. "Shithole Station," he growled under his breath. He turned his eyes to Mongo Barnes, who stepped down beside him, leaving the other members of their group standing beneath the canvas overhang that flapped up and down in the hot breeze. "Whose idea was it to meet Blake Carly here, Mongo?" There was a testiness in his tone.

Mongo Barnes said with no hesitation, "It was *your* idea, boss. You and Blake come up with it on your own."

"Oh . . ." Creed relented, looking Barnes up and down, seeing that the big yellow-haired gunfighter was in no mood for taking any guff and knowing full well that when it came down to where the bullet met the bone, Mongo Barnes didn't have to take any guff off anybody.

"Yep," said Barnes, "as sorry as I am to inform you of it, Blake and you decided this was the best place to meet."

"Jesus, I must've been awfuly drunk," Creed whispered, running a shaky hand across his sweaty forehead.

"As I recall, you both was drunk," said Mongo, looking out across the Sangre de Cristo Mountains. "A couple of us tried to say something, but all you two could think about was Blake killing that lying sheriff and making it look like it was just some spur-of-the-moment thing."

Creed nodded. "Yeah, well, as long as that went all right, I expect we can stand to wait here another day or two for Blake. Killing Ed Tarpin has given me a whole new level of respect for Blake Carly." He glanced darkly at the men standing on the boardwalk behind them and said in a raised voice, "Especially at a time when it appears that guts is getting to be *scarce* in this line of work!"

The men milled about and looked down, avoiding Creed's harsh stare. Barton Creed's temper was unpredictable at best, drunk or sober. With a hangover he was even worse.

But Mongo didn't seem too concerned. "I hope you ain't aiming that remark in my direction, boss," he said coolly, leaving enough room for Creed to either settle himself or let his temper rage.

Creed mopped his wet brow again, then said sideways to Mongo, "Naw, forget it, Mongo. If I had more men like you riding with me I wouldn't have

to put up with some of these low-life poltroons." He
jerked a nod over his shoulder toward the rest of the
men but kept his voice low so they couldn't hear
him. He'd said enough to keep them wondering
where they stood with him. Then he said to Mongo,
again raising his voice for the rest of the men to hear,
"Pay no mind to what I said. I've got a hangover
that's got me seeing little devils run along the
rooflines."

A weak laugh came from the men.

Mongo Barnes smiled to himself. He'd been right
about Barton Creed. The man wasn't nearly as explo-
sive and out of control as he acted. Creed knew when
to blow up and when not to. This was good to know,
Mongo thought, resting his hand on his pistol butt.
In this business you never knew when the time might
come to take things over. He gave the men on the
boardwalk a look, making sure they saw how he'd
just handled Creed. "Well, boss," he said to Creed,
"I reckon we all get a hangover now and again. I
just wanted to keep the air clear between us."

Creed leveled his gaze on Mongo, seeing what he
was doing. Changing the subject, he turned to the
men and said, "If Blake ain't here by tonight, come
morning we're headed on to Taos. If we got to wait,
we can at least wait somewhere where we can tell
the liquor from kerosene."

A short cheer arose from the men.

"And where we can tell the women from the don-
keys," Mongo added.

"Yeah, that too," said Creed, not liking the way
Barnes included himself in addressing the men. Even
in his hungover condition Creed was starting to see
more and more clearly that Barnes was testing him,
making him look bad in front of the men. All right,

he told himself, maybe he'd let himself go lately—
too much drinking, too much sitting back, not kicking enough behinds, not keeping his shooting as
sharp as he should. But that was all about to change.
"Get all your drinking and such done today and tonight. Starting tomorrow we leave the whiskey behind us and get back in shape to take care of
business."

"What if Blake shows up?" asked a surly young
Texas gunman named Billy Drew, his black-beard-
stubbled face shadowed by his wide hat brim.

"If he shows up, we go on to Taos anyway," said
Creed. "Either way, we're sobering up and getting
back to what we all do best." He looked from face
to face among the men, then added in a lower tone,
"Do I have to remind anybody what that is?"

Heads shook back and forth in unison.

"What about you, Drew?" he asked, singling out
the young gunman. "Do I have to remind you what
it is we do best?"

"Nobody has to remind me of a damn thing," said
Drew, giving Creed a serious look. "I just asked so
I'd know what's going on."

The men fell silent.

"Well—do you?" asked Creed.

A tense silence passed, then Billy Drew said,
"Yeah, now I know." He offered a slight grin, a trace
of arrogance in his voice. "We're going to get sobered
up and go make some money."

Creed said, "There now, good for you! I knew it
wasn't too much for you." He also offered a slight
smile, letting everybody know that he was in good
humor, under control and not about to fly off the
handle. "All of you get whatever you need together,
ammunition or whatnot. When we leave here I want

us looking like a military unit, not like some bunch of saddle tramps looking for leftovers."

Creed and Mongo watched as the men dispersed and headed off along the boardwalk and across the narrow street.

"Just between you and me, boss," said Mongo, "if everything went well for Blake, why ain't he already here by now?"

Creed stood silent for a moment, then said, "We've got to give him time. He's the only one who knows where Ed Tarpin and Earl Hedgepeth buried that gold."

Mongo shook his head slowly and regretfully. "We never should have trusted that damned sheriff and his deputy. There are some lines you just don't cross. Working with dirty lawmen is the worst of all."

"It's too late now to go sounding off about what we should or shouldn't have done," said Creed. "The deal is, Blake finds out where the gold is buried, then kills the sheriff. As soon as we see Blake come up over the horizon we'll know that Tarpin is dead and we'll know that we've got seventy thousand dollars worth of gold waiting for us. It's that plain and simple."

"*If* he comes riding up over the horizon," said Mongo. "As it stands, I ain't counting on ever seeing Blake Carly again. He might have met his match with that sheriff." He seemed to consider another option, then said with a shrug, "Hell, he might have found out where the gold's buried and gone there on his own."

"Blake Carly would sooner cut his tongue out and swallow it before he'd ever try to double-cross me," said Creed.

"Alls I'm saying is it pays to look out for the worst

sometimes," said Mongo. "I have nothing but respect for Blake Carly. But every man riding the trail is a one-eyed jack as far as I'm concerned. You seldom see the face on the other side of the card until it's too late."

"You tell Blake all that when he gets here," said Creed, cutting the matter short. "I'm sure he'll want to hear it."

"I don't give a damn to tell him," said Mongo. "He knows it's true. It's the same thing he'd say about me if it was the other way around. I'd expect no less of him."

Dismissing any further talk on the matter, Creed rubbed his sweaty palms on his trousers and said, "Come on. I need a drink or two to get the devils settled."

"I thought you just told everybody that it's time for them to get sobered up," said Mongo, eyeing him.

"That's right, I did," said Creed. "But I gave them the rest of the day to drink their fill. Come morning I'll be chewing hide off any man who can't sit in his saddle sober as a judge. But right now I got to throw back enough rye to keep my hands from shaking." He returned Mongo's stare and added, "This life I live, I never know when I might have to shoot myself a snake."

Chapter 3

For the rest of the day the ranger and Carly rode silently along the narrow paths and winding trails toward Taos. Every few hundred yards the ranger stopped to look down from some high point and check their trail to make sure no one was following them. The Carly twin sat slumped in his saddle, now and then brushing flies away from his brother's blanket-wrapped corpse. When dusk settled on the western horizon the two rode their horses down to a wide stretch of shallows along the eastern bank of the Rio Grande. The Carly twin stood beside the dun at the river's edge, his hands still cuffed in front of him, staring grimly into the river's slow swirling current. Sam observed him from a few feet away as he made a small fire and boiled a pot of strong coffee.

The ranger had set both saddles on the ground beside the sun-bleached trunk of a downed cottonwood that lay partially buried in river silt and bits of washed-up driftwood. He secretively unloaded his Winchester repeating rifle and slipped it back into the saddle boot while the twin appeared to be lost in his thoughts. "Come get some hot coffee and beef in your belly, Carly," he said, hunkered down beside the fire, heating strips of jerked meat in a small skillet. "Maybe you'll feel a little better after you eat."

The twin turned and walked slowly to the campfire, his head bowed, passing less than three feet from the rifle without giving it a glance. "I ain't hungry," he murmured. "I don't know if I'll ever feel like eating again." He plopped down beside the fire and stared at his brother's body, lying no more than fifteen feet away. Flies droned and soared in short circles above a wide, dark bloodstain.

"Some coffee, then," said the ranger. He studied Carly's grim expression as he lifted the pot with his gloved hand, filled a tin cup and set it in front of him. The twin loosened a bandanna from around his neck, wrapped it around the hot tin cup and raised it to his lips with cuffed hands. He blew on the steaming coffee and sipped it carefully.

Half facing his prisoner, Sam set the skillet between them and said quietly, "It's best you keep your strength up if you can."

Carly nodded, but he turned his face from the food and only sipped his coffee while Sam ate a strip of the jerked meat in silence. When he was finished, he stood up, walked over to the rifle, slipped it from the saddle boot and carried it out of sight to the other side of the horses. When he returned with the rifle loaded, he kept it in his hand, picked up his cup of coffee and sat down a little farther away from his prisoner now that darkness had set in. He noticed that the twin was holding a piece of the jerked beef between his fingers, chewing it halfheartedly and washing it down with a sip of coffee.

Sam sat quietly until out of nowhere the twin said

as he stared across the river, "When we were kids my brother and me, if one of us got sick it wasn't no time until the other had the same illness."

"I expect most children can say the same thing," Sam offered, observing him closely, paying particular attention to the young man's eyes as he spoke.

"That's so," said the twin, "for two kids living under the same roof in close quarters. But with us it was more than that. I could feel a cold or a fever come upon him if it happened to get to him first. I might go a day or two feeling his illness before it even got to me. But then it always got to me."

"I don't understand," said the ranger, to keep Carly talking and gather more information to draw upon in deciding which twin this was. "If *you* felt ill, it must've been *your* illness you felt, not his."

"No," said the twin, sipping his coffee. "It's hard to explain, but it was different somehow when I felt what was ailing my brother. I felt his illness through him some way."

"Oh . . ." The ranger let his words trail off, hoping the man would continue talking. If this was actually Blake Carly impersonating his brother, he would slip up eventually. The ranger had to listen closely for any sign, any telltale clue. The man hadn't made a play for the rifle, Sam reminded himself, but maybe he hadn't been as wrapped up in his grief as Sam had thought.

"It was the same when we got older," the twin said. "I could be all the way across the territory, working for one of the ranchers, not giving my brother a thought. All of sudden I'd have a strange dark feeling come over me—and I'd know my brother was in trouble again. I'd just know it." He shrugged.

"That's interesting, Carly," said the ranger. "And what about your brother? Did he have the same things happen to him?"

"He always said he didn't believe in it—didn't like to talk about it. But I know he went through the same strange feelings. He just didn't want to admit to it." He looked over at the blanket-wrapped corpse for a moment in silence, then said, "I always said we were one man with two bodies. He always said we were the two exact opposites. He said he was made up of all the bad things a person can have inside them and that I was made up of all the good that can go into a person."

"I believe there's good and bad in all people. What about you?" said Sam, watching his eyes even though the twin looked away from him out across the Rio Grande.

"Yeah, that's what I always thought," said the twin. "But not Blake. I hated to hear him say it, but he swore there was no good in him, only meanness. He had a notion that there was no use in him trying to be good because the bad in him would always stop him. He said we were freaks. He never believed in God, but he said that whatever created us screwed things up, caused us to not get the proper balance of good and evil."

"That's a bad attitude to carry through life," said the ranger, still observing, still searching in every word, every slight change of expression. So far he hadn't seen anything to dispute the twin's claim that he was Abel Carly. *The good twin.*

"I know," said the twin, "but that was his thinking and he couldn't change it. He once said the only way it would change was if one of us died. When one of us died the other would get the portion of good or

evil he'd missed out on." He looked again at the
corpse and fell silent for a moment. "If that was true
I reckon I'd know it by now." He took in a breath
and let it out in a long, quiet sigh. "Whatever meanness my poor brother had in him is gone from now
on—whatever goodness too. I just wish he could
have seen some sign of goodness in himself before
he died. It would make me feel better about his im-
mortal soul."

The ranger sipped his coffee, not knowing how to
respond to such a statement. There were other things
he wanted to hear from the twin, questions he
wanted ask in order to watch his eyes and hear how
he answered them. But these things would keep until
daylight. He didn't want to push too hard all at once
and put the man on guard. In a moment, when the
twin had stopped talking about his brother, Sam
stood up and slung the coffee grounds out of his
cup. "I'm not going to cuff you around a tree tonight,
Carly," he said. "I'm going to trust you to behave
yourself."

"Much obliged, Ranger," the twin said. He watched
Sam walk over to the saddles, slip the rifle into the
boot and carry both saddles back to the campfire.

"Here," said the ranger, pitching the other saddle
over beside the twin. "Make sure you stay on this
side of the campfire. If you get up in the night without saying something first, or come around this
campfire thinking I'm asleep, it will cost you a toe
at the very least."

"Ranger, I'm who I said I am. You don't have to
worry about me trying anything like that. All I want
to do is to get back to Benton Wells, clear this up
and get this cloud of suspicion off my shoulders. I
want to hold my head up like I always have."

"That's good," said the ranger, fanning a blanket out and wrapping it around his shoulders as he sat down and pulled his sombrero low on his forehead. "Now just do like I told you and you can go back holding your head high."

The twin smiled slightly. "You can count on it, Ranger. I'm not leaving this spot before morning." He watched the ranger settle beneath the sombrero. In a moment he could have sworn he heard the ranger snore quietly. But only once, then it stopped. Was he asleep? Carly asked himself, or was he just being wily? Was this just one more way the ranger was testing him? Was the ranger trying to set him up, the same way he had tried to set him up with the rifle? Well, all he had to do was bide his time. He smiled to himself, looking the ranger up and down, checking the Winchester rifle in its boot and the Colt holstered on Sam's hip. Sooner or later the ranger would see that he was Abel Carly, the good twin. It shouldn't be hard convincing the ranger who he was. After all, he knew Blake Carly like the back of his hand. A part of him had been Blake Carly all his life.

Sam raised his head just enough to watch his prisoner in the glow of firelight through half-closed eyes without the twin knowing it. In moments he saw Carly spread his blanket on the hard ground with his cuffed hands, lie down on it and roll it around him. Using his saddle for a pillow, the twin soon fell asleep. Or so it appeared, Sam cautioned himself. He watched his prisoner and managed to rest himself without falling sound asleep, a wise practice he'd learned over the past two years while transporting prisoners to the territory prison in Yuma.

Twice in the passing night Sam perked up at the sight of the twin rising slightly in his blanket, but then he relaxed when he realized it was nothing more than a man changing his sleeping position. When first light mantled the line of rugged hills, Sam stood up, walked around the campfire and nudged the twin with the toe of his boot. "Up, Carly. We've got a stout ride ahead of us," he said.

Carly groaned and sat up in his blanket, rubbing his face with his cuffed hands. He gathered his wits, then looked over at the still form of his brother and shook his head. "I hoped I'd wake up and this would all be a bad dream."

The ranger didn't answer. He walked to the horses and began inspecting and preparing them for the long hard day ahead. The twin joined him, and when they finished with the horses they had a quick meal of the same thing they'd eaten the night before. They filled their canteens from the Rio Grande, closed the camp and mounted up, riding the first few hundred yards at a slow walk. But then they came to a fork in the trail and turned onto a narrow path too steep and treacherous to climb on horseback. For the rest of the morning they led the animals along a fast little stream that raced down from among towering boulders and tall, clinging pines. They traveled steadily upward, the roar of water beside them raging down, at times in a sheer drop of a hundred feet, then racing on, crashing against rock and leaving a high, cool spray in the morning air. At points along the steep path the stream forked and raced off in other directions, all of which spilled at some point into the winding Rio Grande.

"We'll stop here," Sam called out above the roaring water. He took a canteen from his saddle horn and handed it to the twin. Looking up, he judged they likely had another two miles to cover before reaching less hostile land. "When we get up there we'll noon in some shade and rest these horses before pushing on to Taos."

The twin nodded, sipping from the canteen in his cuffed hands and passing it back to the ranger. Twice before when they had stopped, they had moved the dead twin's body from one animal to the other, rotating the burden equally between the horses. Now, knowing what to expect, the twin dropped down onto a rock and held the reins of the big dun, watching the ranger raise each of the Appaloosa's hooves in turn and inspect them as he had at the other stops. When the ranger finished checking his stallion and walked over to move the body from the dun to the Appaloosa, the twin stood up to help him. But as the ranger stepped closer to the horse, the twin suddenly slammed into him from the side. The two tumbled down off the path, and behind them the ranger heard the dun whinnying in panic.

Instinctively the ranger rolled atop the handcuffed prisoner as they came to a stop against the side of a rock. Grabbing the twin by his cuffed hands, Sam shot a hard right to his jaw and turned him loose, limp on the ground, no longer a threat. Then Sam turned quickly back toward the path just in time to see the whinnying dun rearing high and writhing wildly. On its back the body of the dead twin flapped like a bundle of loose rags, a stiff arm protruding from the blanket. On the dun's front shoulder a six-foot rattlesnake sank its fangs in and whipped back and forth.

The ranger drew his pistol, cocking it on the upswing. But then he stopped, realizing that the shot would kill the horse as well as the snake. His eyes flashed to Black Pot. The stallion sidestepped away from the dun, but Sam knew that the snake might be hurled loose at any second and land atop the Appaloosa. His gaze returned to the dun with resolve. The shot resounded amid the roar of water. The snake's head exploded in a spray of blood, its own and that of the dun. Sam watched with regret as the horse faltered sideways and plunged down over the rocks, tumbling and sliding along the raging waterway.

The ranger hurried to the edge of the stream, running along it, and saw the corpse come loose and roll free of the blanket it had been wrapped in. Then horse, corpse and blanket all raced out of sight around a bend in the stream. Shaking his head, Sam glanced toward Black Pot, making sure the stallion was all right. Then he hurried back to where he and the twin had rolled off the path. He stood five feet from the unconscious twin and looked around the rough ground for his rifle, his Colt still in his gloved hand. Behind him he heard a groan as the twin pulled the rifle from beneath him and said, "Here it is, Ranger. Turn around easy-like—" Sam turned around easy-like, but he had the Colt out, cocked and aimed, the barrel pointing squarely at the twin's forehead. "—I don't want you shooting me by mistake," the twin continued.

Sam saw the rifle pointed at him, but he could read nothing of the man's intentions in his eyes, nothing to tell him whether or not he should drop the hammer on the Colt.

"Drop it, Carly," Sam said quietly.

The twin nodded at the rifle in his cuffed hands and said, "Take it—and give me a hand up from here."

Sam kept his gun hand tensed on his Colt, but he

reached out with his free hand, took the rifle barrel, carefully moved its aim away from his belly and gave a strong pull on it. The twin came to his feet with a grunt, then turned the rifle loose. His cuffed hand went to his face, his right hand nurturing his already swollen jaw.

"No hard feelings, Ranger," he said. "I know you thought I was making a move on you. But I wasn't. I saw that snake was too close and I couldn't do anything except shove you out of its way. That's all I knew to do at the time."

"Much obliged," said the ranger, uncocking and holstering his Colt. "I apologize for hitting you, but that's all I knew to do *at the time.*"

He wasn't about to take all of this at face value. Watching the twin for a reaction, he leveled the rifle twice, throwing two live rounds out on the ground, letting the twin know the rifle had been loaded, in case he'd had any doubts and those doubts had caused him to stop whatever play he might have been making. Yet, when the twin saw the bullets in the dirt, Sam could see nothing revealed in his eyes.

"I understand, Ranger," said the twin, looking up from the bullets into his eyes. "Like I told you, no hard feelings." As if dismissing the matter, he nodded toward the raging stream and said, "How are we going to get my brother's body back?"

"Sorry," said the ranger. "We're not getting his body back. Not now, anyway. If the judge turns you loose, you can outfit yourself and come back. It's up to you."

"Ranger, I can't leave him out here this way," said the twin. "Judge or no judge! It's bad enough that I killed him. Don't make me live with the thought of turning his body over to the wilds."

"We've got no choice," said the ranger. "There's dozens of directions this water could have taken him in between here and the Rio Grande. It could take days to find him—if we found him at all. We're down to one animal. Even if we found his body before it reaches the river and floats away, we've got no way to pack him to Taos."

"I've got to do something," said the twin, as the two of them walked together to the edge of the stream and looked down it to see the water rumbling out of sight.

Sam let out a breath. "We'll backtrack along the path as far as the last falls. But if we haven't found him by then, we'll have to move on. Fair enough?"

The Carly twin didn't answer. Instead, he turned and started walking away down the path, intently searching the stream and the rocks along the other side for any sign of his dead brother. Sam let him go, but kept an eye on him as he walked to where Black Pot stood waiting. Picking up the Appaloosa's reins, the ranger led him along the path, helping the twin search the rumbling waterway for any sign of the body.

They went around the first turn and found nothing. Fifty yards farther they saw the stream fork to the right and seem to disappear. The ranger stood in silence as the twin looked back and forth along the other bank, hoping beyond reason to see the body lodged in the rocks along the shoreline. "If he and the horse took that fork—there's no telling where it goes before it finds the river," Sam said quietly.

"I know," said the twin. He turned and walked on. The ranger followed. They searched closely for the next three hundred yards until they reached a waterfall that dropped more than thirty feet and

raced away into a sharp, rocky turn. Still there was
no sign of horse, man or blanket.

"This is all we can give it," the ranger said. "Let's
get on to Taos."

"No, wait, please!" said the twin. He looked wildly
up and down the rolling, shimmering water. "I think
I saw something!"

"Oh? Where?" the ranger asked, realizing that des-
peration had begun to overcome him.

The twin's eyes darted downstream. "Down there!
I think it's the blanket!"

"Come on, Carly, we've got to go," Sam said
softly, letting him know there was no use trying to
kid himself.

"No, Ranger, I swear, I did see something!" cried
the twin. He pulled away from the ranger's hand
on his shoulder and hurried along the river's edge,
stumbling with his cuffed hands held out as if grasp-
ing for his brother. "Blake? Blake! I know you're out
there!" he called out loud to his dead brother. Sam
looked on, sympathetic yet careful not to let the man
get too far away from him, lest this whole thing be
a ruse, an attempt to escape. In spite of the incident
with the rifle, he still wasn't going to trust a man
who had a murder charge hanging over his head,
especially the murder of a lawman.

He allowed the twin a moment alone at the water's edge.

"Blake!" the young man shouted to the roaring
water. "Please forgive me! I wish to God things had
been different for you! I wish to God I could have
done something to make all your trouble go away!"
He sank to his knees, his cuffed hands held out to
the river, folded tightly as if in prayer. "I wish to
God I could give your life back to you! I'd do any-

thing to! Anything!" He sobbed aloud, painfully, until at last he lowered his cuffed hands and sat slowly shaking his bowed head.

"Come on, Carly," the ranger said softly, walking up beside him and resting his hand on the man's trembling shoulder. "What's done is done."

The twin stood up, nodding slowly and wiping his eyes on his shirtsleeve. "I'm ready to go now." He didn't face the ranger as they turned and walked over to where Black Pot stood waiting. Sam picked up the reins and led the stallion back up along the narrow path, keeping the Carly twin a few steps in front of him.

When they had traveled a few yards, the twin said over his shoulder, "Ranger, I apologize for breaking down like that."

"Think nothing of it, Carly," the ranger said, a sympathetic tone to his voice.

Carly smiled slightly to himself and stared straight ahead. "I know it looked weak on my part, crying that way."

A brief silence passed as he waited for the ranger's reply. When it came the twin felt a slight sting in it.

"Oh?" said the ranger. "I didn't *see* you cry."

The twin's expression grew grim as he looked up the winding path ahead of them. "You have a suspicious, untrusting nature, Ranger," he said.

"I know," Sam replied. "It came with a badge pinned to it."

Chapter 4

Standing naked beneath a loose-fitting man's shirt that lay open down her front, Millie Tristan gazed out the window of the crumbling abandoned relay station. For a moment she contemplated what to do as she watched the two figures and the horse come over a distant rise in the wavering evening heat. Then, as if she had come to a decision, she looked over at Arvin Peck, the last remaining station hostler, who sat snoring, drunken and shirtless, his large belly still sticky and wet with sweat and whiskey. "Jesus," said Millie under her breath. The hostler was sprawled in the wooden chair, his head thrown back, his gaping mouth turned up to the ceiling. A fly walked around in the glistening beard stubble on his chin.

"You filthy son of a bitch," Millie whispered, deciding not to wake him.

Once he was awakened, Millie was certain, he'd be up half the night before passing out again. She was also certain that if she woke him he'd be all over her. Her skin still crawled from earlier in the day when he'd laid her down roughly atop the wooden table, spread her dress open and mounted her, the bottle of whiskey in his hand sloshing all over her bare breasts. She'd had to wash her dress and her personals and bathe herself as well. Her gingham dress and other belongings still hung drying in the sun out back. Looking again at the two figures on the horizon she said to herself, "Whoever you are, you can't be no worse than this bucket of guts."

After another quick glance at Arvin, she went to the water bucket hanging on a wall peg, took it down and carried it out through the back door to the well, sending the chickens into a frenzy of clucking and batting wings as they sped out of her way. She estimated it should take the two men another twenty minutes to arrive. She dipped the bucket down over the low stone wall of the surface well, scooped up some water and poured it into the same pan she'd bathed in earlier. Reminding herself that she had plenty of time, she sat down on her bare bottom on the wall of the well, crossed her legs and took a leather pouch of chopped smoking tobacco from her shirt pocket, along with some wooden matches and thin papers. Expertly rolling herself a smoke, she ran it in and out of her lips, lit it and took a long, deep draw. Whatever these two might have to offer, she would be ready for it, even if it was no more than an escort back to Taos. She looked around, telling herself that anything beat the hell out of this.

From the low rise, the ranger and the Carly twin stared ahead at the relay station and walked on across the hot sand through low clumps of cactus and mesquite until they stopped a hundred yards away to take the canteen from the saddle horn and finish the last of the tepid water. The ranger took the empty canteen from the twin, capped it and hung it back on the saddle horn. He studied the relay station through the heat, noting the corral where three horses and a donkey stood under the shade of a wide white oak.

"Any chance of you taking these cuffs off of me before we get there?" the twin asked, raising his hands.

Sam just looked at him.

"Come on, Ranger," the twin said. "How do you think it feels, being cuffed this way in front of people? I told you who I am, and I haven't done anything to make you think otherwise. Can't you give me the benefit of a doubt? Just while we're here?"

The ranger considered for a second, staring at the adobe station and seeing what he thought was a woman's face peep around the side of the crumbling structure. "All right," he said finally, stopping and pulling the key to the cuffs from his vest pocket.

"All right?" The twin looked surprised.

"Yes, that's what I said. Hold them up here," Sam said.

"Thanks, Ranger," said the twin. "Ranger, you're not going to regret this."

"I know *I'm* not," said Sam, giving him a warning look. "See to it that you don't."

He unlocked the cuffs with his left hand, keeping his right hand close to the pistol on his hip as he watched Carly take them off.

"I have to tell you, Ranger, that's the worst feeling in this world, being cuffed like that, knowing that you're helpless to do anything for yourself." He rubbed his wrists as he spoke.

"That's the whole point of cuffs," the ranger said, putting the warm metal cuffs behind him on his gun belt. "Now, keep yourself ahead of me about four feet—and keep your hands at your sides so I can see them at all times."

The twin shrugged slightly, offering a trace of a smile. "Sure thing, Ranger," he said. "But I hope you remember all this once that judge realizes who I am and sets me free."

"I'll remember it," said the Ranger, "and if the judge calls it your way, I'll beg your pardon, tip my hat and go my own way—wishing you the best of luck."

"Fair enough," said the twin, walking through the hot sand toward the station. "I'll wish you the same."

The ranger watched him closely from behind, still not sure how he felt about the earlier incident with the rifle. How would things have gone if the twin had known the rifle was loaded? Had seeing the Colt pointed at his face caused him to change his plan and ask for a hand up from the ground? Sam considered it. On the other hand, he told himself, if this was Blake Carly, why did he even ask the ranger to turn around slowly and take a chance on looking down the pistol barrel? Why hadn't the twin just shot him with no warning and left him lying in the rocks? These were questions he could not answer with any satisfaction—not with his life on the line. Walking on, the ranger again caught another glimpse of someone at the corner of the building. This time the twin saw it too.

"Somebody sees us coming, Ranger," the twin said over his shoulder. "Don't know why they can't step out and show themself."

"I saw them too," Sam replied. "Probably just being cautious." Deftly he slowed a step, long enough to pull his rifle from his saddle boot and switch it to his right hand, holding it around the small of the stock, his thumb over the hammer. They walked on.

When they stopped out front of the relay station, Sam stepped to one side, still behind the twin, and called out, "Hello, the station." A silence passed beneath a hot, billowing breeze. Then he called out again. This time when no answer came, he nudged the prisoner forward and slightly to the side, the two of them stepping through the wide open doorway together.

"There's a handsome sight," the twin said quietly, staring at the snoring station attendant, the fly having walked its way up to the tip of his nose. "Want me to wake him up?"

"No," Sam whispered, shaking his head, smelling the strong odor of whiskey. "If he was sober he wouldn't be sleeping this time of day. There's somebody else here." He gestured with his rifle barrel toward the back door.

Walking a step ahead of the ranger, the twin heard the sound of a woman's voice humming pleasantly as they neared. He paused and gave the ranger a look, but the ranger nodded him forward.

"Oh, my!" said the twin, stepping through the rear door and seeing the naked woman standing beside the well, washing herself with a wet cloth from the pan of water. He ducked his hat brim, hiding his face.

The woman gasped in apparent shock and surprise, her hands going alternately to her breasts and her lower belly. With a short scream she gave up on trying to cover herself with her hands and instead turned and snatched up a man's shirt and fumbled with it for a second until she got it on and held it closed in front. The ranger had modestly turned his gaze away from her, but the twin had looked on bemused until she closed the shirt and said, "Who—who are you men? How long have you been standing there?"

"Begging your pardon, ma'am," said the ranger. "We just got here. I called out hello to the station from out front, but nobody answered. Sorry to have frightened you. We're in need of a horse to get us on into Taos."

"Well—you shouldn't have just barged on in here that way." She looked upset, yet she seemed to be recovering quickly. The shirt clung wet against her flat belly and her round breasts. She seemed satisfied with her attempt to cover herself. "I'm afraid Arvin is alseep right now. He's the one who runs this place, or at least he did. This station is shut down now."

"Yes, ma'am, we can see that," Sam said. "From the whiskey smell, I'd say Arvin is going to sleep for a long while."

"I'm only his guest. My name is Millie Tristan," she said, ignoring the ranger's remark about the whiskey. "I rode out from Taos just to see the place, get one last look before it's taken over with mesquite and lizards." She smiled. "So, you boys are headed for Taos?" She looked back and forth between Sam and the twin. The ranger started to reply, but as her eyes went to the Carly twin the twin raised his hat brim, revealing his face to her.

Millie's smile widened in delight. "Blake! Blake Carly!" she squealed, running to him and throwing her arms around him before he could stop her.

"Whoa, ma'am!" said the twin, trying to settle her down.

"Ma'am?" Millie replied, looking a bit hurt as she

tried to press herself against him. "Since when was I ever *ma'am* to you?"

The twin peeled her arms from around his neck. "The thing is, ma'am, you're mistaking me for my brother! I'm not Blake. My name is Abel!"

"Sure it is," Millie laughed aloud. "And I'm not Millie, I'm the queen of France!" But in a second, when she saw she was laughing alone and realized that the twin's resistance to her was genuine, she stepped back and closed the front of the shirt again. "You're serious, aren't you?" she said, looking at the young man in disbelief. Her eyes then went to the ranger, as if seeking confirmation.

"Yes, ma'am," the ranger said. "He's serious—or so he says." As Sam spoke, Millie caught her first glimpse of the badge that lay partially hidden under the lapel of his duster. "I'm Arizona ranger Sam Burrack," he said. "How well did you know Blake Carly?"

"Sam Burrack!" said Millie, looking impressed. "I've heard of you! You killed Junior Lake and his pa! His whole gang! Or so I've been told!" She grinned broadly. "You are a famous lawman, even over here in New Mexico." But then, as if it had taken a second for the ranger's words to sink in, her demeanor changed to a more somber one. Her eyes took in both men again, noting the rifle in the ranger's hand. "*Knew* him, you said?" she murmured, with a look of curiosity and dread coming over her face.

"Yes, ma'am," the ranger replied. Seeing how the news had stricken her, he said, "I'm sorry to tell you, but if this man really is *Abel* Carly, then Blake is lying dead back somewhere along the banks of the Rio Grande."

"Oh—" Millie stepped backward as if in a trance and sank down onto the low stone wall surrounding the well. The shirt fell open in front again, exposing her breasts. She didn't bother closing it. "I—I knew Blake Carly well. I mean, *very* well," she said with emphasis. "We were as close as a man and a woman can get. We might have been in love with one another, if you can imagine such a thing." Her hands trembled as she took out the tobacco pouch and tried to roll herself a smoke.

"I can imagine that easily enough," said the twin.

"Thanks," she said, taking his words as a compliment. She ran her fingers through her long auburn hair. "Fellows, this is all quite a shock to me. I never even knew Blake had a *brother*, let alone a twin!"

Seeing the difficulty she had holding the paper steady between her fingers, the Carly twin stepped over, saying, "Here, let me help you." He took the paper and tobacco from her and rolled a smoke. The ranger looked on with interest.

"Much obliged," Millie said, her eyes turned to him in curiosity. She took the smoke, firmed it up, struck a match along the stone wall beneath her and lit it without taking her eyes from the twin's face. "You are Blake's spitting image, I swear you are!" She puffed on the cigarette. "I wonder why he never mentioned you?"

"I don't know, ma'am," said the twin. "My brother and I didn't see one another much these last few years, but I can't imagine why he wouldn't tell somebody about me, especially somebody he was close to."

"Oh, yes, we were close," said Millie. "Let me tell you. We just about ate each other up for a whole summer, back when he was riding with the—" Her words stopped short as she suddenly remembered that a lawman was standing nearby.

"It's all right, ma'am," said the twin. "Nothing you say is going to cause my brother any trouble from now on." His expression saddened.

Millie smoked idly and looked back and forth between them again, trying to get a better idea of their circumstances. "So, what happened to Blake? What are you two doing out here, one horse short?" she asked.

The ranger only watched and listened.

"A rattlesnake got our other horse," said the twin, giving her the quickest version of what had happened. "As for my brother . . ." He hesitated, then said, "I'm afraid I'm the one who shot him."

Millie stared at him blankly for a moment. She shook her head as if to clear it and get refocused. "You shot him? You killed Blake? Your own brother?"

"Yes, ma'am, I did," said the twin.

"Please quit calling me ma'am," she said. "It feels unnatural for some reason, you looking so much like Blake." She looked at both of them. "Call me Millie— everybody else does." Then as an afterthought she said, "Blake sure as hell did."

"Yes, ma'am, Millie," the twin said in a low voice.

Millie puffed her cigarette and whispered, "I'll be damned." She stared down at her bare feet in reflection as she continued to smoke.

"It wasn't something I wanted to do," Abel said quietly.

"Wasn't that supposed to be the other way around?" Millie said, paying no attention to his words.

"Ma'am?" said the twin.

"In the Bible," she said. "Wasn't it Blake who killed Abel, not Abel who killed Blake?"

The twin and the ranger just looked at one another. "It wasn't Blake, Miss Millie," Sam said. "It was *Cain*."

"Huh?" Millie looked confused.

"In the Bible," said the ranger. "It was *Cain* who slew Abel—not Blake."

"Oh, well." Millie shrugged, dismissing it. "Same thing either way, though—one brother killed another. My pa was a preacher. He beat a lot of that Bible stuff into me and my brothers and sisters." She grinned and blew out a long stream of smoke. "Reckon he didn't beat hard enough, huh?"

Neither man commented. They watched her smoke, her nervous hand finally closing the shirt slightly.

"He used to beat us and say, 'The beatings will continue until you grow to love the Lord.'" She shook her head. "I never understood that line of thinking."

The ranger said, "Miss Millie, look at me."

Millie raised her face. The ranger saw a tear glisten at the corner of her eye. "You've looked at this man, and you've heard him say who he is. Now tell me, in your opinion, is he or is he not Blake Carly?"

Millie took her time thinking about it, looking up into the twin's eyes. The ranger watched them both intently, looking for any sign or signal that might pass between them. He saw none.

"No," said Millie at length. "Now that I think about it, this isn't Blake Carly. I thought it was—I reckon anybody would, they look so much alike. But now that I know he had a twin, I realize this is not him."

"You're certain?" the ranger asked, still searching for something between them. He wasn't foolish enough to think that this young woman would give up Blake Carly if she knew this *was* him standing before her. Sam just wanted to see the interaction as he put the question to her. So far there was nothing to make him think this twin had ever been her lover.

"I'm *almost* certain," said Millie. She nodded toward a small hay barn. "If you'd like for me and him to walk off together for about ten minutes or so, I can tell you for sure."

The ranger looked at the two of them. "That won't be necessary." He looked toward the corral where the horse stood in the shade of the cottonwood tree. "I'll need to wake up the hostler and see about a horse."

"So you fellows are going to Taos?" Millie asked again. "I'm thinking about going there myself. Could sure use some company."

Sam noticed her hand loosening on the front of the shirt, allowing herself to be seen. "Why don't you get yourself some clothes on, Miss Millie?" As he spoke he removed his glove and reached down to her.

She took his hand and stood up. "I'm waiting for my dress to finish drying right now." She nodded toward the open rear doorway leading into the adobe. "That filthy pig soiled all my clothes with whiskey."

As if her words had summoned him up, the drunken station hostler staggered into the doorway with shotgun in hand. "Who the hell are you?" he demanded drunkenly, staring at the twin and the ranger.

"Easy with that scattergun, Mister," the ranger said. He slowly raised his hand and spread his riding duster open, revealing his badge. "I'm Ranger Sam Burrack. I'm transporting a prisoner back to the territory."

"So what, you've got yourself a shiny badge?" the man said in a slurred voice. "Any sumbitch can find a way to pin a badge on his chest these days. It don't mean squat to me."

"See how stupid he is?" Millie blurted out.

"Quiet, ma'am," said the ranger. His thumb slipped unnoticed over the rifle hammer. "I'm in need of a horse," he said to Arvin, ignoring both the drunken comment and Millie's response to it. "I'm paying top dollar."

"Oh, are you?" The hostler relented, lowering the shotgun a bit. "Well, I'll tell you right now, these horses cost me plenty. They're going to have to bring an awful lot—out like this, away from town, no water to speak of twixt here and Taos."

"Those horses didn't cost you a plug nickel, Arvin!" said Millie. "You lying stack of shit! You told me they were left here by the stage line when they quit this route!"

"That doesn't matter," said the ranger, trying to keep things from overheating. "I'm still buying." He leveled his gaze at the hostler. "Now how about lowering the scattergun and let's talk business."

"This ole ten-gauge has got you nervous, huh?" The drunk grinned and jiggled the shotgun in his hands.

"Only because I don't want to kill you, Mister," said Sam, tightening his grip on the rifle hammer, ready to cock and fire the weapon at any second.

"Kill me? Ha!" said the hostler. "I'm the one who's got the drop on *you* here." He looked past the ranger and the twin to the woman. Then he looked back at

Sam and said, "I'll tell you right now, the whore ain't going nowhere, horse or no horse. If you've got designs on her you'll have wait till I'm finished."

The ranger bristled, but caught himself and said, "Mister, why don't you put down the gun and let's talk horses. That's all I came here for."

"No drunken pig son of a bitch is telling me when I can or can't *leave!*" said Millie Tristan. "I came here by choice, and I'll leave the same way. You got better from me than you've ever had in your miserable life!"

"Everybody take it easy," the ranger cautioned, seeing the hostler's knuckle turn white as he gripped the shotgun.

"Yes, please take it easy," the twin pleaded, staring at Millie.

Ignoring the ranger, Arvin Peck said to Millie, "Not until I've taken my fill of you, you ain't! I paid you a twenty-dollar eagle to come out here! You'll stay till I wear the hide off your ass if I tell you to!"

"That's it!" said Millie. "I'm leaving right now!" She turned and jerked her dress down from a strip of cord holding it. "Whatever you thought you were doing to me, you can go do to yourself, you sour-smelling pig!"

"Damn you, whore!" Arvin's shotgun started up toward her. Sam saw the man's thumb cocking both hammers, saw the killing look in his eyes.

"Mister, don't do it!" Sam shouted, hoping to distract him while he lifted his Winchester to fire.

But Arvin didn't give him a glance. The shotgun came up level with Millie's naked midsection. But instead of firing, the ten-gauge tumbled from the hostler's grip as a shot exploded from a Colt Thunderer in Millie Tristan's hand. Arvin fell dead in the dirt, a bullet hole in the center of his forehead, a strange, suddenly sober look frozen onto his face.

"Nailed him," Millie said firmly. Her dress lay on the ground. She stood with her feet spread shoulder-width apart, the front of her body completely exposed, the barrel of the Colt Thunderer tipped up in her hands, curling gray smoke into the still air.

"Yes," the twin said in an awestricken tone, "you did, sure enough." He looked baffled and added, "Where did that pistol come from?"

"But I had to do it," Millie said matter-of-factly, not answering him. "It was him or me." She lowered the barrel toward the ground, both hands still wrapped around the butt. She cocked her head to one side, curiously studying the bullet hole in Arvin's head.

"Miss Millie," the ranger said calmly but firmly, "lay the gun down on the well and step back away from it."

"Why?" Millie asked, seeing no need for such a move. "It's *my* gun. I carry it all the time. You saw what happened. It was self-defense."

The ranger and the Carly twin looked at one another.

"Millie," said the twin, "the ranger here is concerned that if I'm not really Abel, but my brother Blake, we might cause him harm on the way to Taos. Right, Ranger?"

Sam kept his rifle pointed loosely in Millie's direction. "That's close, Carly," he said, "except for the *harm* part. I'm not nearly as concerned about either of you harming me as I am that I'll have to kill you for making some foolish mistake." He reached behind him, pulled out the handcuffs and pitched them to the twin, making sure Millie got the message about who was in charge. "Put those back on," he said firmly. Turning to Millie he said, "I'm not going to tell you again to lay that gun down. I've seen you're good with it, and I see you're not afraid to use it. Does that tell you where you stand with me?" The rifle hammer cocked with a sound of finality to it.

"All right, Ranger, I'm laying it down," Millie said quickly. "Here, see? It's down!" She laid the gun down, patted it as if to keep it in place, and stood up with her hands chest high, the shirt open even more than it had been. "All I want to do is get along with you. I'm not going to be any problem if you take me along to Taos." She smiled. "It could even turn into a fun ride if you give it half a chance."

The ranger eyed them both closely, the cocked rifle still in his gloved hands. He didn't like the way things were shaping up. "Back away from the well," he said, ignoring her words. As she backed up, he picked up the pistol and shoved it down into his belt. "From now until we reach Taos I want the two of you in front of me at all times. Now get yourself dressed," he said to Millie, "and do it without turning it into a stage show."

Chapter 5

Dayton Clifford had only partially unrolled the map. He consulted it briefly, then rolled it up and put it away. He sat poker straight in his saddle, scanning the land behind them through his binoculars while Mazzel and Rawhide Hale sat flanking him. Behind him sat Lon Pence and Kenny Brewer. The four looked at one another, stifling their laughter as Clifford asked, without taking the binoculars from his eyes, "Didn't we pass these ridges from this same direction over two hours ago, Rawhide?"

"Well, now, it might appear so," said Rawhide Hale, keeping himself from laughing out loud long enough to explain, "but that's just your imagination."

"I see. So I'm only *imagining* we've gone in a wide circle the past two hours?" Dayton Clifford asked calmly.

"Well, yes, so to speak," said Rawhide. "You see, the land is awfully tricky up here. Sometimes it looks like you're just riding in circles when actually you're gaining ground hand over foot."

"I see . . ." Clifford repeated in contemplation, puffing on his pipe. He lowered his binoculars and urged his horse forward a few feet then turned it sideways to the others while he studied the land with the naked eye, looking a bit puzzled. He looked at the four faces, each man struggling to keep from laughing at him. "Like many newcomers I suppose I have a lot to learn about this land, its harshness, its temperament."

"Yeah, that's it, all right," Mazzel said, not trying too hard to conceal his grin. "You'll need to get used to the land's *temperament*." He passed a glance to the others, then said to Clifford, "I always say a man shouldn't go nowhere till he knows the *temperament* of the land. Right, boys?"

"Right as rain," said Rawhide Hale, his own grin starting to surface, seeing that Dayton Clifford was now at his mercy out here. "Now that you've learned that, what say we camp here for the night, get that advance distributed, to sort of give us all something pleasant to dream about, and come morning we'll get right back on the trail."

"I would like to do that very much," said Clifford, "but I'm afraid we've wasted too much time today. We'll need to travel all night just to get back on schedule."

"Schedule?" said Mazzel, barely holding back his laughter. "This is the first we've heard about any schedule."

"Oh, yes," said Clifford. He tapped his forehead with his black-gloved finger. "I keep a running account of progress right here. If I feel we haven't put in a good day, then we have to make up for it by traveling all night."

The faces lost their mirth. Mazzel frowned. "You're

out of your mind, Clifford! We can't travel this trail
at night. Look at it. It's high, slim and dangerous up
here! Rawhide can't lead us up in the dark!"

Clifford turned his gaze to Rawhide Hale and
asked, "Is that true, Rawhide? Can you not lead us
after dark?"

"That's the hard, cold truth of it," Rawhide said,
crossing his wrists on his saddle horn. "I ain't about
to even try it."

"I see," said Clifford in an understanding tone. "In
that case I'm afraid you're fired."

Rawhide chuckled and looked at Mazzel and the
others. "Damn, boys, I've been fired! Can you believe
that, as hard as I've worked, as much as I've done—"

His words stopped short as Dayton Clifford's big
Colt roared once. The shot swept Rawhide out of his
saddle and flung him backward off the trail. He
sailed two hundred feet down, bouncing off of protruding boulders and through the tops of swaying
pinyons. The sound of breaking branches echoed
sharply up to the stunned men. "Jesus! Good God
Almighty!" Mazzel shrieked. "You just killed him!
You killed old Rawhide!"

"Yes, so I did," Clifford said quietly, still holding
his Colt, the tip raised slightly, gray smoke curling
from it. He eased his horse closer to the edge of the
trail and looked down curiously. "Is that one of Rawhide's arms stuck to a broken branch—or am I only
imagining again?" He gave Mazzel and the other men
a frosty stare.

Mazzel backed his horse up a step, his mouth
agape. The other men wore the same expression.

"Let me ask you something, Mazzel," said Clifford. "Do you think you can lead us up this trail in
the dark?" He wagged the Colt idly back and forth.

"Yes! I can," said Mazzel in a hushed tone.

"Now be very honest about it," said Clifford, with a cruel smile. "I wouldn't want to make demands on you that you aren't capable of fulfilling." He cocked the Colt slowly and let the barrel tip toward Mazzel.

"I—I can do it!" Mazzel stammered in panic. "I know I can! Absolutely! Please! Just let me show you that I can!"

"Very good, then," said Clifford, letting the gun hammer down with his thumb. "I have faith in you." He looked around at the others and added, "I have faith in every one of you. I feel like the more men work together the better they begin to understand one another. Wouldn't all of you agree?"

The men nodded in unison.

"You make me proud," Clifford beamed. "After you, then, Mister Mazzel . . ." His words trailed off as he backed his horse up a step and gave a sweeping gesture with his hand, motioning Mazzel and the others ahead of him. "I'll just ride back here for a while, make sure we all keep going in the same direction, eh?" Now it was his turn to chuckle.

The men rode upward, in stunned silence, single file without a glance back down at the spot where Rawhide Hale's dismembered body lay on a broad flat rock in a widening pool of blood.

For the next hour they climbed the long, meandering trail as darkness closed around them. When they reached the top the men formed a semicircle and Clifford said, "There, now, that wasn't so bad, was it?"

The men groaned and murmured. "Olla Sucia is another couple hours' ride," said Mazzel, being as helpful as he could, having seen how Clifford fired people. "It'll be late when we get there, but we can take on some water—and maybe some hot grub if it's all the same with you, Mister Clifford."

"Sounds like a splendid idea, Mister Mazzel," said Clifford, seemingly unfazed by the grueling ride. "But first, men," he said, raising his voice for the others to hear, "let's drop down long enough to rest these horses for a few minutes. What say all of you?"

The three men nodded and silently stepped down from their saddles. Squatting in a close circle, Kenny Brewer whispered—after first making sure that Clifford couldn't hear him—"This sonsabitch is a raving madman!"

"We know it, Kenny," Lon Pence whispered in reply. "Now shut up before you get us all killed."

"Did you see what he did to poor ole Rawhide?" Kenny whispered.

"Hell, yes, of course we seen it!" whispered Lon, having a hard time keeping his voice down. "We ain't blind!"

"Then I'm sure we all know we're going have to kill him," Kenny said with resolve, glancing at each man in turn.

"I don't know that we are," said Lon. "I for one ain't too eager to go making that man mad at me. Like you said, look what he done to Rawhide. He's crazy, there is no doubt. But by God we knew he was a gunman when we agreed to take this job."

"What are you saying, Lon?" Kenny asked. "That we ain't going to do a damn thing about him killing poor Rawhide?"

"Nothing against our pard Rawhide," said Lon, "but the truth is he was long overdue for killing anyway."

"I come near killing him myself a time or two,"

said Mazzel. "Not that one thing has anything to do with another."

Kenny just looked at the two in disgust. "I can't believe what I'm hearing. In other words, we don't avenge one of our own?"

"That's it as far as I'm concerned," said Mazzel. "I've seen what this man will do at the drop of a hat. Alls I want is to get this job finished and get away from him. Maynard Aubrey is going to get a piece of my mind when it's all over. You can damn sure bet on that."

"Yeah," said Lon Pence. "I'll go along with that. Tell Maynard Aubrey he can go straight to hell if he ever asks us to do anything again." He nodded firmly.

"You two sorry sonsabitches," Kenny Brewer said, staring in disbelief. "You make me want to puke!" He clenched his fists in anger.

"Oh," said Lon, "well, what about you? I didn't see you do anything when he shot Rawhide plumb out of his saddle. Seems like that woulda been a dandy time to declare yourself and get down to it."

"I'll get down to it," said Kenny. "Don't think I won't. I'm making that a sacred vow to Rawhide's spirit right here and now, that by God, I am going to kill this man."

"Well, good luck," said Mazzel.

"Go get him," said Lon.

Kenny ducked his eyes and said, "Not right now. I didn't mean this very minute."

"When, then?" asked Lon.

"Before this is all over, that's when," said Kenny.

"I think that's all bullshit," said Lon Pence. "You sat here chastising us for not doing anything, then come to find out all you're doing is shooting your mouth off anyway."

"I'm not shooting my mouth off!" said Kenny, his voice getting louder as he spoke. "I said what I'm going to do and by God I'll do it." He stopped and cleared his throat. "When the right time comes, that is."

Lon Pence and Ben Mazzel guffawed.

"To hell with both of yas, then," said Kenny, no longer whispering. He stood up and started toward his horse.

"Is there something on your mind, Mister Kenny?" Dayton Clifford asked quietly.

Kenny heard the other two mumble and chuckle under their breath. He gave them a hard stare, then turned to Clifford, saying, "Yeah, now that you mention it, there damn sure is something on my mind."

"Come on, then, out with it," said Clifford. He faced Kenny squarely, his feet shoulder width apart. "It's not good to keep something bottled up inside you."

"All right, then," said Kenny. "It's about that advance money. You said we'd be getting it distributed out between us tonight when we stopped to make camp."

"You are absolutely right, sir," said Clifford. "That is what I told all of you." He shrugged and added, "Unfortunately though, since we have to make up for the time Rawhide cost us, and we won't be making a camp tonight, we'll have to postpone distributing the money until tomorrow night." He looked from man to man, his expression turning grave. "I hope that doesn't displease anyone?"

"No, sir," said Mazzel, standing up and heading for his horse. "I'd rather wait till tomorrow, to be honest with you."

"Me too," said Lon Pence, standing and hurrying to his horse. "There's no place to spend it out here anyways."

Clifford smiled and turned back to Kenny. At the same time he put his hand up on his stomach near the holstered Colt. "How does this set with you, Kenny Brewer?"

Kenny watched the other two mount up and pull their horses back a step. "I'm with them," he said. "I was just curious is all."

"Never forget what curiosity did to the poor cat, Kenny," said Clifford.

Kenny looked puzzled. "What was that?" He looked from Clifford to Lon Pence and Ben Mazzel, a bewildered expression coming to his face.

"It *killed* it, you dumb sumbitch," said Mazzel.

"Oh!" Kenny ducked his head, raised his hands in a show of peace and hurriedly climbed into his saddle without another word.

Clifford grinned as he mounted his horse. "At first I thought I might have a hard time adjusting to this country after all those years on the streets of Chicago. But you know, I'm beginning to feel right at home here."

The ranger halted his stallion at a narrow spot in the trail above a stretch of flatland that reached the last few miles into Taos. "Hold up here for a few minutes," he said to Millie Tristan and the Carly twin riding in front of him. The two stopped their horses and looked back at him. "We'll rest these horses some before riding in."

"Why?" Millie asked. "We're almost there."

"I never ride a tired horse across open land," said the ranger.

Millie stared blankly, as if she had no idea what he meant.

The Carly twin explained. "If a man gets riders hot on his trail crossing open land, he wants his horse to be fit to outrun them. It's a cavalry practice. Right, Ranger?"

The ranger gave him a searching gaze. "Yes, or an *outlaw's* practice."

The twin smiled and said, "Or a *lawman's*?"

"Or a *whore's*, from now on," Millie cut in, tired of the suspicion she saw the ranger had for the twin. Shaking her head, she took the canteen from her saddle horn, stepped down from her saddle and stretched her back. Sam waited until the Carly twin stepped down before dismounting himself. He led his Appaloosa forward, gathered the reins to the other two horses and led all three aside. While Carly and Millie plopped down on a flat rock sticking out of the steep hillside, Sam checked each horse's hooves.

"So, tell me, Ranger," Millie called out, "will you have to write a report on me shooting that skunk? I mean, I won't get in no trouble, will I?"

"It was self-defense, like you said," Sam replied. "If you were in any trouble you'd be wearing cuffs right now. I'll write a report, give it to the judge, and that'll be the end of it."

Millie shrugged. "He never takes himself a real break, does he?" she said to the Carly twin, loud enough for the ranger to hear her. She sipped from the canteen and passed it to the twin.

The two looked over at the ranger a few yards away.

"He hasn't yet that I've seen," the twin replied in the same tone of voice. He sipped the tepid water and wiped one of his cuffed hands across his mouth.

Sam only glanced at them and continued his task.

The two sat in silence for a moment, then Millie whispered to Carly, barely moving her lips, "How the hell did you come up with this twin malarkey?"

Carly whispered in reply, "It's not malarkey. I guess Blake didn't want anybody to know about it—even you."

"You can quit playacting with me, Blake," she whispered. "I know better."

The twin stared at her intently. "Millie, this is not playacting. Seriously. I'm not Blake Carly. I'm Abel, his twin brother."

"You don't have to worry, Blake," she whispered. "He can't hear us. It's me, Millie, you're talking to. I'm on your side. I always was. If I hadn't been you would've been dead long ago. Remember the night Raymond Phelps made the mistake of telling me he was gunning for you? Who tipped you off, huh?" She turned toward him, her face only a few inches from his, her eyes searching his closely.

"Millie, I—"

Before the twin could speak, her lips were pressed upon his. She threw her arms around him and held him to her, not allowing him to pull back. She kissed him long and deeply. At first he tried to stop her, but the warmth in her lips soon caused him to give in. While he did not return her kiss completely, he found himself no longer resisting.

At length Millie turned him loose and gave him a puzzled look, as if now unsure whether or not this was the man she had known so intimately. After a moment, she gave him a halfhearted shove and whispered, "You bastard. I can't believe you're acting this way to me."

"Millie, I'm sorry," the twin whispered, looking past

her face, seeing the ranger watching them. "I almost wish I could tell you that I *am* Blake!" he said, his lips glistening wet from her mouth. "All I can say is, if I *was* Blake, I wouldn't be denying it to you." He smiled, lightly touching his fingers to his lips. "Only a fool would do that. I might not be the wild, daring man my brother Blake was—but I'm no fool."

"Don't you worry, hon." She patted his chest. "Twin or no twin, first chance we get, this dress is coming up and you're going to prove something to me once and for all. That's a promise!"

The Carly twin just stared at her. "Yes, ma'am," he said.

When Sam had finished checking the horses' hooves and allowed both riders and animals a few minutes of rest, the three were back on the trail. An hour later they rode into Taos and found the streets bustling with commerce. Hardly anyone gave a second glance at the twin's handcuffed wrists, but all eyes turned toward Millie, who had switched to a sidesaddle style before they entered town. She rode smoking a cigarette, her legs crossed, revealing a good length of creamy white flesh. Men stared at her from the darkened doorway of the Rose Negra Cantina, and one even called out her name and waved a floppy dust-caked sombrero.

"Well, fellows," Millie said to the twin and the ranger, "looks like business is beckoning me." She grinned. "Now if you two will pardon me." She backed her horse up to the ranger's and held out her hand. "I'd like my gun back now, *por favor*."

"Yes, ma'am," said the ranger, lifting the Thunderer from his waist and handing it to her butt first. "I unloaded it before we got here." He held out his gloved fist and dropped the cartridges into her hand.

Millie smiled. "You untrusting man, you." She put the cartridges into her dress pocket and said, "Thank you, Ranger, for allowing me to ride back here with you."

"You are welcome, ma'am," Sam nodded, touching the brim of his sombrero.

The twin looked at Millie with disappointment. "What about your promise to me?"

Millie had cut her horse away a few feet toward the hitch rail in front of the cantina, but now she reined it back beside the Carly twin, reached out and cupped his cheek for a second and said playfully, "I'm not leaving you—and I haven't forgotten my promise! But I'll have to work tonight to raise enough stage fare to get me over to Benton Wells, won't I?" She looked at the ranger and said, "That is where you're taking him, right?"

"Yes, ma'am," said Sam.

"Then that's where I'm going too," Millie said. "First thing come morning." She smiled at the two of them and said, "Adios, for now."

The ranger and the Carly twin watched her ride her horse to the rail and slip down from her saddle into the waiting arms of two dusty cowhands who had stepped forward from the doorway of the cantina to assist her.

"Let's go, Carly," said the ranger, gesturing the twin forward toward a low-standing adobe hotel twenty yards away.

"Why can't she ride to Benton Wells with *us*, Ranger?" the twin asked, nudging his horse forward. "Instead of having to spend money for stage fare."

"Don't even think about it," the ranger replied.

Chapter 6

Young Julio Luna, his mother, Deanna, and his blind grandfather had pressed hard taking their small herd of goats across the stretch of flatland along the Rio Grande. At dusk the three made a camp near the water's edge and built a fire of dried driftwood that had washed down from the rugged hills towering above them. When Deanna had prepared food and set the old man's wooden bowl in his lap, she called out for Julio to join them. No sooner had her words echoed across the hills above them, then Julio came running wildly toward the camp from farther up the riverbank. He bounded barefoot over rocks and driftwood half his size, sending nervous goats bleating in all directions.

"Mother, Grandfather! Come quickly!" he blurted in Spanish, his face flushed, his breath heaving in his chest. "There is a dead man in the water!" He held up a wet boot—the expensive hand-tooled boot that had belonged to the Carly twin. "I tried to pull him from the river, but his boot came off in my hands!"

"Let me feel it, Grandson," said the old man. Setting his wooden bowl aside he reached out gropingly until Juilo handed the boot to him. Deftly the old

man's brittle fingers traveled over the boot, taking in
the stitching, the shape of the heel, the slight wear
on the sole.

"Come, Julio," said Deanna, knowing her son to
be a serious young man, not doubting him for a moment. "You must take me to him!"

As the woman and her son hurried away, the old
man held on to the boot and stood up slowly, taking
his time. Reaching for his long wooden staff beside
him, he felt his way through the rocks behind them,
knowing by their scent and the smell of the goats
and the sound of the river that he was headed in the
right direction. But before he caught up to his daugh-
ter and her son, his senses discovered something else
in the drifting air. He stopped and stood still as a
stone for a moment, his cloudy white eyes seeming
to search from deep within their dark shell. "Sante
Madre," he whispered, crossing himself. Then he
turned and hurried back through the disgruntled
goats to the campsite.

At the water's edge, Deanna hiked her dress up
and waded out ten feet, following Julio across the
sharp, rocky river bottom to the body lying facedown
between a protruding boulder and a pile of driftwood, bobbing steadily in the silty water. She gasped
at the sight of the gaping hole in the back of the
corpse's head.

"Perhaps we should go and leave him for someone
else to find," she said, thinking out loud.

"But we must bury him, Mother," Julio replied.
"Grandfather says we must honor the dead no less
than we honor the living."

"Yes, this is so," said Deanna. "But sometimes perhaps it is better to let things be as they are and not
interfere." She looked back quickly along the river,

wondering why her father had not yet caught up to them. Her eyes went back to the corpse as her son leaned over it and struggled to turn it onto its back.

"Help me, Mother," said Julio. "We must see who this man is so we can describe him to people in Olla Sucia."

"Yes, of course." Deanna leaned down and helped him after quickly gathering her dress above her knees and tucking it into her waist. When she and Julio felt the body give way and flop the rest of the way over on its own, Deanna stepped back and gasped, her hand going over her mouth as she saw the purple-white flesh surrounding the bullet's exit hole in the man's forehead. Julio also jumped back at the sight of it.

"Mother! He has been killed!" the boy said in awe. "Look at the hole! Look at the color of his skin!"

"Yes, I see, Julio!" said Deanna, feeling a sudden urge to turn and leave this place quickly. "Let us take a look in order to identify him—then we must leave here!"

"We must wait for Grandfather," said Julio. "Grandfather will want to bury this man!"

"No, Julio! Do not disagree with me," said his mother. "We must hurry and leave this place. We will make camp farther up the trail. Take a good look at this man so we can remember his face."

Dutifully, the boy forced himself to stare intently at the dead man's face for a moment. Grimacing, he said, "I think he has been in the river a long time. He looks terrible."

"Yes, he looks terrible," the woman agreed. She crossed herself. "A violent death is an ugly death."

Behind her at the river's edge a voice called out, "He never was *real* pretty to begin with, ma'am."

Stunned by the sound of the voice, Deanna and Julio turned and saw the horsemen gathering their mounts along the water. At the center sat Barton Creed, smiling at her, his wrists crossed on his saddle horn as his horse lowered its muzzle into the water. In Creed's right hand he loosely held a long-barreled Colt.

Deanna reached out, grabbed Julio by his shoulders and pulled him close against her, lest he attempt to do something brave and foolish. As the two stood, frightened and helpless, Creed stepped down from his saddle and handed his reins to Billy Drew, who had just pulled his horse up beside Creed's. Next to Creed, Mongo Barnes stepped down and did the same thing, causing Drew to frown as he now had two sets of reins in his gloved hands.

Wading out through the shallow water toward the woman and her son, Creed said in disgust to Mongo Barnes as he stared at the corpse's pasty face, "I'll be a son of a bitch if he ain't gone and got himself killed!"

"There goes all our plans, then," Mongo said with equal disgust. Finally, after staring at the pale, dead face with its shattered skull and its eyes partly open and staring blankly, the two men looked at one another, then at the woman.

"What happened to him?" Creed asked her flatly in a demanding tone.

"We do not know what happened to him," Julio responded quickly before his mother could answer. "I only found him here a few moments ago."

"Did I ask you anything, you little nit?" said Creed, stepping in close and tapping his pistol barrel on Julio's head.

"Por favor!" cried Deanna, drawing Julio back a

step and placing her hand on his forehead. "He is telling you the truth! We found him like this. We are not killers! We did him no harm!"

Creed cut a mirthless grin to Mongo Barnes and said, "Hear that? They ain't killers, these two."

"They sure could have fooled me," said Mongo. His eyes roamed over Deanna's bare legs and her breasts, her frightened breathing causing him to smile. Over his shoulder he called out, "Billy Boy, do these folks look like killers to you?"

Billy Drew said sullenly, "Nobody ever called me 'Billy Boy' in my life, so don't even try to get it started."

Ignoring Billy, Mongo called out to the other four, "Dick? What about you boys? Don't you think this woman looks like a killer, this dress hiked up and all?"

Dick Spivey, Arnold Prather, Denton "The Blade" Ermy, and Ray Hightower stared hungrily at the woman.

"I can't speak for Blake Carly, but she's damn sure killing me," Dick Spivey replied. He looked back and forth along the riverbank, then said to Mongo, "Ask the señorita if she and this boy are traveling alone."

Thinking quickly about her blind father, Deanna said, "No, we are not alone. We have a large herd of goats, and my husband and all of his goat herders are coming up the trail right now. They are armed and they are mounted—!"

"Whooeee!" Mongo Barnes laughed, cutting her off. "You get her started, she sure knows how to lay it on hot and heavy!" He laughed, stepped in close, jerked Julio away from her and shoved him off his feet. The boy landed in a splash beside the corpse. Staring hard at the woman up close, Mongo said, "I ain't never seen a goat herder who could afford a donkey and a bolo, let alone a gun and a horse!"

Knowing what would come and dreading it, Deanna nevertheless stood firm, her feet planted beneath her in the silty river bottom. "It is true. If you do not leave right now, my husband will kill every one of you!"

"Oh!" said Mongo. "Then I expect maybe you are a killer!"

On his back in the water, Julio saw the men move closer to his mother, like wolves surrounding a wounded doe. The ones on horseback, including Billy Drew, stepped down from their saddles and let their reins fall to the ground. Julio scooted backward in the shallow water until he could rise to his feet and slip unnoticed to the riverbank.

Deanna smelled sour whiskey and chewing tobacco in her face as Mongo Barnes snatched the front of her dress and gave her a hard jerk forward, pulling her against him. "Answer me right now, killer woman. Are you going to give it up easy like, or do we have to take it from you the hard way?"

"My—my dress—it is the only one I have," Deanna said in defeat. "*Por favor*, let me take it off and put it on the rock." She gestured toward the boulder beside the corpse. Behind the men she had seen her son slip away toward their horses. Her only hope was that she could keep them distracted. She prayed silently that Julio would run away, but she feared he would not.

"Hot damn, boys!" said Dick Spivey, watching Deanna loosen the drawstring at her bodice and pull the dress down off her shoulders and below her firm breasts. "I'm sorry as hell ole Blake is dead, but this ain't no bad way to end the day!"

For a lingering moment Deanna stood naked before them, allowing their eyes to touch her as she folded her dress and laid it down. She could no longer see Julio, and she could only pray that he had left. She turned back to the men and spread her arms slightly. "If I lay down with each of you, will you not hurt me or my son?"

"Hurt you?" Barton Creed reached out and took her hand. "Well, maybe we'll hurt you just a little bit," he chuckled, turning her toward the riverbank, leading her along, the rest of the men following, each eager to take his turn with her.

As Creed walked her past the horse toward a stand of young saplings, Dick Spivey looked at his horse and said suddenly, "Hey! Where the hell's my rifle?" He glanced down and saw the bare footprints on the sandy riverbank. Then he swung around quickly, his eyes following the footprints off along the shoreline. "Where's that damned kid?"

He'd hardly gotten the words out of his mouth when a shot sounded and a bullet slammed into his shoulder, twisted him around and flung him backward into the water.

"What the hell?" shouted Creed, turning the woman loose and ducking with the rest of the men, his Colt up and ready.

"There!" shouted Mongo. Fifty yards away they saw the old man staggering back and forth blindly, waving his staff in one hand and a battered Walker Colt horse pistol in the other. The pistol had no direction until Mongo's voice seemed to draw it toward him. Stunned by the spectacle, the gunmen didn't respond instantly. Another shot thundered, this one aimed at the sound of Mongo's voice but stopped by

Spivey's big dun horse, which stood between him and the blind man. The horse went down with a long, screaming whinny, and the rest of the horses fled in terror.

"He's killing our horses!" Creed bellowed. "Shoot him!" He fired three shots as he shouted, but his bullets could not hit the weaving, staggering blind man. Nor could the bullets of the others as the old man homed in on the sound of Creed's voice and leveled a shot at him. Creed's hat was lifted from his head and sent spinning away. Bullets sliced through the air, danced wildly off of rocks and thumped into driftwood all around the elusive old goat herder. But none of them found their target.

Mongo Barnes shrieked loudly at the men, "Damn it! Either shoot him or run in and beat him to death with your gun barrels! He's got to die!" Knowing now that the old man would aim at the sound of his voice, Mongo crouched, taking close aim, ready to fire as soon as the man stopped staggering long enough to pull the trigger. "I've got you now, you blind old son of a bitch," Mongo said under his breath.

The goat herder staggered backward a step when the bullet sliced past him. To the men it appeared the bullet had hit him. They held their fire and stared in disbelief, expecting to see the old man crumple to the ground. Instead, he staggered back and forth, the big horse pistol still waving wildly above his head. Billy Drew said to the others, "What the hell is this?" Then they saw the blind goat herder stagger toward the cover of the rocks.

"Jesus!" said Ray Hightower. "He ain't human! No wonder his eyes are all white!"

"He's just blind, damn it!" said Denton the Blade, discounting Hightower's claim. "He's as human as you and me!"

"Oh, yeah?" said Hightower. "Then maybe you better explain why a bullet in the chest didn't kill him!"

"Shut up and shoot him before he gets away!" shouted Mongo Barnes. "Or do I have to do everything all by my damn self?"

The men turned to aim at the old man, but before any of them could get a shot off, rifle fire exploded from the stand of trees behind them along the riverbank, and the old man vanished into the hillside.

Shot after shot came from the trees. Finally Creed caught a glimpse of the boy, who had taken the rifle and was making good use of it. "It's only that kid!" Creed shouted. "Rush him!"

"Rush him, hell!" said Spivey, gripping his wounded shoulder. "Those bullets don't know who's firing them! They'll still punch a hole in your belly!"

"I'll be a son of a bitch," Creed cursed, looking around and seeing that the old man was gone. When he turned toward the water he saw that the woman had also vanished. From the trees the rifle fire stopped. "Blake Carly is dead. We've lost our horses and been ambushed and outshot by a blind man! I've got to go somewhere and do some serious thinking about what in the living hell I'm doing here!"

Realizing that the woman, the blind man and the child had disappeared into the hills above them, Creed and the others spent more than an hour rounding up their horses. When they were finished they gathered around the campfire that the woman had prepared earlier. Billy Drew, Arnold Prather and

Ray Hightower dragged the Carly twin's corpse out of the river and watched Creed search its pockets thoroughly. Mongo Barnes stood back a few feet and said sarcastically, "You don't really think Blake Carly was stupid enough to write down directions to that hidden gold, do you?"

"I don't know if Blake was *stupid* enough to do that or not," said Creed, raising his voice in anger and disgust, "but I'd hate like hell to look back someday and realize we was all too *stupid* to search him just in case he *did*!" He stepped away from the corpse, wiping his wet hands on his trousers. Seeing that Creed was through searching the body, Prather and Hightower gave one another a knowing grin.

Prather said, "I reckon we ought to give ole Blake a little send-off, don't you think?"

Billy Drew didn't answer until moments later, when Hightower walked to his saddlebags and came back with a bottle of whiskey. "Now you're talking," said Billy, accepting the bottle.

He threw back a drink and watched the two men prop the corpse up against a rock. As the bottle went from hand to hand, each man gave a short salute and said a few words to the pale, wet body. Once the bottle had drawn all the men together and made its rounds, Prather lightened up the group by finding a straw hat that had fallen from the old blind man's head earlier and placing it on the dead Carly twin. Raising a chuckle from the men, Prather then pulled the corpse's eyes open wide, giving it a comical leer.

"Here, try this," said Hightower. He rolled a smoke, lit it and stuck it in the corpse's mouth.

"All right, let's show some respect," said Creed. "Blake was one of our own." But he couldn't help but smile at the ridiculous look on the corpse's face.

Finishing off the bottle of whiskey, Creed cocked his head slightly and said to the corpse in a raised voice, "Blake Carly, you dead son of a bitch! Where's that gold? Huh? Can't you come back to life just long enough to tell us that?"

Prather took the empty bottle from Creed's hand and stuck it in the hand of the dead Carly twin, wrapping the cold, stiff fingers around it and propping it on his knee. "There, that's more like it," he chuckled.

"It ain't right messing around with the dead like this," said Mongo, who was seated on the ground three feet from the corpse. As he spoke, the body began falling slowly forward. Mongo didn't see it until it landed facedown in his lap. He let out a shriek and jumped up from the ground cursing, his hands trembling. The men hooted with laughter, all except Dick Spivey, who sat nursing his wounded shoulder and avoiding the flat stare of his dead comrade.

"Damn it!" shouted Mongo, "this ain't funny!" He slapped water and the burning bits of tobacco from his trousers and stomped away, not wanting the men to see how rattled he was by the incident.

"This beats all," said Prather. "As many men as Mongo's killed, still he gets spooked by a dead man falling on him!"

Again laughter roared through the night.

Before dark, Denton the Blade had snatched up a young goat, slaughtered it with his long boot knife, stuck it on a spit and hung it above the flames. By the time darkness had surrounded the campsite, the blackened goat carcass sizzled and dripped juice into the fire. When the round of laughter had played itself out, Denton the Blade carved a slice of meat, blew on it, tested it, then said, "Damn, boys, it ain't as sweet as that naked woman, but it's still mighty good. Dig in!"

"It's about damn time," said Prather. "I'm near starved to death."

The men came forward, sliced themselves some of the hot, tender meat and sat down to eat. They set cups of boiling hot coffee beside them to cool.

"Speaking of that woman, I hate like hell letting her get away," said Denton the Blade, *"especially* after seeing her naked." He whistled under his breath, then looked at the dead Carly twin, who Prather and Hightower had righted and reequipped with a burning cigarette and a cup of steaming hot coffee. "Ain't that right, Blake, ole pard?"

"We all hated it, but it's too late to worry over it," Creed said firmly, not wanting to dwell on the fact that they'd let her slip right through their fingers.

"They're still up there somewheres," said Billy Drew, peering into the darkness of the jagged hill line. "Probably laughing at us. And they have every reason to, far as I'm concerned." He shook his head in disgust. "We ought not call ourselves outlaws after letting something like that happen."

"That's enough, Billy Boy," said Mongo Barnes, as upset as Creed was about losing the woman and having their horses scattered.

Billy Drew took a long, patient breath and let it out slowly. Rising from the ground, he dusted the seat of his trousers and said, "I told you once before as politely as I could not to call me Billy *Boy*. Get on your feet, Mongo. It's time we decide which dog has the bite and which one has the growl."

"Whoa, now. Hold on, both of yas," said Creed, standing up quickly.

"Suits the hell out of me," said Mongo, rising into a stance, his feet spread, his hand near his gun.

"Huh-uh," said Billy Drew, shaking his head. He moved his hands slowly to his gun belt, unfastened it and let it fall. "I ain't looking for no gunfight with you. I'm just going to hang a frog on both your eyes for all of us to look at the next week or two. Maybe then you'll start taking me more serious."

Mongo grinned cruelly and dropped his own gun belt and kicked it aside with the toe of his boot. Stepping forward with his fists balled and half raised, he said, "There ain't nothing I like better than teaching a young Texas punk-wood like you how a real man fights—"

But he barely got the words out of his mouth before the young Texan hammered his jaw with a hard straight left that staggered him backward a step.

Mongo caught himself, shook his head and tried to recover. But Billy wouldn't allow it. He charged in, hitting him once, twice, three times with a fast, jabbing left. Each punch resounded with the dull thud of knuckles against bone. The men winced as blood flew from Mongo's nose and split eyelids.

"Billy! He's had enough!" shouted Creed.

"Almost," said Billy Drew. He stepped in close enough to grab Mongo by the front of his shirt, steadying the staggering man while he launched a hard, rounding right hook that sent Mongo flat on his back, knocked out cold.

"Jesus!" Denton the Blade said in awe.

Prather stepped over and looked down at Mongo's limp form, lying crumpled and bloodied. Chuckling, he shook his head and said, "Damned if he don't look worse than Blake Carly over there!"

"He's not dead, is he?" Creed asked, moving beside Prather.

"No," Billy Drew said confidently, wiping his bloody knuckles on a wadded-up bandanna, "but he'll wish he was for a day or two." He looked around at the others. "It's a serious thing calling a man a name he doesn't want to be called."

"Billy, I think he was just doing it funning with you," said Hightower.

"They always try to say they're only funning with you," Billy replied. "But making up a nickname and hanging it on you is their way of making you look small. I won't tolerate it. I hope everybody understands that." He looked from one face to the next, stopping at Barton Creed.

"Yeah," said Creed, sounding a bit irritated with the young Texan. "I believe we all see that you're serious about it." He and Prather stooped and lifted Mongo to his feet. "You better hope he doesn't decide to settle this score with a gun."

"Let him," said Billy Drew. "I'm better with a gun than I am with my fists any day."

The men just looked at him as Billy reached down to pick up his gun belt.

"Speaking of guns, leave that one where it's laying," said a voice from the outer edge of the firelight. Billy Drew froze at the sound of a hammer cocking. So did the others, their eyes turning to the four men standing in a semicircle around them.

"I'll be damned," Creed whispered, realizing they had been caught completely off guard. "Is there *anybody* who can't ambush this bunch?" he asked in disgust. He shot the other men a look of outrage and disbelief. They all were stunned. Mongo stood limply

between him and Prather, his arms looped around
their shoulders, his head hanging to his chest. Billy
Drew stood poised but made no move toward his
gun belt. Hightower and Denton the Blade saw the
spot they were all in and raised their hands in
surrender.

"I won't tell you again," said Dayton Clifford,
stepping forward with his Colt cocked and pointed
at Billy Drew from fifteen feet away and growing
closer with each step. Billy straightened up and took
a step back, his hands also rising. "That's very pru-
dent of you, sir," Clifford said to him. Turning his
attention back toward Creed and Prather, he said,
"Raise your free hands, gentlemen."

"Can we sit him down?" Creed asked. "He's getting heavy."

"No," said Clifford. "Both of you remain as you
are." He motioned for Lon Pence to come forward
from the outer edge of the firelight, saying, "Lift their
guns and drop them in a pile, Lon."

As Lon moved forward cautiously and did as he
was told, Clifford looked at the corpse sitting against
a rock. While he and his men had watched from the
cover of darkness, they'd seen the corpse fall over on
Mongo Barnes. "Did I hear someone say that this is
Blake Carly?" he asked. Looking closer at the body,
Clifford saw that the cigarette had burned down to
within a fraction of its blue lips.

The men stood silent for a moment. Finally Creed
said, "Mister, he's dead."

"I can see he's dead," said Clifford, turning his
gun barrel toward Creed. "Are you going to make
me ask again?"

Creed said quickly, "He *is* Blake Carly. Leastwise

he *was* Blake Carly. I reckon there's no harm in saying so now."

"No harm at all," said Clifford. He motioned for Ben Mazzel and Kenny Brewer to come in closer. The guides had wanted no part of sneaking up on Creed and his gang, but the vision of Rawhide Hale being torn apart in the tips of the pine trees still stood out vividly in their minds. Dayton Clifford expected his orders to be obeyed. Mazzel eased forward first, coving the gunmen with his rifle. Kenny Brewer followed suit, a few feet away from Mazzel, both of them with their rifles aimed and ready.

Moving over in front of the dead Carly twin, Clifford reached out with the tip of his pistol and flipped the straw hat off the corpse's head, then stepped back, bemused at the sight of the bullet hole in the forehead. "Uh-oh! He must've made someone angry." He gave a short grin over his shoulder to the men standing with their hands raised. "I trust none of you had anything to do with this?"

Creed started to answer, but then he thought better of it and said, "That all depends—is there a price on his head?"

"No," said Clifford, taking out a folded poster from inside his duster and opening it. "At least none that applies to the general public."

"The general public?" Creed gave him a curious look as Clifford compared the face on the poster to the pale, blank face sitting before him.

"This is Blake Carly, all right." Clifford smiled in satisfaction without answering Creed. Mazzel, Pence and Brewer looked at one another in relief, hoping that now they could get away from Clifford and return home.

"Who are you men?" Creed asked. "You don't sound like you're from around here."

"Thank you," said Clifford. "I'm not."

"Back East?" asked Creed.

Clifford didn't answer.

Emboldened, Creed said, "I didn't see no badge on you, did I?"

"No," said Clifford, still studying the dead man's face as he leveled his Colt more intently at Creed, "but that doesn't really matter, does it, since we all have loaded firearms pointed at your bellies?"

"That's true enough," said Creed, easing back, "but I would like to know who's standing behind those *loaded firearms*, if that's not being too pushy on my part."

"Of course," said Clifford, stepping away from the corpse. He folded the poster and put it away. "I'm Dayton Clifford, a man hunter from Chicago, in the employ of a prominent gentleman who wishes to remain anonymous." He smiled. "I hope you'll understand."

Creed shrugged and raised his free hand, the knocked-out Mongo getting heavier by the second. "Hell, sure, why not?"

"Very good," said Clifford. He made a sweeping gesture toward Mazzel and the other two. "These gentlemen are trail guides—Mister Mazzel, Mister Brewer and Mister Pence."

Creed and his men nodded in unison, not sure how to take the words or the mannerisms of Dayton Clifford. "If you don't mind my asking," said Creed, "how much is this *prominent* fellow paying for ole Blake here?"

"Not enough for us to share," said Clifford. He looked at Mazzel and the others. "Right, fellows?"

"Yeah, that's right," said Mazzel. "So don't nobody go getting any ideas. We're not sharing what's ours."

"There. You see?" said Clifford.

"It doesn't seem right," said Creed, taking on an attitude as he passed his men a guarded glance. "Ole Blake there and us have been pals for a long time. You've got to give us something for our trouble, dragging him out of the river and all."

Clifford said, "You are in no position to make demands, Creed."

Creed looked stunned. "How did you know my name?"

Patting his duster lapel, Clifford said, "I know your name because I have your picture right here." He grinned. "Do you care to see it?"

Creed looked even more stunned. Fear clouded his brow. "Is there anybody *else* here that you're hired to hunt down?"

"No," said Clifford. "Believe me, if I were hunting you, Creed, you would be *very* dead right now."

"Just thought I ought to ask," Creed said, looking relieved as he saw Clifford uncock his big bone-handled Colt and lower it slightly.

Noting the change in the outlaw leader's expression, Clifford said, "But don't get too relaxed, Creed. I might kill you anyway if you don't give me a straight answer about the hidden gold."

Creed's eyes widened. "*What* hidden gold?"

"The gold I heard you talking about while we sat watching from behind those rocks," said Clifford, gesturing toward the rocky perimeter of the campsite. Quickly he cocked the Colt again and leveled it at Creed's belly.

"Wait a minute, damn it!" Creed pleaded. "You

caught me by surprise! Hell, I'll tell you about the gold!" He glanced at the others. "Why not? Nobody's ever going to find it now! Blake was the only one who knew where it was." He shrugged. "I ain't even sure he found out where it's at!" He nodded toward the wide-eyed corpse. "Somebody opened his skull before he got back to us!"

"I see your lips moving, Creed," said Clifford, "but so far you haven't said a word that makes any sense to me."

Creed saw the man's gloved hand tighten on the Colt. "All right, I'm trying to!" he said. "There was a crooked sheriff in Benton Wells, over in the territory. Him and some banker was in cahoots on having a shipment of government gold stolen. The sheriff killed the four men who did the stealing. Then he hid the gold for safekeeping until the heat died down and the army quit searching for it!"

"And what was Blake Carly's hand in all this?" Clifford asked, his expression revealing nothing that was going through his mind.

"Blake knew the sheriff was crooked. The two had been owl-hoots together up in Wind River country a few years back. Blake had the goods on him and was threatening to turn him in to the law if the sheriff didn't show him where the gold was hidden."

"That sounds weak to me," said Clifford.

"I can't help how it sounds," said Creed. "But ole Blake there could be awfully persuasive with a gun in one hand and a cutting knife in the other. I've seen him nut a mustang quicker than you could say 'Help Sally up.' It's my guess that the sheriff showed him what he wanted to see. But now I reckon I'll never know for sure." He gazed over at the dead body sitting with its cold, stiff fingers wrapped around the whiskey bottle.

Clifford chuckled slightly and shook his head as he uncocked the Colt again and lowered it a couple of inches. "I expected to hear a few saddle bums tell some good trail yarns once I got out here, but I never thought I'd hear one this good, this soon." He took his pipe out of his duster, filled it with tobacco from a small leather pouch, then held it in his teeth, smiling. "Let's see—" he reflected, "we've got a hidden treasure, a crooked sheriff, a crooked banker, and a dead outlaw who is the only person who may, or may not, have learned where the gold was hidden— before he died, of course."

"Mister, I'm no saddle bum and this is no trail yarn," said Creed, trying to maintain some self-respect now that it appeared that Clifford wasn't interested in killing him. "You said tell you the straight-up truth, and that's it."

"All right, if you say so," Clifford replied as if dismissing the matter. "Out of curiosity, though, who is this crooked sheriff and banker?"

Creed looked even more relieved. He lowered his hand a few inches and said, "The banker is a fellow named Aubrey. The sheriff is Ed Tarpin. Can we please turn this man loose? He's getting mighty heavy."

"Sure," said Clifford. "Drop him."

Prather and Creed turned Mongo loose at the same time, and he fell to the ground with a solid thud. Creed rubbed his shoulder. "Much obliged," said Creed. Seeing Clifford eyeing the sizzling goat meat, Creed decided to try to get on the man's good side. He gestured toward the coffeepot and the meat above the fire. "Boys, where the hell's our manners?" he said to Denton the Blade, who stood nearest the fire with his long boot knife hanging loosely in his hand. "Mister Clifford, have you fellows et yet?"

"Thank you." Clifford smiled. He studied the meat on the spit, took out a sulphur match, struck it, and lit his pipe. Then he took the long knife from Denton the Blade's hand, stabbed it up to its hilt into the meat and lifted it off the fire. "Here," he said to Mazzel. "Carry this to the horses for us."

"Hold on," said Creed. "I meant for us to share it with you!"

"I know," said Clifford, "and we appreciate it." He wagged his pistol barrel toward Denton the Blade and said, "Pour that coffee into a canteen and hand it to Lon here." Turning back to Creed, he said, "We're going to pack Carly's body on one of your horses and spook the rest of your horses away."

"Damn," said Creed. "We just rounded them horses up a while ago!"

"I know," said Clifford, showing no sympathy. "We're going to bag up your guns and take them with us too."

"Hold on now!" said Creed. "This ain't Chicago! You can't leave a man *unarmed*. That ain't how things are done out here. It ain't civilized. We can't defend ourselves against whatever might come upon us!"

Clifford puffed his pipe and said, "Apparently being *armed* hasn't helped you much so far," he said, gesturing toward the pile of guns lying on the ground. "When you get your horses collected, I hope you won't come looking for us. If I thought you might, I'd have to kill you right now." He raised the Colt, tensing his hand on the butt.

"No, we won't come looking for you," said Creed,

now mortified and defeated before his men. "You've got my word on it."

On the ground Mongo Barnes moaned and struggled into a sitting position, while the rest of the men stood silently watching the guides load the body onto a horse.

"What hit me?" Mongo asked in a groggy voice, wincing as he touched his swollen eyes.

"Billy just beat the living hell out of you, Mongo. Now sit still and shut up," Creed said in a hushed tone, not wanting Clifford and his guides to come back to the campfire.

But then Mongo saw the three men loading the body while Clifford stood looking back at the outlaws with his Colt trained on them. "Who's this? What are they doing with our horses?"

"They're taking them," said Creed in disgust and shame. "Now shut up."

"Like hell," said Mongo. His hand went to his empty holster.

"My gun's gone!" he said.

"Yeah," said Creed. "They took it."

His head clearing a bit, Mongo began to realize their situation. "What are we going to do?" he whispered.

"What can we do?" Creed whispered in reply. "We're going to wait till they leave, gather our horses and rearm ourselves somewhere." He stared flatly at Dayton Clifford and his guides as they mounted up and rode away, Mazzel carrying the roasted meat and a canteen full of hot coffee. "That pushy Chicago son of a bitch ain't seen the last of us."

Chapter 7

Two hundred yards along the trail, Lon Pence hurled the bag full of guns out into the Rio Grande with a hearty laugh. "I've heard of Barton Creed and his gunmen for the longest time, but damned if I thought I'd someday be pointing a gun at his belly. They weren't so tough, were they, Mazzel?"

"Hell, no," said Ben Mazzel, riding behind him and Kenny Brewer. "I'll never forget the look on their faces when they watched us shoo their horses away!" He laughed aloud. Riding away from the disarmed outlaws with the young roasted goat held up on his knife had Mazzel feeling better than he had since they'd met up with Dayton Clifford. The canteen of coffee hanging from his saddle horn was warm against his leg. Looking back over his shoulder in the darkness at the body of Blake Carly lying face-down across the saddle, Mazzel said to Kenny Brewer and Lon Pence, "Whoeeee, boys! That was slicker than socks on a rooster!"

Lon Pence grinned and nodded in agreement. Riding a few yards behind the three, Dayton Clifford only smiled to himself.

"I hope you remember to mention to Mister Aubrey just how quick we managed to get this situation taken care of," said Mazzel. Then, recalling the incident with Rawhide Hale's murder, he added, "I realize we had what you might call some minor misunderstandings till we all got used to one another. But hot damn!" He grinned again, looking back over his shoulder. "I believe we could bring most anybody in now that we're working together as well as—"

Cutting him off, Kenny Brewer said, "I don't call Rawhide getting ripped apart by them big pines a minor misunderstanding!" He didn't look back at Dayton Clifford, but Clifford got the message. "Far as I'm concerned, Rawhide was my friend and I ain't forgetting him."

"Hush up, Kenny, damn it!" Lon Pence whispered harshly. "We've done what we set out to do. Let's leave well enough alone!"

"Yeah," said Mazzel in the same low tone. "Don't go aggravating the man. We've still got to ask him for our money."

"Why do we have to *ask* for our money?" said Kenny Brewer, letting his voice become louder with no regard for Clifford riding behind them. "We earned the money! There's Blake Carly's body, the job is done! We shouldn't have to go asking for our money with our hats in our hands!"

"What's the trouble up here?" asked Clifford, riding up beside Ben Mazzel.

"Nothing, Mister Clifford," said Mazzel. "Just some talk amongst us about where we're heading now that this job is finished."

"Nonsense," said Clifford. "I heard someone mention the money you have coming." He stared straight at Kenny Brewer.

Brewer slowed his horse until he and Clifford were side by side. "That's right," he said, feeling confident now that they had proved themselves capable of standing up against the likes of Barton Creed and his men. "I told Mazzel and Lon here that we need to get our money from you and push on. The job's over, we did what was expected, Blake Carly is dead. What more is left to be done?"

Considering Kenny's words, Clifford took his pipe from his mouth and said, "You're absolutely right." He nodded toward a flat clear spot along the riverbank where the water glistened and shimmered black in the light of a full moon. "Let's stop, eat our goat meat and drink our coffee. I'll get the money from my saddlebags and we'll settle up." He looked back and forth between the three. "How does that sound to everybody?"

"Sounds good to me," said Kenny firmly. Mazzel and Pence only nodded, recalling how quickly and casually Clifford had killed Rawhide Hale.

"What about you two?" Clifford asked, looking at Mazzel, then Pence, forcing them to share their opinions.

"Whatever you want to do, Mister Clifford," said Mazzel. "You're the boss. I'll go along with whatever you think is best."

"Same here," said Pence. "It's been a pleasure riding with you. However you want to settle up suits me to the top of my head."

Listening to Mazzel, Kenny grumbled under his breath and spit in disgust. "Settle up with me, Clifford," said Kenny, dropping the "Mister." "The sooner the better."

"Indeed, then . . ." Clifford said quietly, letting his words trail off as he veered toward the clearing. Behind him Kenny Brewer gave Mazzel and Pence a smug look. But when he faced forward again, he saw Clifford turn in his saddle and point his big Colt at his chest.

"Wait!" Kenny pleaded. But his voice was drowned out by the fiery explosion. The shot lifted him from his saddle and flung him dead onto the ground.

"Good God!" Mazzel shouted, having to struggle to keep both his horse and the horse he led from bolting. At the same time he struggled with holding the roast on the knife blade while behind him the body of the dead Carly twin flopped up and down wildly until he got the horses under control.

"Can you handle those animals?" Clifford asked harshly, with no apparent regard for having just killed Kenny Brewer.

"Yes, sir, Mister Clifford!" said Mazzel, seeing the barrel of the big Colt glistening in the moonlight, pointed in his direction now. "I've got them settled, don't you worry!"

"That's right! We're all settled here!" Lon Pence said in a shaky voice, jerking his own horse by its reins to keep it under control.

"All right," said Clifford, "let's eat and get this money distributed."

"We ain't concerned with the money, Mister Clifford," said Mazzel. "Money never was the main thing for me. The most important thing for me was to make sure I done a good job." He shrugged nervously. "Hell, you can pay me later on, whenever it suits you."

Clifford tuned his gaze to Pence. "What about you, Lon?"

"Me too! Sure enough," Lon said quickly, smelling

a waft of burnt gunpowder drifting on the still night air. "Alls I wanted was to be of service. There's more to being a guide than how much money is in it—I believe this world is getting too damned concerned with how much money folks can make and they've forgotten what it means to do a job they can be proud of. Far as I'm concerned—"

"I agree," said Clifford, cutting the frightened man off. He gestured toward the river with his pistol barrel. "Now let's eat."

But the two men hesitated, looking down at the body lying in the dirt.

"Oh, him?" said Clifford. "Don't worry, you can drag him off the trail after we've eaten."

"Mister Clifford," Mazzel ventured warily, "me and Lon here don't want to die. We'd rather you just keep the money and we'll call it even."

"Don't talk foolish," said Clifford. "You men have done your job. I'm going to see to it you get what's coming to you." He looked down at Kenny Brewer. "That young man had a terrible attitude. I had to kill him. I hope you both understand that. He even made an obscene gesture toward me."

The two stared, stunned and silent until finally Mazzel said, "He did?"

"Certainly he did," said Clifford, "unless you think I killed him for no *good* reason."

"No, sir, we *never* thought that!" Mazzel said quickly, his eyes widening. "Not for a second! Did we, Lon?"

"Not us! No-siree!" said Pence. The two were willing to say anything to keep Clifford from killing them too.

"Yes, it's true," Clifford continued. "The day we met he made an obscene and disrespectful gesture with his finger. He did like this." Clifford raised his middle finger and pushed it up the bridge of his nose. "He pretended to be adjusting his shade spectacles. But it was pretty clear what he was doing."

Mazzel and Pence looked at one another for a second, fear shining in their eyes. "Well, then by God," said Mazzel. "What else could you have done but killed him? That's what I want to know!"

"Me too!" said Lon.

Clifford smiled slightly. "Let's go eat."

"Yes, sir," said Mazzel, gigging his horse forward, Lon right beside him. Looking back at Clifford, Mazzel gratefully watched him shove the big-bellied gun back into its holster. "Just out of curiosity, Mister Clifford," he said, "I hope me and Lon here ain't done nothing disrespectful, have we? God knows if we did, we sure never intended to, did we, Lon?"

"No!" Lon said sharply, a slight tremor in his voice. "I know I sure never!"

Instead of replying, Clifford chuckled and stuck his pipe back in his mouth. "Don't forget what curiosity did for the cat, fellows," he said quietly.

"Jesus, Mazzel, what are we going to do?" Lon whispered when they'd gotten far enough ahead that he thought they might be out of hearing distance.

"Shut up!" Mazzel hissed in reply. "That man has hearing sharp as a trailing hound! Just do like he tells us, is all I know to do!"

"Should we rush him?"

"Not me," whispered Mazzel. "I never seen a man as fast as him with a gun!"

"I never seen him draw it," said Lon, "so I can't say."

"I never saw him draw it either," Mazzel whispered. "That's how I *can* say!"

"How the hell did he get to be that fast with a gun living in Chicago?" Lon asked, as the two stopped their horses at the clearing and stepped down.

"I don't know and I don't care to know," said Mazzel. "Now shut up before he thinks we're plotting something!"

When Clifford stepped down from his horse and joined them, Mazzel asked, "Would you like us to build a campfire, Mister Clifford?"

"No, don't bother," said Clifford. "There's enough moonlight." He carried his sleeping blanket under his arm. "Lon, unsaddle my horse and bring my saddle over to me," he said.

"Right away, Mister Clifford," said Lon, hurrying to his task.

"Oh, it's no bother at all, Mister Clifford!" said Mazzel, still concerned with the fire. "If you want a fire we'll sure work one up!"

Clifford smiled to himself and puffed his pipe. "The food's already cooked, the coffee's already boiled. I think we're fine."

"Are you sure, Mister Clifford?" Lon Pence asked, stepping in with Clifford's saddle in his hands. "Because we can have one going in no time if you—"

"Damn it, Lon! You heard him," said Mazzel, cutting Lon off. "We're fine. He ain't wanting no fire!"

Clifford smiled to himself and whispered as he plopped down onto the blanket he'd spread and looked up at the stars, "Yes . . . we're doing just fine."

They ate and sipped coffee, Mazzel and Pence sitting as if at attention, ready to jump quickly at Clifford's command. When Clifford finished and lay back on his blanket and flipped half of it over himself, he said in a sleepy voice as he rested his hand on the bone-handled pistol butt across his chest, "Don't forget to drag your friend off of the trail."

"No, sir, we won't forget," said Mazzel, he and Pence giving one another a worried look. They sat staring silently at Clifford for a moment, then got up without a word and walked up to the trail in the moonlight.

Out of hearing distance, Mazzel said, "I'd make a run for it, but I swear I believe he's already thought it out and knows a way to stop us!"

"Yeah, and kill us for trying," said Lon.

"Then we better put all of that kind of notion out of our minds and wait until we get to Olla Sucia," said Mazzel. "Once we're around a whole town full of witnesses, he ain't apt to pull that gun so quick and kill us."

"So that's our plan?" Lon asked.

"That's *my* plan, Lon," said Mazzel. "You're welcome to work out one of your own if it doesn't suit you."

"No, I go along with you," said Lon. "We keep quiet and do like he says till we get to Olla Sucia."

They took Kenny Brewer's body by his boots and dragged him out of sight behind a thick stand of mesquite. "Seems like we ought to bury him," said Lon.

"You can if you want to," said Mazzel. "I'm saving up all my strength to wait on *Mister* Clifford when he hollers for us."

Returning to the campsite, they walked softly to keep from disturbing Dayton Clifford and dropped onto their own blankets, exhausted and shaken by the day's events. Within moments they were both asleep, neither of them waking until well after dawn when the morning sun grew warm on their faces.

"Oh, no!" said Mazzel, sitting bolt upright as if stricken by a strange premonition. "Jesus, Lon, he's gone! Wake up! Clifford's left us!" Standing up, Mazzel staggered drunkenly, his head pounding painfully. He almost fell before catching himself and shaking his aching head. "Lord have mercy, I feel like I've been drinking all night!" He staggered over to the empty blanket lying on the ground and just stared down at it for a second as if not believing his eyes. "Damn it, Lon! Wake up," he finally shouted.

"Huh?" Lon sat up, rubbed his eyes, then staggered over beside Mazzel. "My head feels like a blacksmith's hammering iron inside it."

"Mine too," said Mazzel. The two looked at one another, then at the blanket again. In the center of the blanket lay Clifford's leather tobacco pouch. Mazzel reached out warily and picked it up and jiggled it in his hand. The two looked around the campsite as he opened the bag.

"He's run our horses off and left us stranded afoot," said Mazzel.

Rubbing his head, Lon said, "How the hell come us to sleep so late?"

"I don't know," said Mazzel, also rubbing his forehead, "but it's something that devil done to us, you can bet on it."

"It's twenty miles or so to Olla Sucia," said Lon.

"I don't know about you," said Mazzel, "but I'd rather walk that far than be around Mister Clifford. That son of a bitch is crazy if crazy ever needed another name!"

"Yeah, but twenty miles," said Lon, looking

around as if their horses might appear from behind a rock.

"Twenty miles ain't near as apt to kill us as he was," said Mazzel. "Besides, look at this!" He nudged Lon to get his attention. In his hand Mazzel held a roll of bills he'd taken from the leather tobacco pouch.

"I'll be damned," said Lon. "Our money?"

"You bet it is." Mazzel grinned, then shook his head. "See? After all that craziness, acting like he was going to beat us out of our money—he turns around and pays us after all."

"Beats the hell out of all I've ever seen," said Lon, running his fingers through his disheveled hair.

"I believe he had every intention of killing us and keeping our money," said Mazzel, staring off in the direction of Olla Sucia. "Something must've come to his mind to make him think otherwise."

At daylight Dayton Clifford rode into Olla Sucia, one hand resting idly on the big Colt across his stomach, the other hand leading the horse with Blake Carly's body lying over the saddle. Sheriff Roland Masden stood watching from the boardwalk in front of his office, a mug of steaming coffee in his hand. The sheriff saw the horses turn toward him and pull up at the hitch rail ten feet in front of him. "Good morning to you, Sheriff," said Clifford, removing his pipe from between his teeth.

"Morning," Sheriff Masden replied, staring intently at Clifford's hand resting on the big Colt. The other men nodded and touched their hat brims. "What can I do for you?" he asked, without taking his eyes off of Clifford's Colt.

Clifford let his hand drop clear of the gun butt.

"I'm Dayton Clifford," he said. Nodding back over his shoulder at the body of the Carly twin, he said, "I'm a man hunter from Chicago. This man is an outlaw from over in Arizona Territory."

"Yeah? What's his name?" asked Masden, stepping down from the boardwalk and walking around to take a closer look. The first thing he noticed was four bullet holes, exit wounds in the corpse's back where Clifford had stopped on the trail, opened the dead man's shirt and shot him four times in the chest.

"He's Blake Carly," said Clifford, without dismounting. He watched the sheriff raise the corpse's head by the hair and wince as he examined the bullet hole in its forehead.

"Those holes in his back were put there after he died," the sheriff said matter-of-factly.

Clifford gave him a smug grin. "Do tell, Sheriff. How perceptive of you." His smile disappeared. "But it isn't against the law, is it?"

"No, I reckon not," said Masden. "If a bounty hunter wants to show everybody what a thorough job he's done, it's no skin off my nose."

"I'm pleased to hear that, Sheriff," said Clifford, his hand easing away from his pistol butt as he smiled again and relaxed.

"Blake Carly, eh?" said Sheriff Masden, letting the corpse's head down and swatting at flies as he walked back to the front of Clifford's horse.

"Correct, Sheriff. He's a real hardcase outlaw—or was anyway," Clifford said, looking down at him from his saddle.

Masden thought about it for a second, then said, "Seems like I've seen some paper on him from around here as well. If this Blake Carly is wanted in New Mexico Territory, you might collect yourself a bigger bounty here and not have to pack him all the way back with you."

"I'm not concerned with the bounty," said Clifford.

"You're not?" Sheriff Masden eyed him closely. "You don't sound like any bounty hunter I ever seen, then."

"I never said I'm a bounty hunter, Sheriff," said Clifford. "I said I'm a *man* hunter."

"That's not the same?" the sheriff asked.

"No. At least not this time," said Clifford. "I'm employed by a private party. As far as I'm concerned you can have this man's body and whatever bounty New Mexico Territory has on him. All I want is his photograph and a ticket on the next stage headed west." He looked back and forth along the wide, dusty street. "Do you have a photography shop here?"

"Sure do," said the sheriff, pointing toward the other end of town. "Bowles Photography, right down there next to the barbershop. And we've got that stage you're wanting too. It leaves here at noon, if you can get that photograph taken and cured in time. Harvey Bowles is not a man you can rush. He's one of them kind who thinks his work is some sort of gift from God."

Clifford smiled slightly, his pipe between his teeth, his right hand resting deftly on his Colt without him realizing it. "Oh, I'm sure I can appeal to his sense of good reasoning."

Sheriff Masden stood watching as Clifford tipped his hat and rode off along the dusty street. In front of the photography shop, Clifford stepped down from his saddle, hitched both horses and walked inside. Moments later the sheriff heard the commotion as Harvey Bowles came stumbling out the door, his coat half on and his camera and tripod under his arm. He almost fell hurrying out into the street, where he quickly began setting up his camera. Behind him, Clifford stepped out of the shop, slipping his Colt back into the holster across his chest.

"Noon can't get here quick enough to suit me," Sheriff Masden whispered under his breath, watching Clifford step down to the horses, drop the corpse onto the street and prop it against the edge of the boardwalk. Clifford opened the dead man's shirt in front, revealing the four bullet holes in his chest. Sheriff Masden shook his head. Walking toward the photographer's shop, Masden watched a few early pedestrians start to gather on the boardwalks on either side of the street, taking an interest in what was going on. "Bowles, get this over with quick," said the sheriff as he drew closer.

"This wasn't my idea in the first place," the photographer said nervously. He hurriedly adjusted his camera and handed the sheriff a flash pan. "Here, fill this and help me out, if you're in such an all-fired hurry!"

Within moments three photographs had been taken of the corpse and Bowles began taking down his equipment as Clifford stepped forward puffing his pipe. "Now then, Clifford," said Sheriff Masden with a trace of sarcasm in his tone, "is there anything else we can do for you?"

Clifford smiled slightly. "Much obliged, Sheriff, but I think this will be all."

"Good," said the sheriff. "Then I expect you'll be taking that body to the undertaker and arranging to have it put in the ground?"

As the sheriff spoke, Clifford reached into his

pocket, took out a gold coin and flipped it to the photographer. "You, there, Bowles," he said. "Take care of the corpse when you're all through here."

Bowles caught the coin in a reflex reaction. But then he just stared at it in his palm while Clifford turned to the hitch rail, gathered his two horses and led them toward the Running Horse Saloon a half block away. In front of the Running Horse, the saloon owner, Dennard Franki, stood watching while his new partner, Floyd Percy, swept the boardwalk free of cigar butts and broken glass from the night before. Looking up at the sound of Franki chuckling, Percy stepped over beside him and asked, "What's so funny?"

Franki nodded toward the scene in the street in front of the photographer's. "Looks like Bowles and the sheriff have their hands full this morning." Sheriff Masden and Harvey Bowles had picked up the body by the heels and shoulders and packed it away.

"Yeah," said Percy, tossing the matter aside and going back to his broom. But Franki, staring at Dayton Clifford, said over his shoulder, "Take a close look, Percy. Here comes a hired gun if I ever saw one."

Percy stopped again, propping his hands atop the broom handle. "How can you tell?" he asked, scrutinizing the man and the two horses.

"It's just something you learn over time, partner," Franki said quietly.

Chapter 8

Walking into Olla Sucia in the noonday heat, Barton Creed and his men didn't see Dayton Clifford sitting inside the stagecoach puffing on his pipe and observing the haggard outlaws on foot while the stage rolled past them on its way out of town. Clifford grinned to himself, then tugged his hat brim down and relaxed back in his seat in a halo of gray pipe smoke, the pictures of the dead Carly twin safely tucked into the leather travel bag sitting at his feet. "Some are born to win, some are born to lose," he chuckled to himself, being the only passenger. "Some are born to only stare in *wonder* at the game . . ."

On the hot street, headed for the Running Horse Saloon, Creed grumbled to Mongo, who staggered along beside him, a wet, bloody rag pressed beneath his left eye. "I know those sons of bitches are here—they had to come here before going anywhere else. No tenderfoot from a big city like Chicago could stay away from a town for long."

Behind Mongo the rest of the men walked single file, Dick Spivey at the end, straggling along painfully, his good hand gripping his wounded shoulder. Mongo started to remind Creed that the *tenderfoot* had left them riding in style, while they were the ones on foot, having to come to town to re-outfit themselves. But he decided not to mention it at that moment, not with his face swollen twice its size and his vision still blurry from the beating he'd taken from Billy Drew. Creed was in a sour mood. There was no point in aggravating him any further.

On the boardwalk in front of the Running Horse Saloon stood Dennard Franki and Floyd Percy, who had stepped out for a breath of fresh air. Seeing the outlaws walking toward the saloon, Franki said in a whisper to Percy, "Uh-oh. Here comes seven of the worst devils ever spit out of hell." He nodded at the two in front and said, "Those two are Barton Creed and Mongo Barnes. I know you've heard of them." He looked at the next man, the young Texan Billy Drew. "I don't recognize that one, but the other four are Dick Spivey, Arnold Prather, Denton 'The Blade' Ermy, and Ray Hightower."

Floyd Percy gave Franki a look. "You sure came up with their names pretty fast. Sounded like you had them memorized."

"It always pays to know your customers," said Franki. He drew on his long cigar, took his timepiece out of his vest pocket and checked it. "Like I've told you, in this business you get all kinds—killers, robbers, rapists. You have to treat them all the same. As long as they've got money to lay down for whiskey and gambling, they're the salt of the earth, far as you and I are concerned. It's our obligation to see to it they leave with their thirst quenched and their pockets empty." He offered a wry smile.

"Would they be coming here on foot if they had any money?" Percy asked.

Franki shrugged. "I suppose that all depends on

why they're on foot. Something could have happened to their horses. They could have plenty of money, just no horses."

Seeing the outlaws turn away from the saloon and head across the street toward the Red Lady Sporting House, Percy said, "I suppose it doesn't matter. It looks like they're not coming here. They seem to be more interested in the womenfolk right now."

"Yeah, for now maybe," said Franki, not to be discouraged. "But these men only want women for a short while. It's hard drinking and all-night gambling that keeps their hearts beating. Give them an hour, an hour and a half at the most. Once they've got a hot bath, had themselves a woman and got a shot or two under their belts, they'll start getting fidgety, start wondering how their luck's running. That's when we'll see them." He grinned and puffed his cigar.

"Then I guess I'd better go help the bartender get some extra bottles out of the back room and get ready for them," said Percy.

"Yes," said Franki, "why don't you do that? I'll take myself a nice rest for a few minutes and get prepared to do some dealing and poker playing." He stuck his watch back in his vest pocket and patted it. "I'm predicting a long but very prosperous night here at the Running Horse."

"I hope so," said Percy. "Seems like since I became your partner profits have fallen off considerably. I spoke briefly to DeLyle Lambert about it. He suggested the three of us sit down and go over the books, see if all the money can be accounted for."

Franki looked stunned, but quickly recovered. "You sound as if you think I have been mishandling our funds!"

"No, I didn't mean it that way," said Percy. "It's just that DeLyle Lambert has lots more business experience than either of us, him being an attorney and all. Maybe he can help us get things back on track, profit-wise."

"Just between you and me," said Franki, "DeLyle Lambert has never impressed me much. And just because he's an attorney doesn't mean he's got enough sense to count all his toes with his socks on as far as I'm concerned. But if it will make you feel better, then by all means let's get together with him. I want you to feel good about throwing in with me. That's what counts in my book."

"I'm glad you feel that way," said Percy. "I'm just hoping he can show us why it looks like business is booming but still we're losing money."

Franki shrugged innocently. "I'm afraid that's the way it goes in this business. Sometimes it looks like business is booming when it isn't, other times business looks slow when we're actually making money hand over fist."

Percy look confused by his partner's slick talk.

"But don't you even think about it for now, partner," said Franki, giving Percy a pat on his back and a nudge toward the front door of the Running Horse, "My job is to do all the thinking and look after our investment. You get right in there and take care of the *hands-on* part of the business. We'll both get rich here, just wait and see. It's just a matter of time. DeLyle Lambert will be asking *you* for financial advice." He smiled, watching Percy walk back inside the saloon.

Once his new partner was out of sight, Franki stuck his cigar in his mouth and looked over at the Red Lady Sporting House, where a tinny piano had started up and the sound of squeals and laughter burst from every window and door. Damn DeLyle Lambert! he fumed to himself. He wasn't about to let some weasel like DeLyle Lambert snoop around, keeping watch on how he ran the business. This was something he'd have to nip in the bud. He hadn't figured on Floyd Percy being smart enough to notice that profits were down in spite of a huge drinking crowd almost every night. Now that Percy had noticed—well, that sort of changed things, Franki thought. Something had to be done quick. "This son of a bitch has got himself a lawyer," Franki growled under his breath.

Puffing his cigar and leaving a wake of smoke behind him, Dennard Franki walked along the boardwalk until he reached an alleyway that ran behind the Running Horse Saloon. He quickly walked to the rear of the building, slipped along a path littered with whiskey bottles and cigar butts and circled around the back of the town. He came back to the main street three blocks from the Running Horse, ducked his head slightly to avoid being seen and crossed the street. Again taking to an alleyway, he hurried to the rear door of the Red Lady Sporting House and slipped inside.

"Well, well, look who we have here," said Victoria Bright, owner of the Red Lady. She grinned widely, showing gold-capped front teeth designed in the shape of two hearts, and hiked a hand on her waist. "I thought there were no women here at the Red Lady skinny enough to please you, Franki."

Beside her a young golden-haired woman with diagonal red, white, and blue stripes painted on her face chimed in, saying, "I knew you'd soon tire of dealing yourself the same *hand* every night!" She squealed with laughter at her little joke.

"Shut up, Polly Ann!" said Franki, red-faced. Addressing Victoria Bright he said, "I didn't come here for a woman—not this time."

"Uh-oh," said Polly Ann. "Somebody better tell the piano player he's got a long night ahead of him!"

"Damn you, Polly Ann," said Franki. "Victoria, can you shut this whore up?"

"Shut up, Polly Ann," Victoria said to the young woman. Victoria's flaming red hair stood high atop her head, interwoven with pearls and bouncy white silk ribbons. Her low-cut brocade dress exposed large breasts adorned with colorful cherub tattoos. "Now then, what can we do for you, Franki?"

"I came to talk to Barton Creed," said Franki.

"Talk to Creed? What about?" Victoria asked.

"If it was any of your business, Victoria, I already would have told you," said Franki.

"Oh," Victoria said coldly. "Well, it appears that Mister Creed is indisposed at the moment. Perhaps you'd like to come back another time?"

"This can't wait," said Franki. He fished out a thick roll of bills, peeled one off and held it out to her. "Tell him I've got to see him right now."

"Tell me yourself, barkeeper," said Barton Creed, stepping in from the other room flanked by two half-naked young women, his arms draped over their shoulders, a bottle of rye hanging from his left hand. Staring at Franki, he lowered his right arm from one woman's bare shoulder and rested it on his gun butt.

Before Franki could pull back the bill in his hand, Victoria snatched it and stuffed it down her dress.

"There, all done," she said, patting her bosom as she stepped back farther from Franki.

"Barton," said Franki, "can you and me talk in private?"

"I expect we can, if you make it quick," said Creed, nodding at the two women. "I've made some promises to these two young doves that I intend to keep."

"Of course," said Franki. "This will only take a moment." He followed Creed as the gunman stepped away from the women and carried his bottle toward a small room down the hall.

"Last time I saw you, Franki," Creed said over his shoulder, "you needed my help with some investors you were hiding from down in Brownsville."

"Yes, that was a most unfortunate situation," said Franki. "Luckily I finally got it settled to everybody's satisfaction." They walked into the room and Franki closed the door behind them.

"All right, let's hear it," said Creed, handing Franki the bottle of rye. "Who is it you're wanting killed this time?" He grinned. "Another partner, I bet."

"As a matter of fact it is," said Franki, red-faced.

"The big fellow I saw standing out front of the Running Horse with you?" Creed asked.

"Correct," said Franki.

"Well, hell, why not?" said Creed, scratching his beard-stubbled jaw. "Give us time to get the trail dust off our backs." He gave Franki a close gaze. "It's going to cost you eight hundred dollars this time, though."

"*Eight* hundred?" Franki looked shocked. "Last time it was only five hundred!"

"This ain't the last time." Creed grinned. "This is the time after the *last* time. I'm getting tired of killing partners for you. *Next* time it could be a *thousand* dollars."

"All right, then, eight hundred it is," said Franki. "Just hurry up and get it done. Come see me for your pay."

"I need half that money right now, Franki," said Creed.

"Why? Don't you trust me?" Franki asked. "I've never skunked you."

"It ain't about trust," said Creed, lowering his voice. "The thing is, me and the boys came in here without ten dollars between us. We got our horses stolen and our guns taken away from us. We came to get a stake." He lowered his voice even more, into a whisper. "I figured I could muscle enough from Miss Victoria to outfit us and get us on the man's trail who did this to us."

Franki gave him a stare of disbelief. "You were going to *rob* Miss Victoria?"

"Keep your voice down," said Creed. "It was either her place or the Running Horse. Which one would you rather?"

"Oh, I see," said Franki, quickly turning the subject away from the Running Horse to keep Creed from getting any ideas. He jerked out a roll of bills, peeled off four hundred dollars and handed it over. "Come around tonight after you and your men get caught up here."

Creed took the money, fanned it, folded it and put it away. "Just have my other four hundred ready. If he's your partner he won't be hard to spot. I always look for the man who's sweating the hardest."

Franki chuckled and said, "That's a good one, Creed. I'll have to remember that." He turned to leave.

"Not so fast, Franki," said Creed. "I got a question for you. Did you see four fellows come through here with a dead man over a saddle?"

"Are these the men who stole your horses?" Franki asked, not wanting to say anything that might distract Creed from killing Percy for him, especially now that he'd already been paid half up front.

"Yeah, they're the ones," said Creed. "Have you seen them?"

"No," said Franki, giving a thoughtful look as he answered. "There hasn't been four riders come through town together for over a week. If you happen to see these men are you getting right onto their trail?"

"Damn right," said Creed.

"Then what would that do to our deal?" Franki asked.

"If I knew which way those snakes went, our deal would have to wait until I hunted them down and killed them," said Creed. He eyed Franki closely. "Are you sure you haven't seen them?"

"I'm certain I haven't seen them," said Franki, not about to mention that a lone rider had come through, had a photo taken of a dead man, then left town on the noon stage. "If I see them, I'll come running and let you know," he added, backing away to the door. He turned and left, leaving Creed once again scratching his beard stubble.

On his way down the narrow hall, Franki passed Mongo Barnes. Mongo gave him an evil stare through his swollen eyes, neither man acknowledging the other. When Franki was out of sight, Mongo stepped into the room with Creed and said, "What's that tub of guts want now, another partner killed?"

"Damn, everybody in the world must know what

Franki's up to," said Creed, grinning. "But now that you mention it, yep, that is what he wants!" Creed took out the roll of bills and fanned them for Mongo to see. "Don't this beat all. We ain't been in town long enough to get a bath and already Dennard Franki's sticking money in my face, wanting us to kill some poor bastard for him!"

Mongo gave a swollen, crooked grin. "We're like a couple of damn cats. No matter where we get dropped from we always land on our feet."

"Ain't it true!" said Creed. The two roared with laughter.

"What are we going to do about the bastards who stole our guns?" Mongo said, when their laughter stopped.

"We're going to kill them, of course," said Creed. Lowering his voice, he said, "What are you going to do about Billy Drew beating you the way he did?"

"Kill him, *of course*," said Mongo, mimicking Creed's words.

"Good enough," said Creed, slapping Mongo on the back. "I just wanted to make sure we're both of the same mind here. Now let's go get ourselves some guns and horses." The two walked out of the room together and toward the back door of the Red Lady.

Seeing them leave, Victoria called out, "Hey! Where are you headed, Creed? The party's right here!"

Creed grinned over his shoulder. "The party is wherever I'm at!" He flipped a handful of dollar bills into the air. "Take care of my boys until I get back!"

"How do you want to handle killing Franki's partner?" Mongo asked through swollen lips.

"We'll keep it plain and simple," said Creed. "He insults one of us, starts a fight, and we shoot a bullet or two through his belly. I'll even pick up a small hideaway pistol in case he ain't armed."

"Want me to be the one to shoot him?" asked Mongo.

Creed shrugged. "Sure, go ahead. I killed Franki's last two partners."

It was after dark when Creed and Mongo returned to the Red Lady Sporting House with a string of horses and gun belts filled with pistols and ammunition hanging from their shoulders. Creed carried a Spencer rifle across his lap. At the rear door of the Red Lady, the men gathered, some of them only half dressed, and listened to Creed. "Boys, I just want you to know that me and Mongo has been looking out for you." He dropped the gun belts to the ground, saying, "Take your pick!" and stepped his horse back as the men hurried forward and snatched the weapons up. "These horses will be waiting for you when you're all finished up in there!"

Dick Spivey wore a bandage one of the women had made for him. Feeling better with his shoulder treated, he asked Creed, "Where are you going now?"

Turning their horses to leave, Creed replied, "We've got some business to take care of at the Running Horse. We'll meet all of you there later tonight and throw a spree like this town has never seen!" Touching his hat brim in a grand gesture, Creed spun his horse and rode away to the saloon, Mongo right beside him.

The two were still laughing when they reached the Running Horse, hitched their mounts out front and swaggered through the bat-wing doors. But they stopped in their tracks and cut their laughter short

when they looked down at the end of the bar and
saw the two trail guides, Mazzel and Pence, staring
back at them with expressions of horror on their
dirty faces.

"Oh, Lord," said Ben Mazzel.

Lon Pence started to turn and bolt for the back
door, but Creed's voice caused him to freeze in place.
"Hold it right there!"

The Running Horse had only started to fill up with
the night drinking and gambling crowd. A few miners at the same end of the bar slipped cautiously out
of the way, giving Creed and Mongo clear shots. The
two guides saw there was no escape. They continued
to stare as Creed and Mongo walked over to them,
their hands on their newly acquired Colts.

"Mister Creed, please!" said Mazzel. "Dayton Clifford forced us to do what we did! The man's the
most cold-blooded killer I ever saw!"

"Really?" Creed gave a cruel grin. "Well, I'm here
to change all that."

"Please, mister!" said Lon Pence. "We got jackpotted too! He left us in the same fix! He left us
afoot, same as he did you fellows! We're not your
enemies! He is!"

"But I see he left you with guns," said Creed. He
and Mongo stepped up close, realizing that the two
worn-out guides were no threat, even with pistols on
their hips. "Where is he?" Seeing that the threat of
a shooting had diminished slightly, the miners eased
back to their spots at the bar, not about to slow down
their drinking.

"I wish to hell we knew where he is," said Mazzel.
"I'm going to put a bullet in him soon as I lay eyes
on him." Mazzel knew he was only blowing hot air,
but if it kept him and Pence from getting shot he

saw no harm in it. "I know he came through here, though. That's why we came here, to blow the hell out of him."

"How do you know he came through here?" asked Creed, getting interested in what they could tell him.

"Because we walked into town through the back way and saw Carly's body in a cooling box out back of the undertaker's."

Creed and Mongo looked at one another. "Franki, you lying son of a bitch," Creed whispered under his breath. Looking around wildly, he called out to Floyd Percy, who stood sweating behind the bar, "Where's Dennard Franki?"

Percy hurried down to the end of the bar and nervously set up two glasses and a newly opened bottle of whiskey. "He—he's in the back in his office, sir!" Percy stammered. "Shall I go get him for you?"

"That won't be necessary. We know our way," Creed growled. "Are you his new partner?" he asked with a dark stare.

"Yes, I'm Floyd Percy, sir," the sweaty man said in a trembling voice.

"Quit sweating, Floyd Percy. This is your lucky day!" said Creed. He swatted the two glasses away with the back of his hand, picked up the bottle of whiskey and swigged from it.

Stomping to the office and kicking the thin door open, Creed and Mongo caught Dennard Franki climbing out the back window—he had overheard part of the conversation about the body behind the undertaker's.

"Please, Creed!" Franki begged. "I didn't know who you meant! You said *four* riders and a body! There was only one rider!"

"You knew you was misleading me, you word-twisting son of a bitch!" said Creed.

At the bar the drinkers heard Franki scream, but his scream was silenced beneath a blast of gunfire. A deathlike quiet fell upon the Running Horse, broken only by the sound of Creed's and Mongo's boot heels walking slowly back across the floor. Creed took his time, raised the bottle to his lips while Percy, the guides and the rest of the drinkers stared wide-eyed. "He pulled a hideaway gun on me. I had to shoot him," Creed said in a raised voice. Jerking his head toward the office door, he added, "Go look for yourself. It's still in his hand."

One of the miners stepped forward defiantly. "He never carried a hideaway—"

Creed shot him dead before the words got out of his mouth.

Beside Creed, Mongo pulled his gun instinctively. "We might have pulled it off if you didn't shoot this fool," he said.

"To hell with it," said Creed. "It don't matter what we do. We're like cats, remember? We'll land on our feet!" He raised his gun and leveled it in Floyd Percy's face. "I came here to collect four hundred dollars Franki promised us for killing you! You want to give me my money now, or do you want me to finish my work first?"

Without a second's hesitation, Percy hurried to an ornate brass-trimmed cash box to get Creed's money for him. Creed and Mongo turned to the two guides. "What did you do with our guns?" he asked Mazzel.

"Clifford made us throw them in some shallows along the Rio Grande," Mazzel replied, still looking worried.

"Do you remember where?" Creed asked.

"Sure do," said Mazzel. "Right, Lon?"

"Yep," said Lon Pence, both guides showing their eagerness to help.

"Then what are you waiting for?" said Creed. "It ain't every day men like you two get a chance to ride with the likes of us." He turned a cold stare on the stunned faces of the other drinkers, saying, "Tell your sheriff to come looking for us if he's tired of living."

Lon Pence whispered to Mazzel, "Are you thinking what I'm thinking?"

"Oh, yeah," said Mazzel. "First chance we get, we've got to make a run for it."

PART 2

PART 2

Chapter 9

Eight days later Dayton Clifford arrived at Maynard Aubrey's office in Benton Wells and plopped the pictures of the dead Carly twin onto Aubrey's polished oak desk. He turned down a cigar that Aubrey offered him from a gold-inlayed mahogany box and instead settled into a wingback chair, filled his pipe and lit it. He studied the expression on Aubrey's face closely as the banker went from one picture to the next. "My goodness, Clifford," said the banker, "I certainly do not envy you your profession."

"Gruesome, eh?" Clifford said flatly. "He died hard. I finally had to put that last bullet through his forehead just to get him out of his misery." There was no reason for Aubrey to think he was lying, Clifford reminded himself, so he could use this conversation as an opportunity to squeeze some information out of the banker. "If you think he looks bad, you should see some of the ones that made me angry." His gaze intensified. "You know? The ones who lied to me or tried to keep information from me. I have been known to take a man apart starting at his toes."

"I shudder at the image," said Aubrey, getting uncomfortable under Clifford's stare but not sure what the gunman was getting at. He reached inside a desk drawer, took out an envelope filled with cash and slid it across the desktop. Clifford arose from his chair, picked up the envelope, riffled the contents, then put it in his suit coat pocket.

"I could have shot Blake Carly once and been done with him," Clifford said, sitting back down. "Instead I shot him a total of five times." Clifford shrugged, continuing with his details. "I didn't think it was necessary to get a picture of the other wounds, just so long as you could see he's dead. That's what you paid me for."

"Indeed so," said Aubrey. "He is as dead as anybody I've ever seen." He offered a tight, smug grin. "You are an efficient gunman. I commend you, sir." Aubrey considered the gunman's words for a moment, then said, "But five times? Whatever did he do to provoke you?"

Clifford continued to stare flatly, saying, "He stopped talking in the middle of a story he was telling me—one hell of a story."

"Oh?" Aubrey's brow clouded slightly. Clifford caught it before the banker managed to change his expression. Clearing his throat, Aubrey fidgeted with his hands. "Well, at any rate he's dead, and the world is a better place for it. I'm sure you must have things to do."

Puffing on his pipe with one leg comfortably crossed over the other, Clifford asked, "Aren't you curious as to what the story was about?"

Aubrey's face looked suddenly drawn and anxious, but he tried to hide behind a forced smile and a wave of a hand. "Oh, whatever it is, I'm sure I would have no interest in it."

"But I bet you would," said Clifford. "It's all about a large sum of hidden gold that was stolen right out from under the government's nose. He told me all about it before it was over with. He said you played a big role in it."

"I have no idea what you're talking about," Aubrey said, but his left eye gave a slight twitch. That was all Clifford needed to see to know that he had just struck a nerve.

He pressed the banker by rising from the chair and walking slowly but deliberately to the office door. He locked the heavy oak door and stared at Aubrey for a second before walking back to his desk.

"Now see here, sir!" said Aubrey, stepping sideways to pull a long sash that connected to a bell in the outer lobby. "Whatever I might know, I'll never tell!"

But Clifford moved quickly and caught his wrist just as the banker made his move. Aubrey felt his chin tilt upward above a sharp edge of steel, the knife in Clifford's hand having appeared out of nowhere. "We both know you're not going to hold out for long, Aubrey. Either you'll spill your guts or I'll spill them for you." He ran the flat edge of the blade down the banker's vest, giving Aubrey an idea of what he would do. His voice dropped to a whisper. "You've seen my work." He gestured toward the dead face of the Carly twin staring up at them from the photo atop the oaken desk. As he did so he applied a bit more pressure on the knife blade, making sure the banker understood what lay in store for him.

"Wait!" said Aubrey. "You're right! I can't hold out! I'm no hero! I'll tell you whatever you want to know!"

Clifford eased the pressure off the knife blade. "I

want to know everything," he said, nudging the banker back down into his chair and standing over him with the blade pointed at his left eye. "If I see a twitch I'll know you're lying. You don't want to hear what I'll do then."

Aubrey swallowed a tight knot of fear in his throat and said, "Sheriff Ed Tarpin and his deputy, Earl Hedgepeth, were in on it with me. They set up a gang of outlaws to pull the robbery, then they hired the four guides, Mazzel and his pals, to lead them into the old stone ruins north of here. That's where it's been hidden all this time. I knew they were taking it to the ruins, but Tarpin decided to extort money from me until we could reclaim the gold. He kept promising to reveal the location to me, but he never would. He kept playing me along."

"Wait a minute," said Clifford. "You mean to tell me that all the while I was with Mazzel and those other idiots, they knew all about the stolen money?"

"No, of course not," said Aubrey. "They thought they were leading a hunting party when they took us into Stone Valley toward the old ruins. They never realized our supply wagon was carrying close to a million dollars in newly minted gold coins. While they escorted me off to track a large elk, Tarpin and Hedgepeth took the wagon into the ruins and hid the gold. Those poor stupid guides actually thought Deputy Hedgepeth was some sort of foreign dignitary."

"Where did Blake Carly fit into all of this?" asked Clifford, the blade still pointed unwaveringly at Aubrey's eye.

"He knew some dirt on Sheriff Tarpin. I hired him to put the heat on Tarpin and get the information I needed to go find the gold."

"If you were stupid enough to trust a man like

Blake Carly with that kind of information, you deserve to get skunked on the deal," Clifford chuckled darkly. "What the hell were you thinking?"

Aubrey looked embarrassed. "I was thinking that you would find Carly and kill him for me before he got to his gang and told them where the gold is hidden."

"Well, that part worked out," said Clifford, his eyes going to the picture on the desk again. "But what were you going to do about finding the gold after that?"

"I don't know," said Aubrey. "I was desperate. I couldn't bear to see the likes of Carly and his friends getting that gold. I suppose that was all I thought about." He gave Clifford a questioning look. "Perhaps I felt like someone would come along whom I could trust and we'd go partners on the gold and find it. Does that sound too foolish to you?"

Clifford grinned flatly and puffed a couple of times on his pipe as if considering it. "What about Hedgepeth?" he asked. "He still knows where to go."

"I'm afraid Hedgepeth is dead," said Aubrey.

"Killed by someone you hired, no doubt," said Clifford.

Aubrey only gave him an innocent look, saying, "All I can tell you is that he's dead. I have no idea who killed him or had him killed. But I can tell you that together you and I can find that gold and split it."

Clifford puffed on his pipe. "There sure seems to be an awful lot of dying surrounding that hidden gold." As he spoke his eyes traveled up the long bell pull running from the floor to the ceiling. Bending sideways, he picked up the loose end.

Aubrey's eyes widened in fear. "Don't be a fool,

Clifford!" he said quickly. "You'll need my help! You'll need to finance the hunt from back here! You'll need me to channel the gold into circulation if you ever find it!"

"Those guides can show me where they took you among the ruins." With the knife still in his hands he wrapped a two-foot length of sash between his hands and tested its strength. "From there I'll figure where it's hidden."

"That's impossible, Clifford!" said Aubrey, shaking at the realization of what Clifford was about to do to him. He looked ready to bolt from his seat, but his fear kept him pinned in place.

Clifford said soothingly, "Don't make this hard, Aubrey. Look, I'm not going to shoot you full of holes—I'm not even going to stab you and leave a mess on this beautiful rug." He stepped around sideways to the terrified banker. "This will be just like going to sleep—consider it sort of a *gentleman's* way of hanging."

In the outer office of the bank, Aubrey's assistant, Brerton Embry, sat busily addressing a stack of paperwork. When he heard a muffled gasping sound come from beyond the closed door to Maynard Aubrey's office, he stood up from his desk, walked over and quietly knocked on the door. "Mister Aubrey? Is everything all right?"

"Don't worry about it. Go on back to work," said a voice that the young assistant could not recognize as belonging to his employer. But with a look of concern toward the locked door, he walked dutifully back to his desk.

Inside the office, Dayton Clifford turned loose of the length of sash, unwrapped it from around Aubrey's neck and let it fall back into place down the wall. He straightened the dead man's collar and tugged it up, hiding the darkening marks on his throat. "There now, who can tell anything?" he said to the blank, bulging eyes as he lifted one of the thick hands and adjusted it so that it looked as if Aubrey had died clutching his chest. He straightened a couple of items on the desk, picked up the picture of the dead Carly twin, tucked it inside his coat and looked all around before letting himself out through a window into a deserted alleyway. Pulling the window closed behind him, he murmured, "Too easy." Now all he had to do was go find that gold.

Maynard Aubrey's body had been in the ground three days before Millie Tristan arrived in Benton Wells by stage. The day after her arrival the ranger and the Carly twin came into town on horseback, the twin riding right beside him. Had it not been for the twin's handcuffs no onlooker would have guessed the pair to be a lawman escorting his prisoner. Seeing the two veer toward the sheriff's office, Millie hurried along the boardwalk and stood awaiting the twin as he stepped down from his saddle.

"Did you miss me?" Millie asked, throwing her arms around him, kissing him shamelessly in public.

"More than I can tell you," the twin replied, looking a little embarrassed. Unable to return her embrace, he could only hold his cuffed hands to one side. The ranger watched intently, making sure nothing passed from Millie to him.

"Millie, are you still carrying that Thunder somewhere out of sight?" Sam asked, already feeling like he knew the answer.

"If I say I'm not, are you going to search me all over?" she asked playfully.

"No," said the ranger, "but when I ask you a serious question I expect a serious answer. Now, let's try again—"

Cutting him off, she said, "Yes, I am still carrying it, Ranger Burrack." Still staring into Carly's eyes as she spoke to the ranger, she continued, "Is there a law against it?"

"We both know there's not," said Sam. "But there is a law against drawing it and trying to help somebody escape the law."

"Any fool knows that," said Millie, sounding indignant.

"But it doesn't hurt to be reminded of it now and then, does it?" the ranger said with a trace of a smile. "Sometimes it keeps the air from growing too thick."

"No, I suppose it doesn't," said Millie. Turning loose of the Carly twin, she faced the ranger. "I heard someone in the saloon last night say that the *honorable* Territorial Judge Leonard Persons is in town." A measure of sarcasm came into her voice.

"You have something against Judge Persons?" Sam asked her as he gave the prisoner a nudge toward the door to the sheriff's office. Rather than have Millie behind him, Sam motioned her ahead of him through the door.

"No, I have nothing against *His Honor*," she replied coyly. "But he does snore like a pig, and he can't go to sleep unless he's pulled both of his socks down over the bedposts."

"That's enough of that," the ranger chastised her.

Inside the office, a young man wearing a frayed suit coat and a battered bowler hat stood up and hurried around a wide littered desk to meet them. "You must be Ranger Burrack," he said, nervously scurrying to a cell door and opening it as Sam trailed the Carly twin across the dusty wooden floor. "I'm Jasper Farley, the town barber. I'm the temporary sheriff here until the town board hires somebody who knows what they're doing."

Millie stepped to one side and watched the twin walk into the cell and turn to the ranger to have his cuffs taken off.

"Yes, I am Sam Burrack," said the ranger as he unlocked the cuffs and took them off of Carly's wrists. "This is—"

"Blake Carly," said the young man eagerly, cutting the ranger off. "I know! I've seen him around here for a long time. I've cut his hair more than once." He looked Carly up and down as he talked, scrutinizing his hair as the twin removed his hat and wiped his sleeve across his forehead.

The ranger took pause at the young barber's words as he closed the door to Carly's cell. "Are you certain this is *Blake* Carly, not his twin brother, Abel?"

"Yes, I'm certain," said Farley.

Carly and Millie both started to speak, but the ranger raised a hand, silencing them. "Hush, both of you. Let's hear what the barber's got to say." He asked the barber, "What makes you *certain* this is Blake?"

Now the young barber felt himself on a spot. He looked back and forth between the ranger and the Carly twin. He raised a finger to his lips in contemplation. His look of certainty clouded as he looked the twin up and down closely. "Come to think of it, he does look a little different somehow."

The ranger sighed to himself. "Different how?"

"I don't know, his clothes perhaps?" said the barber. "Blake Carly wouldn't be caught dead wearing worn-down cavalry boots." He pointed at the twin's feet.

Millie Tristan giggled under her breath at the look on the ranger's face.

"Did I say something wrong, Ranger Burrack?" asked the barber. "Perhaps if I looked at him a little longer?"

"No," said Sam. "I don't want you changing your mind because you think it's something I want to hear. That's not what I'm looking for."

"But what *are* you looking for? What *do* you want to hear?" asked the young barber. "I'm sure if I knew . . ." His words trailed off.

"Never mind," said the ranger. "I'm going to find Judge Persons and let him know we're here. Keep a close eye on these two while I'm gone." He stepped over to a wall peg, took the key to the cell and pocketed it. "For safekeeping until I get back," he said, giving the twin and Millie both a sharp look. "Behave yourself, Millie."

"I will. I promise, Ranger," Millie said, turning from Sam and staring at the Carly twin through the bars. "Tell this *barber* that it's all right for me and Abel to talk," she added.

"It's all right, Farley," the ranger said to the barber turned sheriff.

Hearing Millie, the barber said, "Oh! So, this *isn't* Blake, then?"

Millie giggled.

"It depends on who you want to believe," said the ranger. He turned and left.

As soon as the ranger closed the door behind himself, Millie and the Carly twin stood close to the bars and spoke softly. "I'm sorry, Blake," Millie whispered. "I would have slipped you a gun, but I was certain the ranger would have searched me."

"No, that's not what I wanted from you," said the twin.

Millie continued, whispering quickly, "I would have even pulled this Thunderer on Farley, but Burrack took the key!"

"No, please, listen to me," said the twin, clasping her hands through the bars and holding them close to his lips. "I'm not going to have to break jail. If the law is fair and just, I won't have to. I'll walk out that door a free man." He squeezed her hands affectionately. "Millie, I am who I say I am."

"You don't want my help?" Millie asked, sounding a bit hurt.

"Millie, listen to me," said the twin. "All the way here from Taos I've been thinking about you. I've been thinking about you and very little else, even with a noose hanging over my head if things happen to go wrong for me."

"Don't talk sugar talk to me," Millie said, lowering her eyes. "I'm a whore and a damn good one." She collected herself, then raised her eyes, a hardness returning to her expression. "I'm going to get you out of here, some way. I promise you!"

The twin studied her eyes. "You're not hearing a thing I say to you, are you?"

"I hear you very clearly," Millie whispered, "and I know the spot you're in. I don't give a damn who you say you are. You can say you're Abraham Lincoln as far as I'm concerned, as long as it gets you off the hook."

The twin sighed. "But no matter what I say, you still think I'm Blake, don't you?"

Slicing a glance first toward the barber, who had

walked farther away to the desk, Millie gave the twin a wink and said, "Of course not! I know you're Abel Carly, the *good* twin."

Without returning Millie's smile, the twin said, "Let me ask you something, Millie. Suppose you found out that I really am Abel—not Blake at all. Would you leave? Would that be the last I ever saw of you?"

Millie thought about it for a moment. Before answering, she reached inside her dress, took out a roll of bills and fanned them, then expertly rerolled them. "Here's three hundred dollars I made for us—two hundred of it I made on the way here, at stage stops. A hundred is just what I made last night at the Three-Fingered Lady Saloon. "I'll take care of you, just like I used to."

"You didn't answer me, Millie," said the twin. "Would you leave if you found out that I'm not Blake?" He watched the roll of money disappear beneath the folds of her dress.

"But I won't find that out," said Millie.

"I see," said the twin with resolve. "And nothing I can do or say will change your mind?"

"No," said Millie. "I don't want to change my mind." She smiled as if she had possession of a secret she would share with no one. "Can't you see that?"

"Yes," said the twin. "I see that now."

Chapter 10

———

After explaining the unusual situation with the Carly twins, the ranger awaited the judge's response. "I like to think of myself as a man known for not beating around the bush, Ranger Burrack," said Judge Leonard Persons, the two of them seated at a small round table in the center of his room at the Claremont Hotel. The ranger sat with his pearl-gray sombrero on his crossed knee. He watched the judge take a deep breath and let it out slowly, almost in a sigh. "So I'm going to come straight out and tell you," Persons continued. "Whoever this Carly twin is, he's going to go free unless you can produce a witness against him."

"That's the whole problem, Your Honor," said Sam. "I don't think there's anybody who can say he's Blake Carly anymore than anybody who can say he's not. I don't think the woman with him knows for sure."

"Millie Tristan . . ." the judge said thoughtfully. "We can't take her word for it, especially if she's as stuck on Blake Carly as you say she claims to be. She's as wild as an antelope and unpredictable as a rattlesnake." Catching himself, the judge quickly said with a reddening face, "Or so I've been *told*." He busied himself for an awkward moment with the report the ranger had turned in on Millie shooting the station hostler. "But I agree with you here. This was self-defense." He slipped the one-page report into his desk.

The ranger only nodded. "I'll go to each of the witnesses who saw Carly shoot Tarpin, Your Honor, but I doubt if it's going to do any good."

"I agree," said the judge. "I think it will only serve to raise further doubts. In a case where identity cannot be clearly established beyond reasonable doubt, the court is powerless to bring charges against a man, regardless what crime he's accused of. In this case even you can't identify this man as Blake Carly."

"I realize that, Your Honor," said the ranger. "All I can go by is the way they were dressed, and in clear conscience all I can say is that he's dressed exactly as Abel Carly was dressed when I got onto their trail. If he is Blake Carly he had plenty of time to change clothes with his brother before I got to him."

"But that is all spit in the river as far as my court is concerned, Ranger," said the judge, a troubled look on his face. "I hate to say this, but I'm going to have to order you to turn this man loose. We can't try him for killing Sheriff Tarpin. Any drunken attorney in this territory would rip this case to shreds." The judge seemed to brace himself for what the ranger might do or say in response.

To Judge Persons' surprise the ranger simply replied, "I understand, Your Honor." Half standing up from his chair, he added, "I'll go release the prisoner right away."

"Wait a minute, Ranger," said the judge. "Please sit down."

Sam eased back down into his chair.

"I don't want you going off and doing something rash just because the victim in this matter was a lawman," said Judge Persons.

"That thought never crossed my mind, Your Honor," said the ranger. "You said to set him free, and that's what I intend to do."

"I know we haven't had the opportunity to work together much, Ranger Burrack," said the judge, "but I've heard many things about you—enough that it's hard for me to believe you're taking this so well."

"Your Honor," said the ranger, "whatever else you might have heard about me, I hope you've also heard that I try to be a fair man."

The judge offered a tired smile. "I'm afraid the shootings are always the first thing one hears about a good lawman. News about a man's character travels slower for some reason, especially if it's *good* character." He seemed to relax a bit, seeing how the ranger seemed to be accepting the news about freeing the prisoner. "I have to say I am more than a little surprised at your reaction. Feel free to tell me what you think about my decision."

"My job is not to second-guess you, Your Honor," the ranger said.

"Please, call me Judge Persons outside of the courtroom," said the judge. "And in this case I welcome any comments you might have. Quite frankly, this one disturbs me." He looked closely at the ranger and said, "Nobody in my position wants to let a killer go free. But even *more* importantly, no man in my position wants to hang an innocent man. For my sake, give your opinion, Ranger."

"Don't be hard on yourself, Judge Persons," said the ranger. "That's all I can tell you. I've been trying all this time to figure out who this man is. For all my watching and listening to him, I still have neither a clue nor a hunch. If I can't tell you which twin he is after coming this far on the trail with him, I reckon I can't expect you or anybody else to either." The ranger paused, then said, "So I prepared myself for whatever your decision might be. I told myself that whatever you decided, I'd accept it and go on about my job. If this man is innocent, we'll both have done the right thing. If he's not innocent, then we'll soon know it."

"Oh?" the judge asked curiously. "And how will that happen?"

"If he's Blake Carly, he might fool everybody for a while, but before long he'll run afoul of the law again. Then I'll get him, or somebody wearing a badge will get him. I always figure if a criminal gets by with one thing it just whets his appetite for the next thing. If there's one thing the law has on its side it's time."

"Yes, that's true," said the judge, the ranger's words seeming to ease his troubled countenance. "Another thing the law has on its side is a long memory." He looked the ranger up and down. "I'm glad we agree on this, Ranger," the judge said. "Because to tell you the truth, this one is going to keep me up a few nights. I didn't know Sheriff Tarpin very well. Does he leave a family behind?"

"No, Judge," said Sam. "It was just him."

"It helps, knowing that there's no grieving widow or children to answer to," Judge Persons said reflectively. "What kind of man was Sheriff Tarpin?"

"I can't say, Judge," said the ranger.

But the slight change in the ranger's tone of voice caused the judge to cock his head in curiosity and

ask, "Do I detect that there was some animosity between the two of you?"

"No," said the ranger. "I never worked with the
man." He hesitated for a moment, then said with
resolve, "You asked me for my opinion, so I suppose
I ought to give it you."

"Please do," said the judge.

"Not to speak ill of the deceased," said Sam, "but
from all I've ever seen or heard about Tarpin, he
was no more than a half-step away from being an
outlaw himself."

"I see," said the judge. He considered for a moment, then said, "But that doesn't excuse the fact that
he died serving the law. We have many men wearing
badges who started out on the other side of the
law."

"I only mentioned it because you asked me, Judge
Persons," said the ranger. Dismissing the matter, the
ranger said as he stood up from his chair, "If you'll
excuse me, I'll go release the prisoner."

Seeing the judge nod his head to excuse him, Sam
turned and walked to the door. But as he turned the
knob, Judge Persons said to him, "The law is not
perfect, Ranger. But I'm sure I needn't tell *you* that."

"No, Judge. I learned that early on," Sam replied,
stopping for a moment to let the judge finish whatever he still needed to say.

"Someday we will be, though," Persons said.
"There's a method called fingerprints that I read
about in *Harper's Weekly*. It's based on every person
having a unique set of fingerprints, unlike anyone
else's." He held up his fingers and wiggled them
slightly. "I realize it could take years to develop, but
once this process becomes usable, we'll eliminate this
sort of problem ever happening again."

"I won't pin my hopes on it, Judge," the ranger said, offering a tired smile. He opened the door and left.

Arriving back at the jail the ranger walked right past Jasper Farley, seated at the oaken desk, took the cell key from his vest pocket and unlocked the door to the twin's cell. Jasper arose and came walking over, and Millie Tristan stood back from the bars and watched curiously.

Sam said to the twin, "Carly, you're free to go."

"What?" said Jasper, stopping in his tracks. "How can this man go free?"

"Simple," said the ranger. "No one can say that he's Blake Carly."

As Sam swung the cell door open, Millie Tristan let out a shriek of delight. "Oh, this is *so* wonderful!" she cried, shoving past the ranger into the cell and throwing her arms around Carly's neck.

The twin embraced her, but stared over her shoulder at the ranger with a look that Sam found difficult to read. A trace of triumph came to his face, but he quickly put it aside. He sighed in relief and said, "Thank you, Ranger Burrack." But he made no effort to leave the cell. Instead he stood there with Millie's arms around him.

"Don't thank me, Carly. Thank the judge," said the ranger. "It was his decision. I just uphold the law." The ranger's voice held no bitterness or doubt. "As it turns out, I apologize for having to bring you back here. It was my job."

"I understand, Ranger," said the twin. "No hard feelings." But still he made no move toward the open cell door.

"Well," said Millie, turning the twin loose and tugging his arm, "what are we waiting for?"

The twin resisted her and said, "Before I go, I want to hear the ranger call me by my name, just once."

Looking into the twin's eyes now, the ranger saw victory, the clarity of a man who knew he had just won some sort of contest and now wanted someone other than himself to acknowledge it. Yet, as the ranger looked into that expression he saw it change, as if to keep from revealing itself to him. He allowed himself a trace of a smile, to show Carly that his expression had not changed quick enough to keep Sam from seeing through it. "I still don't know your name, Carly," the ranger said, his stare and his knowing smile unwavering.

"It's *Abel* Carly," said the twin mildly, all other aspects of his expression suddenly having gone back into hiding. "I just want to hear you say it—once, that's all."

"Oh, come on, *Abel*, what does it matter?" said Millie, playing his request off as something foolish or incidental. She emphasized "Abel" in a way that minimized the importance of his request. Again she tugged him toward the open cell door.

Again the twin resisted, standing firm, facing the ranger. "It matters to me," he said quietly, resolutely.

The ranger let a silence hang over them for a moment, then without relenting he stepped back as if prepared to close the door, saying, "All right, have it your way, Mister Carly."

"Wait!" cried Millie. "Don't lock me in here!" She stepped away from the twin and scurried through the cell door.

Reluctantly the twin followed, smiling slightly, saying as he walked out, "He wasn't going to leave us in there. Were you, Ranger? It was just a bluff—

his way of refusing to admit that I am who I say I am. Right, Ranger?"

Sam didn't answer. Instead he turned away, hung the cell key on the wall peg and turned back toward the two, as Millie stood with her arm around the twin's waist. "Think of today as being born anew, Carly. Whoever you are, whatever you are, today the law has forgiven you all your sins. The world starts all over for you."

"Don't think I don't appreciate it, Ranger," said the twin. His manner and tone made the ranger wonder just how he meant his words.

"I hope you're sincere," said the ranger, "because regardless who you are, few men ever get the chance to do what you can do for yourself. You can change your whole life right here today. All you've got to do is *want* to change it."

"My life doesn't need changing," said the twin.

Sam nodded at Millie, standing against Carly's side. "This woman could have jackpotted you, Carly, but she didn't." To Millie he said, "I hope you know how to play the hand you've dealt yourself."

"Don't concern yourself with me, Ranger," said Millie. "I go the way the wind blows." She smiled and squeezed closer to Carly. "Right now it look like it's all blowing *Abel*'s way." Again she emphasized the twin's name as if to make a point to the ranger.

"I understand, Millie," said the ranger.

"I still want to hear you call me by my right name, Ranger," the twin said, a trace of a smile on his lips.

"Don't push it, Carly," the ranger warned. "It doesn't matter what I call you, or even who you really are. It's who *and what* you become once you walk out into the world that counts. If you're Abel Carly, I suppose you won't even feel the difference.

But if you are *Blake* Carly and you just deceived the law and got yourself a fresh start—life is going to get awfully hard for you to handle. If it makes you step outside the law, that's when you'll hear me call you by your *right* name." He deliberately let his eyes turn cold on the Carly twin as he stepped out of the way and motioned the two toward the door. "You've got my word on that."

The twin and Millie walked arm in arm past the ranger and Jasper Farley and out the door, not bothering to close it behind them.

"I've never seen the likes of all this," said the barber turned sheriff, walking over and closing the door roughly. "You brought this man all the way here just to turn him loose?" He shook his head in confusion. "That makes no sense at all in my book."

"It makes sense to the judge," said the ranger. "It was his decision." He turned away as if dismissing the matter.

"Still, I bet you're madder than hell," said Farley.

"No," said the ranger. "The fact is, I don't know for sure who just walked out that door. But I know everything I just told him is the truth. Now that he's free to choose, let's just wait and see which direction he goes in."

Outside on the boardwalk, walking toward the hotel, Millie hooked her arm into the twin's and said just above a whisper, barely able to contain herself, "My God, you were right! You said you'd walk out that door a free man, and you've done it!"

The twin smiled and stared straight ahead. "Easy, Millie. I'm not going to let myself get too excited about this until I've put this town behind me and gone someplace where I can look over my shoulder without some lawman crowding me."

"Why?" said Millie. "There's no reason for any-body to crowd you. Even if another lawman showed up looking for you for something that happened long ago, they have no right to take you in." She grinned and hugged his arm. "You're Abel Carly as far as the law is concerned. What can they do to you?"

Carly just looked at her. "Still, I don't want the law to feel like I'm rubbing their noses in something, even though I *know* I'm an innocent man."

"Well," she said, in a playful pout, "I can see you're not going to be much fun with that attitude. I better go tell the ranger that you really are Blake, just to get some warm blood pumping through your veins."

The twin stopped suddenly and said, "That's not funny, Millie! I killed my own brother. Whether he was an outlaw or not doesn't matter. He's still dead and I still killed him."

"I'm sorry, Bla—I mean Abel," she stammered, seeing the earnest look on his face. "But still, you don't have to bow and curtsy to the law. You've got a right to be wherever you want to be now that you're no longer an outlaw."

The twin saw the look on her face and realized that for all her toughness, deep down Millie Tristan feared him.

What have I done to you to make you so afraid of me? he asked himself. But no sooner had he asked the question then the answer came to his mind in a different voice altogether, and that voice reminded him that he knew everything he'd ever done to cause her to fear him. Things were different when the bars separated them, or his hands were cuffed, or the ranger had held rein over his every move. Now they were on the street. He was a free man. Not only a free man, but a man with nothing hanging over his head. He had to get used to this, he reminded himself. He took a deep breath and relaxed, looking into her eyes.

"Millie, you're right," he said. "I can go where I please. What's there to worry about?" Taking her hand, he quickly led her along the boardwalk toward the hotel. "I like it here," he said over his shoulder to her. "We'll stay here as long as we want to. We might never move on. How would that sound to you?"

Millie giggled, hurrying to keep up with him. "It sounds fine to me—but slow down a little! What's your big hurry all of a sudden?"

"It just came to me that I don't owe the law or nobody else a damn thing," said the twin. "I want to celebrate. First stop is the saloon, next a restaurant, then the hotel." He squeezed her hand knowingly. "I recall you made some pretty bold promises about what will happen when we get to a hotel."

Hurrying even harder to keep up with him, Millie said in an excited voice, "You better believe I did! But none that I can't keep, *Mister* Carly!"

"I like that *Mister* part," said the twin as they walked quickly along toward the sound of a racy tinny piano coming through the bat-wing doors of the Three-Fingered Lady Saloon. "It leaves a person open to a lot of possibilities."

"Oh?" Millie said coyly. "You didn't seem to like it when the ranger called you *Mister* a while ago."

The twin chuckled. "If you were out to do to me what I thought that ranger and the law wanted to do to me, I wouldn't like it now either."

Chapter 11

In the Three-Fingered Lady Saloon, Millie and the
Carly twin set a round for the house at the bar and
spent a few minutes explaining to the drinkers how
he was not Blake Carly, the man who had shot Sheriff Tarpin. Most of the drinkers had already heard
the shooting witnesses say they had seen Blake Carly's twin with him that fateful day, so the twin's
story was easily accepted, especially since he'd
bought drinks all around. After the first few drinks
Millie and the twin sat at a table near the end of the
bar and sent a young man to a restaurant across the
street to bring them both back a steak dinner. While
they ate and drank to the sounds of laughter and
piano music a young tough by the name of Curtis
Lindsay walked over and stood beside the table. As
the twin looked up at him, Lindsay said, "I just want
to thank you again for the drink a while ago."

Grinning, the Carly twin said, "That's twice you've
said thanks, and this is twice I say, 'You're welcome.' " He nodded respectfully and returned to his
steak. Beside him, Millie kept an eye on Lindsay, not
liking the looks of him to begin with.

"That was quite a story you told about you being

Blake's twin," the young man said. "I reckon you feel pretty bad, having to shoot him and all."

"Yeah," said the twin in reflection, "that's the part I didn't dwell on. I'd just as soon not talk about it."

"Oh, I understand," said Lindsay. "But anyway, it was a huckleberry of a tale!" He looked back and forth between Millie and the twin and raised a beer mug slightly as if in a toast. "I can't say I buy one word of it," he added, chuckling under his breath, "but it made for one damn good barroom story all the same."

The twin gave him a level stare. Before he could reply to the man, though, Millie Tristan cut in, saying sharply, "Mister, nobody gives a blue damn if you *buy it* or not! The fact is, it ain't even for sale."

Ignoring Millie, Lindsay leaned in closer to the twin and said, "*The fact is* I know damn well you *are* Blake Carly, and nothing you and this whore say about it is going to make any difference one way or the other." His hand rested on the pistol at his hip.

The Carly twin started to rise from his chair, but Millie's hand on his forearm stopped him. Glancing down, he saw the cocked Colt Thunderer beneath the table edge, out of sight and aimed at Lindsay.

"Any move you make is only going to prove he's right," Millie whispered.

The twin eased down in his chair, knowing she was right. "I don't know anything about you, Mister," he said. "But I didn't come here looking for trouble. If I *was* my brother Blake, I suppose you and I would've already started shooting chunks off of one another. But I'm not him. So pull in your horns and let us be. I'm no gunfighter."

Lindsay, watching his eyes, said, "Neither was Blake. I always figured him for a coward and a back-

shooter." He gave a taunting grin, knowing that if
this was Blake, he would have to defend his honor.

But giving no more than what could be considered
a normal expression of contempt toward a man who
spoke ill of his dead brother, the twin said, "Too bad
you never found time to tell Blake that when he was
alive. You and him would have had a lot to settle
afterwards."

Curtis Lindsay stared at him a moment longer,
then turned and walked away toward the bar.

Millie faced the twin and brushed a lock of hair
back from his forehead. "Not bad! Not bad at all!"
she whispered just between the two of them. She
uncocked the Thunderer and slipped it back inside
her clothes. "Keep acting this way, and you're going
to make a believer out of *me*."

The twin only smiled, picked up his glass of whiskey and tipped it in a salute.

At the bar Curtis Lindsay picked up a fresh mug
of beer Bert Hall had bought for him. As Lindsay
sipped the foam from atop the fresh mug, Hall asked,
"Well? Is that our man or not?"

Lindsay took a longer drink, getting down past the
foam, then ran the back of his hand across his mouth
and said, "To be honest with you, I really can't say
one way or the other. He sure didn't rile the way I
figured Blake would. But that could all be an act on
his part." He took another drink and added, "I took
one hell of a chance saying what I said to him if it
is Blake Carly." He gave Hall a level stare. "You're
going to be paying for my beer all night, after me
doing that."

"Forget about the beer," said Hall, tweaking his
thin mustache with a concerned look on his face.
"This whole thing has me stumped."

"I know," said Lindsay. "There's been some strange things going on around here lately."

"You're telling me," said Hall. "Blake killing Tarpin, then ole Maynard Aubrey dying like that right at his big fancy desk. Now, here's this twin—" He shrugged, looking baffled. "Nobody knows who the hell he is. This whole thing is starting to give me the willies."

"There they go now," said Lindsay in a low voice, the two of them watching as the twin and Millie Tristan stood up from their table and walked toward the doors. "Want me to goad him one more time?"

"No," said Hall. "He's already shown us that if he's Blake Carly he ain't about to admit it. The best you're going to do is get that whore to stick a few bullets in your belly." He kept a level gaze on the Carly twin and Millie until they disappeared through the doors.

"No whore is going to stick a bullet in my belly," said Lindsay. "The more I think about it, the more I'm starting to wonder if I could take Blake man-to-man."

"Don't talk like a fool," said Hall. "A minute ago you didn't even know if that is Blake Carly. Now you're wondering if you can take him in a fight. I think you're starting to get drunk on me."

"I ain't so drunk I can't take care of myself," said Lindsay, patting his pistol butt. With the beer mug in his hand, he reached out and poured himself a shot of whiskey. "Drunk or sober, I can still get a job done."

"Don't go getting too drunk on me, Curtis, damn it," said Hall. "We need to keep our heads clear and do some figuring here."

"Back to business," Lindsay said, shrugging to

change the subject. "What's Creed going to do when he hears that Blake Carly's dead?" Lindsay raised his shot of whiskey, swallowed it, then chased it with a swig from his beer mug.

"I don't know," said Hall, giving a dubious look at the shot glass, knowing that whiskey and beer together made Curtis Lindsay wild and mean. "He had lots of deals cooking with Blake, that's for sure."

"Then I expect we ought to go find him and make sure he hears about this from us before somebody beats us to him," Lindsay said, pouring himself another shot glass of whiskey.

"That's exactly what I was thinking, Curtis," said Hall, looking him up and down. "We ought to try staying sober tonight, and first thing in the morning we'll ride out of here and go find Creed. It's time him and Mongo started taking notice of us. If Blake Carly is dead, he'll need replacing." He finished his own shot of whiskey and refilled his glass from a bottle sitting near his hand. "It might as well be you and me that replaces him."

"We're both thinking along the same line," said Lindsay, grinning, a streak of beer foam clinging to his upper lip.

"Good," said Hall. Hoping to take Lindsay's mind off the whiskey, he jerked his head toward the batwing doors and said, "Now go see where Carly and his gun-toting whore are headed. We're going to keep an eye on them till we leave town."

Outside of the saloon, Millie and the Carly twin strolled arm in arm along the boardwalk until they stepped down, crossed the dirt street and walked out of the evening heat into the Claremont Hotel. Seeing them from the dusty window of the sheriff's office,

Jasper Farley said to the ranger, "I don't know if I'd make a good lawman or not. There sure seems to be too much *whereas* and *therefore* in it to suit me."

The ranger only nodded, his interest going away from Millie and the Carly twin and concentrating instead on the familiar face of Curtis Lindsay standing in front of the saloon watching the two.

"Do you recognize that man?" Sam asked Farley, to see if the temporary sheriff had been watching his Wanted posters.

Farley studied Lindsay's face for a moment, then said, "No, he doesn't look familiar. If he didn't have that hat on I could tell you whether or not I cut his hair—or at least tell you where he last got it cut."

Sam gave him a look, then said, "His name is Curtis P. Lindsay. "He's wanted all over Texas for everything from murder to forging his name on an army voucher. I've got his name on my list for a killing in Tempe, another up near Tipton, and a string of robberies all the way from Cottonwood to Nogales."

"My goodness!" Farley exclaimed. "Do you suppose he's up to no good here in Benton Wells?"

"That would be my guess," said the ranger, not taking his eyes off Lindsay as he spoke.

"Then—I suppose we should go arrest him?" Farley asked, not sounding too eager about the prospect of it.

Sam glanced quickly over at the hotel. "Not just yet. Let's watch him a while. I'm curious as to why he's so interested in Carly and the woman."

"I—I've heard about your list, Ranger," said Farley, his voice sounding a bit shallow. "Am I going to have to help you? That is, will you need me to—"

"No, Farley," Sam said, cutting him off and letting

him off the hook. "I work better alone. He's on my list because it's doubtful he'll allow himself to be taken alive."

"Thank God," Farley said with a sigh of relief. Then, catching himself, he said, "Not that I wouldn't back you up, Ranger. But this is all new to me. I don't know if I can shoot a man if it comes down to it."

"I understand," said the ranger, watching Curtis Lindsay turn around and walk back into the saloon.

In a room at the Claremont Hotel overlooking the main street, Millie Tristan gathered the soft white sheet over her breasts and leaned back on her pillow. Rolling a smoke for herself, she pushed her hair back from her moist forehead, lit the thin cigarette and relaxed, blowing out a long stream of smoke. "Well—if there *had* been any doubt in my mind before, you just removed it, *Blake* Carly," she said.

Standing near the open window in the dark with his trousers back on, the Carly twin said in whisper, "Shhh, not so loud! These walls have a way of talking from room to room." As he spoke he slipped his shirt on.

"Aha," Millie giggled quietly, wagging a finger at him. "So you finally admit it?"

The twin just looked at her in the soft golden glow of a lamp beside the bed. "When we're alone, I'm whoever you want me to be," he said.

Millie cocked her head slightly and said, "Hey! That sounds a lot like something I might say to one of my paying customers."

The Carly twin smiled, stepped over and sat down beside her on the bed. "I've told you who I am," he said, "so from now on you decide who you want me to be." As he spoke he pulled on his boots.

"Where are you going?" Millie asked.

"It's not that late yet," said the twin. "I figured I might walk over to the saloon, have myself a night-cap, maybe bring a bottle back with me."

"You always was restless afterwards," she said, studying him closely.

"Yeah? Was I?" He considered it, then said, "It must run in the family."

"Come here," she said, reaching out, hooking her arms around him and pulling him closer to her. She let the sheet fall away from her breasts. "No man could ever make love like Blake Carly," she whispered. "So you must be him."

"Is that the only trait you see in common?" the twin asked.

"No," said Millie, "but that's a strong one. I see a lot in common between you and Blake. *Too* much for you to make me believe you're not him." Again she studied him closely.

The twin's expression turned reflective for a moment. "You see, that's because with Blake and me, we were always one man with two bodies."

She gave him a playful shove, saying, "Stop saying that! Every time you say that it gives me the willies. It makes me think I just made love with a dead man."

Still reflecting, he murmured, "Sometimes lately I've began thinking it's true."

"I thought you said you always thought it was true?" Millie said, giving him a curious look.

"What? Oh, yeah," said the twin. "I have always thought it. But I suppose lately I've been thinking it even stronger than ever."

"I know who you are. You're Blake Carly to me," Millie whispered, pulling him against her, pressing his face to her warm breasts.

"Whatever you say," he whispered against her skin. "Just as long as you keep it between you and me."

"Oh, it's our little secret," she said, liking the feel of his breath on her bare flesh. "You can count on that." She pulled his face up to hers for a kiss. But suddenly they both tensed at the sound of a gunshot from the Three-Fingered Lady Saloon and the thump of a bullet landing in the clapboard front of the Claremont Hotel.

"No, wait! Stay away from the window!" Millie warned the twin as he hurried from the bed and looked down on the street below.

He stood cautiously to one side of the window and peeped around the window's edge.

"It's the gunman Lindsay from the saloon!" he said over his shoulder.

On the street Curtis Lindsay looked back and forth along the row of hotel windows. "Blake Carly! Come down here and face me, you damn coward! Don't hide behind a whore all your life. Be a man!"

"Jesus," said Millie, coming up from the bed, one hand holding the sheet around her, the other snatching up the Colt Thunderer from the nightstand. "I might have known I'd have to shoot that son of a bitch before it was over!" She went to put on her shoes.

"No, wait," said the twin, stopping her. "He's right. He's got a fight with me. I can't keep ducking him."

"Forget it," said Millie. "I'll walk down there and part his skull with a bullet." She reached for her clothes. But as she laid the Colt on the edge of the bed to get dressed, the twin snatched it up.

"Sorry, Millie," he said. "I can't let you do that. My brother wouldn't have allowed that, and I can't either."

"Oh, just which brother are we talking about now—Blake or Abel?" she asked, standing and hiking a hand onto her hip.

"Either one," said the twin, shoving the Colt Thunderer into his waistband.

From the street Curtis Lindsay called again. "Are you coming down to face me, Blake? Or have I got to go from room to room hunting you?"

"I'm coming down, Lindsay!" the twin shouted from the window.

"Damn it to hell, be careful," said Millie, watching as the Carly twin left the room and closed the door.

The twin hurried down the stairs and eased the front door open just a crack, to take a look before stepping out onto the boardwalk. He saw Lindsay standing in the street, staring straight at him. But farther up the street he saw the ranger come walking toward the gunman with deliberation, his big Colt in his right hand, his thumb over the hammer.

"Curtis Lindsay," the ranger called out, "drop your gun and raise both hands in the air."

The twin eased back and shut the door all but a slim crack and watched.

"Who the hell are you?" Lindsay stared at the approaching figure in the glow of the corner street lanterns. He looked surprised that anyone had shown up to uphold the law in a town that had no law other than a temporary sheriff.

"I'm Ranger Sam Burrack, and you are under arrest," the ranger called out in a firm tone. "Now drop the gun."

"You're not the law here, Ranger!" Lindsay bellowed. "Where the hell is that barber who's supposed to be keeping the peace here? Firing a gun in the streets is the sort of thing a sheriff is supposed to handle. It don't require a damned ranger butting his nose in!"

"This isn't about firing a gun in the streets, Lindsay," said Sam. "You're wanted for murder and robbery, and you know it. I'm surprised you'd even show your face in a town this size. Are you going to drop that gun like I told you?"

"Not until I shoot the living hell out of Blake Carly," said Lindsay. He looked back up along the row of second-floor hotel windows and shouted, "Blake! Blake Carly! Are you going to keep hiding behind whores and lawmen? Maybe I was wrong, maybe you are some weak milksop twin brother! You sure as hell ain't showing any guts, letting everybody fight your battles for you!"

"I'm here, Lindsay!" said the twin, swinging the door wide open and stepping out onto the boardwalk.

"Stay out of this, Carly," said the ranger. "I came to arrest this man on another matter. It's got nothing to do with you!"

"No, you stay out of it, Ranger," said the twin. "He called me down here, and he's threatened my life. I have a right to defend myself." He stepped off the boardwalk and into the street, avoiding the glow of a nearby streetlamp.

"Yeah, Ranger," said Lindsay. "If you want me, I'll oblige you as soon as I kill this snake!"

The ranger noted how the twin stayed out of the light, not giving his opponent any advantage. "That's it for you, Lindsay," said the ranger, drawing closer and closer. "Drop the gun. I'm not asking again!"

"Go to hell, lawdog!" Lindsay shouted, turning squarely toward the Carly twin. "Let's do it, Blake!" he shouted, suddenly raising the cocked pistol in the twin's direction. The pistol exploded in his hand, sending a bullet slicing through the air only inches from Carly's head. But a split second behind his shot came an orange-blue blast from the Colt Thunderer in reply.

"Damn, what a shot!" Millie whispered proudly, watching from the window above as Lindsay staggered backward and sank to his knees. His gun fell from his hands, and he pitched forward onto his face, dead in the dirt.

Seeing the ranger facing him, the twin stooped cautiously and laid the Thunderer in the dirt. "See, Ranger?" He raised his hands slowly, stood up and backed away from the gun. "I'm cooperating with the law every way I can."

The twin stood stone still as Sam approached the body on the ground, looked down at the bullet hole in the chest, then walked closer to him.

"You seem awfully handy with a gun for a cowhand," he said, picking up the double-action Colt from the dirt.

"I can shoot when I need to, Ranger," said the twin. "I never claimed otherwise. And you saw the whole thing. He made the first move."

"I know," said the ranger. "You don't have to explain yourself. You're in the right, plain and simple." He looked at the streetlamp, realizing that anyone might have avoided the light instinctively. But under the circumstances it still brought up doubts. "It looks like things just keep going your way," Sam remarked. He looked at the Thunderer in his hand and gave it back butt first to the Carly twin. "So once again you're free to go," he said. As the twin took the warm gun and shoved it into his trousers, Sam noted a strange look in his eyes. He wasn't sure what was going on in Carly's mind, but he could tell that something was eating at him. "Does it bother you, being in the right? Having the law on your side? Is this hard for you to handle?"

"No, not at all, Ranger," said the twin. "I'm handling things just fine."

From the saloon came curious late-night drinkers, some with their whiskey glasses or beer mugs in hand. From the dark corner of an alley, Bert Hall stood holding the reins of his horse, watching. Looking at the body of his dead friend lying in the dirt, he shook his head and murmured, "Curtis, you stupid sonsabitch." Then he stepped up into his saddle, turned his horse in the alley and rode away in the darkness.

In the hotel room Millie stood waiting with the sheet wrapped around her. No sooner had the twin come through the door, then she said in an excited voice, "Now that was some *kind* of shooting! But if you want people to believe you're not Blake Carly you better learn to keep tricks like that to yourself." She smiled and chuckled slightly under her breath, taking the Colt Thunderer from Carly.

Without returning her smile, the twin said, "Come daylight we're leaving here."

"But I thought we were staying a few days," said Millie.

"No," said the twin. "We're leaving. I thought I could stay around here for a while, but I was wrong.

I've got to go. Are you coming with me?" he asked flatly.

"Yeah, sure," said Millie. "Where are we going?"

"You'll see when we get there. First we'll have to get you some trail clothes. We'll be heading into some rough country."

On the street below, the ranger had walked back to the sheriff's office, where Farley stood holding a lantern, preparing to gather some men and tote Lindsay's body out of the street. As Sam turned and gazed back at the soft light glowing in the hotel window, he said, "I think Carly's having a hard time being legitimate. I wouldn't be surprised if he heads out come morning. Are you ready to handle things here by yourself?"

"I—I believe so," the barber stammered. "Why? Are you going to follow him?"

"Yep," said the ranger. "For a few days anyway. Long enough to see what he does next. If he's Abel Carly there's no harm done. If he's Blake Carly, I've got a feeling I'll soon know it."

Chapter 12

Along the rocky banks of the Rio Grande, Barton Creed stood down from his saddle and picked up one of the wet guns from the open bag lying on the riverbank. Water ran in a thin stream from the gun barrel. Creed looked at it and smiled with satisfaction.

"This is how life works sometimes, boys," he said, jiggling the wet gun between his fingertips. "One minute you're on foot without two bullets to rub together, the next thing you know, you've got enough guns to clear out a border town!"

The men had spent more than an hour probing the shallows for their weapons. Now that they had found them, they gathered around and crowded into a tight circle, awaiting Creed's approval before snatching their guns from the pile. Creed searched out his own gun, shook the water off it and shoved it into his belt. Then he said, "Sort them out, boys—and be quick about it."

While the men pushed and shoved one another to get to their weapons in the pile, Creed drew his new Colt from its holster and held his thumb over the hammer. He looked around for Mazzel and Lon Pence but saw neither of them.

Mongo caught on to who Creed was looking for and as he drew his dry Colt he shouted across the rocky riverbank, "Mazzel! Pence! Come on up here. It's time we had a talk!"

The men all fell silent and looked around. There was no sign of the two guides among them.

"The sonsabitches got away," said Hightower, his wet gun dripping in his hand.

"Look, there they go!" shouted Dick Spivey, still looking weak from his wound. He pointed upward at a stretch of visible switchback trail where the guides' horses struggled along, raising a wake of dust.

Happy to have found the guns, Creed laughed aloud, saying, "I guess those two ain't as stupid as I thought!"

"Want us to go get them?" asked Ray Hightower, already reaching for his reins.

"Naw, let them go for now," said Creed. "We'll run into them somewhere along the trail. It's that son of a bitch Clifford I want to sink my claws into." Just mentioning Clifford's name caused his knuckles to turn white around his pistol grips. "Everybody get this mess sorted out and let's get going. Looks like we're back in business!" He raised his Colt in celebration and bellowed loudly as he fired three shots in the air.

Hearing the shots echo caused Mazzel and Pence to hurry that much quicker, spurring their horses wildly from the riverbank below until they reached the top of a line of hills that opened onto a stretch of open flatland headed back toward Olla Sucia. "Lord have mercy!" Pence said, snatching up a canteen from his saddle horn as they stopped and rested their horses for a moment. "I don't know how we've managed to get into so damn much trouble in so damn little time!"

"Neither do I," said Mazzel, also taking up his canteen. Winded and wiping grit and sweat from his face, he uncapped the canteen and said, "Once we get to Olla Sucia I'm letting that sheriff know that we need the protection of the law! We're hardworking citizens, honest trail guides. We don't deserve to be treated this way."

"I don't know about you," said Lon Pence, taking a swig of tepid water from his canteen, "but I don't plan on being in Olla Sucia any longer than it takes to change horses and get a hot meal in my belly. Then it's back to the territory—back to *civilization*!"

"Hear, hear," said Mazzel in agreement, tipping his own canteen and taking a drink.

When the horses had rested the two men rode through the night, and the first rays of sunlight found them back at Olla Sucia, walking their horses to the stable. The stable tender stepped forward to meet them at the barn doors, saying, "There you boys are. A fellow came by asking about yas last night, said you recently guided him—"

"Oh, no! Dayton Clifford!" said Mazzel, cutting the stable tender off with a worried look.

Lon Pence interrupted, saying, "I hope you didn't tell him we'd been here!"

"Of course he did," said Dayton Clifford, stepping forward from behind the stable man with a flat, mirthless smile wrapped around his pipe stem. "You wouldn't want this man to lie to me, would you?"

"No, sir! I sure wouldn't, Mister Clifford!" said Pence, his voice trembling as he rattled on. "I was only trying to say that had we already left it might make you think we wasn't coming back, which wouldn't be the case at all. Right, Mazzel?" He turned a frightened glance to Mazzel for support.

Mazzel had no idea what his partner had just said, but he cut right in, saying, "That's right, at least for the most part! We're not really here right now, except to change our horses and get ourselves back to the territory. This ain't our kind of country here, we've decided!"

While Mazzel spoke, Clifford all but ignored him. He stepped right past him, took the reins to both their horses and passed them along to the stable man. "Gentlemen, let's take a walk," he said, directing the two away from the barn door and off into the morning light. "I've got some more work for you to do."

Mazzel and Pence exchanged worried looks. "Mister Clifford," said Mazzel, even as they walked along just as Clifford had instructed, "me and Lon here has talked it over, and we've decided it's time we change occupations, so to speak."

"That's a pity, gentlemen," said Clifford, his hand resting on the Colt across his chest. "Because if I can't hire you to work for me, I can't take a chance on you working for somebody else who might decide to do the same thing I'm going to do."

"Huh? What is it you're going to do?" asked Pence.

"No! Wait, don't tell us!" said Mazzel. "We don't want to know!"

Ignoring him, Clifford said, "I'm going after a treasure in gold coins." He gave the two men a knowing grin, pipe smoke rising around his face. "There, now you both know." He wiggled his fingers on his bone-handled pistol butt.

At first Mazzel moaned at hearing the information. But then it caught up to him what Clifford had said. "Gold?" he said.

"Gold?" Pence said at almost the same time. They stared more intently, still frightened by Clifford but wanting to hear more now that the word "gold" had been introduced.

"Yep, gold," said Clifford. "And this is gold that at one time you two hunting *guides* could have reached out and put your hands on if you'd taken the notion."

They looked at one another, both of them thinking that Clifford had lost his mind. Mazzel replied, "I know of no time that we could have been around gold close enough to put our hands on it."

"Of course you don't," said Clifford, stepping in between the two of them, putting his arms around their shoulders and drawing them to him. "But you're about to take us to more gold than you've ever dreamed of!" He grinned back and forth at them. Pulling them along with him, he said, "Come on. We'll have a drink and I'll explain everything to you."

Mazzel stalled for a second. "Wait a minute, Clifford. Let me ask you flat out. Are you going to kill us if we don't go along with you on this?"

Clifford chuckled, staring into Mazzel's eyes. "Oh, yes, absolutely," he said almost in a whisper. After a tense pause, Clifford chuckled and said, "I'm only kidding, of course." But Mazzel took no comfort in his words.

On Clifford's other side, Lon Pence moved out from under his arm and said, "Mister Clifford, I think we ought to tell you that Barton Creed and the rest of the men we disarmed are right behind us. They held us captive ever since we first walked into Olla Sucia. For days they drug us all over the countryside. Finally we got away while they were fishing their guns out of the Rio Grande. They intend to kill us!"

"Oh, Creed and that bunch?" said Clifford, as if dismissing the seriousness of it. "You won't have to worry about them anymore, not with me on your side."

"But they wouldn't have been wanting to kill us in the first place if it hadn't been for you," said Pence.

"Be that as it may," said Clifford, his fingertips again fidgeting on the bone-handled Colt, "do you want to face them alone, or with me by your side?"

Mazzel said, "We don't want to face them at all—"

Wagging a finger, Clifford cut him short, warning, "Careful what you say now. I'd hate to lose one of you before we get under way." He grinned and gestured them forward. "Come on, let's get that drink and talk this over."

The two gave one another dejected looks and walked along in front of Clifford to the Running Horse Saloon. As soon as the three entered the saloon, Floyd Percy, the new sole owner of the place, whispered something to his bartender, then slipped out the back door and hurried to the sheriff's office.

Clifford directed Mazzel and Pence to a table in the far rear corner and motioned for the bartender to bring a bottle of whiskey and three shot glasses. After a few strong drinks Mazzel's and Pence's spirits improved considerably.

"That damned Aubrey stringing us along that way!" said Mazzel, slamming his big fist down on

the tabletop after Clifford told him about the hunting
trip ruse complete with a false European dignitary.
"Wait till I get my hands on that sumbitch."

Clifford grinned knowingly through his cloud of
pipe smoke. "I'm afraid you'd have to have awfully
long arms to get your hands on Aubrey."

"Why is that?" said Mazzel, seeing there was more
coming on the matter.

"I'm afraid Mister Aubrey is dead," said Clifford.

The two guides just looked at one another.

Seeing the look on their faces, Clifford said, "He
died of natural causes, I can assure you."

Mazzel and Pence seemed relieved.

Clifford started to say more, but he stopped talking
when he noticed Sheriff Roland Masden step through
the bat-wing doors and walk slowly toward their
table.

"Good evening, Sheriff," said Clifford, turning his
chair away from the table to face Masden. He rose
halfway, as did the other two.

"Don't get up," said Masden, extending his left
hand as if to hold them down. His right hand rested
on his pistol butt. He looked first at the two guides,
then back to Clifford. "I never expected to see any
of you three back in my town again."

"Oh?" said Clifford. "I hope I did nothing here
that I should be ashamed of, Sheriff."

"No, not you," said Masden. "You were just pushy
and rude, but I figure that's just your nature, being
a *bounty hunter*, being from the city and all." He
pointed his left finger at Mazzel and Pence. "These
two are a different story. They rode out of here with
Barton Creed and his men after a killing." Singling
Mazzel out, he asked, "Where is the rest of your
bunch?"

"Hold on, Sheriff," said Clifford. "These men work for me now, and I can assure you they have nothing to do with Barton Creed and his band of lowlifes."

"They might work for you now, but they rode out with Creed's gang. The last words out of Creed's mouth were 'Tell your sheriff to come after us if he wants to die.'" He frowned at Mazzel. "Isn't that right?"

"Yes, Sheriff," said Mazzel, "that is what he said. But ask anybody who was here if you don't want to believe us. Me and my partner never bothered anybody. The truth is, we got forced to ride along with Creed. It took us two weeks to find a way to cut out from them."

Sheriff Masden seemed to relent a little. Floyd Percy walked up beside him and said, "Sheriff, that's true. These men never raised a gun. I came and got you because I seen them walk in and I knew you'd want to ask about Creed."

"Obliged, Percy," Masden said without taking his eyes off of Mazzel and Pence.

"Sheriff, if I might interject something here," said Clifford, puffing on his pipe in contemplation. "We were going to come tell you shortly, so you could get yourself prepared." He let go of a long stream of smoke, then added, "Right now Barton Creed and his men are on their way here to Olla Sucia."

"What? They wouldn't dare," said Masden, his hand once again clamping around his pistol butt. "They know better than to ride into this town."

Clifford made a gesture with his hand, turning the conversation over to Mazzel. "It's true, Sheriff," Mazzel said. "We slipped away from them and it's a pretty sure bet they're riding after us. We figured the same as you, that they wouldn't ride into Olla Sucia.

But they dang sure will track us as far as they can
and try coming after us when we leave here."

"Yeah?" said Sheriff Masden, starting to get an
idea. "You think so, eh?"

"Well, of course, Sheriff," said Clifford, as if getting impatient with the lawman. "These men and I
took all their horses and left them afoot! We took all
of their guns and threw them in the river! There's
nothing they won't do to get to us and kill us!"

"Are there still seven of them?" Sheriff Masden
asked Mazzel.

"Yep, seven," said Mazzel. "They're well armed,
but I don't think they would be expecting anybody
to be waiting for them around here. They figure
we're too scared to stop running long enough to
fight."

Sheriff Masden stood biting his lip, thinking
things over.

"Sheriff," Clifford cut in, "if I may say so, you
will never have a better opportunity to take these
scoundrels down than you have tonight."

Sheriff Masden nodded to himself as if he had
come to an important decision. "Percy!" he said,
"have your bartender go round us up some men!
Tell them to hurry! I know just the place to lie in
wait for Creed and his men!"

"Good thinking, Sheriff!" Clifford said half sarcastically, poking his pipe stem toward Masden. Settling
back into his chair, Clifford picked up his shot glass
and started to raise it to his lips.

"Don't get comfortable, bounty hunter," said Sheriff Masden. "I'm deputizing you and your two men.
You're going with us."

Clifford started to tell the sheriff in no uncertain
terms that he wasn't doing anything of the sort. But

then he thought it over, looking Mazzel and Pence up and down, seeing the worried looks on their faces. He raised his shot glass, emptied it and stood up, saying to Masden, "Of course, Sheriff! We wouldn't miss this for the world! Right, men?" As he spoke, Mazzel and Pence both noted his hand resting on the bone-handled Colt again.

Like trained dogs with which Clifford had used his hand on his gun as a command signal, Mazzel and Pence both stood up, but without Clifford's eagerness. "Well, yeah," said Pence. "I reckon so." He gave Mazzel a look of defeat.

"You are the boss, Mister Clifford." Mazzel sighed and shrugged. "We're right behind you."

Chapter 13

————

Eight townsmen joined Sheriff Masden, in addition to Clifford and the two guides. One of the eight, an elderly Indian called Iron Tree who had spent most of his life scouting for the army, left Olla Sucia ten minutes ahead of the rest of the riders and rode at a hard pace along the trail that Mazzel and Pence had come in on. Iron Tree's job was to locate Creed and his men and ride back in time to tell Masden where to set up an ambush. Masden and his posse had gone nearly ten miles when they saw Iron Tree racing back toward them.

"Hold up, men," said Masden. "Let's hear what Tree's got to tell us."

When the old scout slid his horse to a halt in front of Masden, he pointed back along the trail and said, "Seven men coming this way—fifteen, maybe twenty minutes."

"They never saw you, Iron Tree?" Masden asked. Seeing the offended look on the Indian's weathered face, Masden answered himself. "Of course they didn't see you. What was I thinking?"

Beside the sheriff, Dayton Clifford asked the scout,

"Is there any better place up ahead for us to surprise them?"

Iron Tree shook his head. "This is good place." He pointed at the high, jagged rocks lining either side of the trail.

Masden and Clifford turned to face the other men. "All right," said the sheriff, "you heard Tree. Let's get up in those rocks and get ready. This might be the only chance we get to surprise these buzzards."

The men pushed their horses up the narrow paths until they had spread out along the crest of the hills a hundred feet above the trail. Following Clifford's lead, Mazzel and Lon Pence dropped down from their horses twenty yards away and tied the animals beside Clifford's in a stand of scrub cedar. Puffing and panting, the two joined Clifford, who stood looking down onto the trail with a repeating rifle in his gloved hand. "This is the kind of fight we like, gentlemen," he said to the pair of trail guides.

Mazzel and Pence gave each other a baffled look. "Mister Clifford," said Mazzel, "Lon and I ain't never been what you'd call *fighters*."

Clifford turned slowly toward them. Disregarding Mazzel's words, he looked them up and down and said, "Both of you sit down there and take cover until I can get something written down on paper."

Mazzel and Pence looked at one another again. "On paper?" Mazzel said.

Clifford took out his pipe, stuck it into his mouth and smiled slightly. "In case you both get killed. I know you wouldn't want your untimely demise to keep me from finding that gold." He turned and walked away.

"Why do I feel like we just jumped from the frying

pan back into the fire?" Lon Pence asked in a low voice while Clifford walked to his horse, reached into his saddlebags and took out a pencil and a folded-up piece of paper.

"Because that's what we've done, pard," Mazzel replied. "I don't know what Kenny or Rawhide or you and I ever done to deserve this devil coming into our lives, but it's clear to me that nothing good has happened to any of us since we first laid eyes on him."

"We know what we've got to do," whispered Pence. "Why don't we come out and admit it?"

"You know I don't like this kind of talk," said Mazzel. "Stop it!"

"We've got to kill him," Pence whispered, leaning in close to his comrade. "It's the only way we'll ever get rid of him before he ends up killing us both."

Mazzel squeezed his eyes shut for a second as if to keep such thoughts from entering his mind. But then he relented and let out a breath. "All right, I admit it. That's what we've got to do. Are you the one going to do it? Because to tell you the truth I don't think I can kill a man."

"Jesus," whispered Pence, "of course you can. I've seen you kill some big critters—elk, moose, bear, cougar, buffalo—that's no different than killing a man, especially if you know that son of a bitch is going to kill you!"

"It ain't the same somehow," said Mazzel, looking away from him.

"Yeah it is," said Pence. He spit and ran a hand across his mouth, staring hard at Clifford. "I figure all I'd have to do right now is jerk this pistol up and empty it into him. Surprise the hell out of him the way he did Rawhide and Kenny."

"Are you *sure* you can do it, Lon?" Mazzel asked pointedly.

"Yes, *hell* yes, I'm sure," Pence stated firmly. But then his voice softened. "That is, I'm pretty damned sure—almost *certain* I can."

Mazzel saw Clifford walking back toward them and said, "Lon, damn it, *almost certain* ain't good enough. *Almost certain* will just get us both killed."

"I'm doing it! Back me up," said Pence, tensing as Clifford drew nearer.

"Don't, please!" Mazzel whispered.

But Pence bolted upright to his feet. "Clifford!" He shouted before he realized that he hadn't intended to say a word, just draw and start blasting. But now it was too late. His hand wrapped around his gun butt and froze there.

"Not so loud," said Clifford. "If Creed and his men hear us up here, that will be the last we see of them." He looked Pence up and down. "And take your hand off of that pistol. We wouldn't want some shooting accident to tip him off either."

Pence trembled; he swallowed hard. He glanced down at Mazzel stiffly.

"He's right," said Mazzel, cutting his eyes toward Sheriff Masden and his men strung out along the rocks a few yards away.

"Now what is it you wanted?" Clifford asked, his own hand resting on his Colt. He puffed on the pipe with his bemused smile. Mazzel could almost swear that the man knew exactly what Pence had had in mind when he stood up. "You look as if you need to go relieve yourself, Pence," Clifford said. "So run along. But hurry it up."

Lon Pence looked dumbfounded. But then he shook his head as if to clear it, dropped his gun hand

and said in a whipped tone of voice, "All right, I'll hurry."

"That-a-boy," Clifford said mockingly as Pence walked away toward a stand of dried brush on the other side of the horses. "Now then, to work," he added, stooping down beside Mazzel and spreading the blank paper out on the ground. Handing Mazzel the pencil, Clifford said, "Draw from memory the farthest spot you took Aubrey's hunting party to the day you separated from the wagon for a while."

Taking the pencil, Mazzel said, "But that would be Dead Man's Canyon."

"Good! You remember!" said Clifford. "Now draw it as best you can."

Mazzel drew a long line halfway across the paper, then stopped and said, "We didn't go into Dead Man's Canyon, only to where it starts. We left the wagon there and took Aubrey off hunting. We got back late that evening."

Clifford patted his shoulder. "Real good! And that was the only day you spent with the wagon out of your sight long enough for anyone to unload the gold coins from it?"

"Yep," said Mazzel. "But you have to understand, Mister Clifford, that is one long, wide canyon. A man could spend his life searching there and never find a cache of gold coins. This is the kind of land that swallows a man up."

"Spare me the big frontier talk," said Clifford. "Just keep writing."

"Mister Clifford, you need to listen to me on this," insisted Mazzel. "We could all three die in that canyon. No supplies, no spare animals—"

"Not to hurt your feelings, Mazzel," Clifford said in a superior tone, "but so far I've never seen you or any of your *late* fellow trail guides say anything worth listening to about this land."

Mazzel nodded, as the gloved fingertips began to tap restlessly on the bone gun handle. "Yes, sir, Mister Clifford, you are the boss."

Darkness had begun to set in when Barton Creed and his men rode the trail between the tall rocky hillsides. They had followed Mazzel and Pence's hoofprints with no sense of urgency, knowing full well that the two would head straight for Olla Sucia and the protection of the law. But when the unshod hoofprints of Iron Tree's little Indian barb showed up on the trail, Creed began searching the shadows along the way. Dropping back and letting Hightower take the lead, Creed pulled his horse to the side of the trail and said to Mongo Barnes as he stepped down from his saddle, "I believe this damn ole hide has picked up a stone bruise."

"Yeah?" Mongo Barnes gave a wary look around the darkening land and the jagged hillsides. "Maybe I better check mine too." He stopped his horse but didn't step down. Instead he watched the other five men fade into the shadowy hills.

"Well?" said Creed, looking up at Mongo.

"Well, what?" Mongo asked, speaking quietly, his eyes still scanning the land around them.

"Ain't you going to get down and check its hooves?"

"Sure am," said Mongo. But when he stepped down, the first hard volley of shots exploded on the trail ahead of them. "Whoa, horse!" Mongo shouted, as his horse tried to bolt before he could get his leg back over its back and drop into his saddle.

"Ambush!" shouted Creed, jumping onto his horse

and yanking his rifle from the boot as he turned the animal sharply. The sound of hoofbeats came at them along the dark trail.

"Get out of here!" shouted Dick Spivey, his horse pounding past them as he fired back over his wounded shoulder at the blossoms of gunfire above the trail. "They're cutting us to pieces!"

Not wanting to give their position away in the darkness, Creed and Mongo held their fire as long as they could, watching the men ride past them single file. Behind Dick Spivey came Billy Drew, cursing and firing back over his shoulder, a streak of blood running down his face from a bullet graze. Next came Denton "The Blade" Ermy, leading Ray Hightower's horse. Hightower was slumped in his saddle, blood spilling freely from a wound in the side of his neck.

"Quick, into the rocks! Take cover!" Creed shouted, still holding his fire. A few more shots rained down from above as the men dismounted and pulled their horses into cover with them. Then the firing stopped as Sheriff Masden called out along the hill line, "Hold your fire! They're ducked in!"

"That damned sheriff!" said Creed to Mongo Barnes, the man huddled nearest to him. "I never thought he'd have the guts to do something like this."

"There must be a dozen guns up there," Mongo speculated. Looking around at Denton the Blade and Hightower, he called out, "Blade, how bad is he shot?"

But it was Hightower who answered for himself. "I'll live long enough to kill the sonsabitches who did this!"

"That's the spirit, Ray," said Creed.

From the rocks above them, Clifford called out in an almost laughing voice, "Barton Creed, you knucklehead, you! This is your *nemesis* of late—Dayton Clifford!"

Creed looked at Mongo, his repeating rifle in his hand. "My *what*-a-sis of late?"

"Nemesis," said Mongo, scanning the high ridges in the dark, looking for a target to shoot at. "It means enemy or opponent or some such shit."

"Then why don't he just say 'enemy'?" Creed growled.

"Ask him," said Mongo, straining upward in his search. "All I want is one good shot at that pipe-smoking *nemesis* turd!"

"Mazzel and Pence told me how badly you want to kill me, Creed," Clifford called out. "So I've decided to accommodate you. I'll have a whole band of sharpshooters riding with me from now on! We're going to stay on your trail until you're dead!"

Whispering to Mongo, Creed said, "Sharpshooters, my ass. All that shooting and all they did was hit Hightower and graze Billy Drew? Ha!" Raising slightly, he called out, "Clifford, you and your sharpshooters come on down here, see if we don't shoot a lot of daylight through you. Don't try bluffing us out, you son of a bitch! You're going to have to answer to us for everything you did!"

On the top edge of the hillside, Clifford sighed and stood up in the darkness. "Well, Sheriff, that's all for us. The guides and I will be taking our leave now. I hope we've been some help."

"What?" Sheriff Masden couldn't believe his ears. "You can't leave us in the middle of this ruckus! That's not the way we do things out here!"

"I don't know about out here, Sheriff," said Clifford. "I'm from Chicago." He grinned with his pipe between his teeth, looked at Mazzel and Pence and said calmly, "Pull up, fellows. It's time to go."

"Damn it, Clifford!" said Masden. "Why did you come if you wasn't going to stay?"

"I could see you had some misgivings about coming out here, Sheriff," said Clifford. "Since we both have an interest in seeing Creed dead, it made sense for us to join you at the time. But since Creed isn't dead—and judging from the way your men shoot I doubt if he's going to be tonight—there's no point in us being here." He tipped his hat, said "Good evening, Sheriff," and walked away, Mazzel and Pence right behind him.

"What do you want us to do, Sheriff?" asked a voice farther down the hillside.

"Damn it!" said Masden, not believing that Clifford had just walked away in the middle of a gunfight. "Fire!"

Twenty yards away, Clifford, Mazzel and Pence mounted their horses as gunfire exploded again. This time the fire was answered from below. Creed and his men had dug in and gotten ready for a fight, managing to get their horses out of the way before the firing resumed. Listening to the battle begin, Mazzel said, "Mister Clifford, are you sure we want to leave these men up here? They ain't gunfighters. They're just mostly hardworking townsmen."

Clifford nudged his horse forward, saying, "Didn't you just tell me earlier that you two aren't fighters?"

"Well, yes," said Mazzel. "I did tell you that."

"Then what good will it do to stay here?" Clifford shrugged. "I just hoped we could get rid of Creed before we made our way over to Dead Man's Canyon. But I suppose that was too much to hope for."

"Dead Man's Canyon?" said Pence. "I never heard nothing about going to Dead Man's Canyon! I ain't riding into Dead Man's Canyon!"

Clifford stopped his horse and turned it to face Pence. "Oh?" he said. "Is that your firm decision, *Lon*—or is it open for discussion?" His hand rested on the bone-handled Colt.

"Wait a minute!" said Pence. "I've got no problem with that! I'll go!" He looked at Mazzel and added, "Whatever you want, Mister Clifford! Just say so!"

"Good," said Clifford, turning his horse again, this time gesturing the pair to go ahead of him. "Let's go get our gold and be done with it."

Behind them the battle raged.

Chapter 14

In the middle of the night when the firing had fallen silent on both sides, Barton Creed crawled over to where Hightower and Denton the Blade lay behind the cover of a boulder. "How bad is he hit, Blade?" Creed asked, seeing in the pale moonlight that Hightower lay propped against a rock, limp and unconscious, a rifle lying alongside him. The Blade had stuck a wadded-up shirt on the side of Hightower's neck to slow the flow of blood.

"He's alive," said the Blade. "That's more than I can say for some of them men up in the rocks. I'm pretty damn sure I hit two of them. I heard a third holler when Billy Drew emptied his rifle at a muzzle flash." He lifted his chin and added, "They know they ain't fighting no newcomers."

"I just wish we had a way of knowing that Clifford is laying up there with his guts spilling out," said Creed. He scanned the upper edge of the hills, seeing only the darker outlines of the jagged cliffs against the purple starlit sky. "I reckon now is as good a time as any to slip out of here real quietlike. The next ambush from the hills will be *us* getting the drop on them."

Above them, Sheriff Masden and Iron Tree moved

quietly along the edge of the hill line, assessing their losses. Near the horses, two bodies lay wrapped in blankets. Sitting nearby, three townsmen sat bowed over, nursing bullet and ricochet wounds.

Harvey Bowes, who had brought along his camera and equipment to photograph the event, moved among the wounded, his sleeves rolled up above his bloody forearms. "Sheriff, these men need the doctor! I can't do them much good."

Masden looked back and forth in the dim moonlight, then said grudgingly, "I know it. These men ain't fighters, they're everyday working folks. I never should have counted on Clifford and his two guides." He looked at Iron Tree beside him and said, "Slip around and let everybody know we're pulling back."

The old Indian nodded and moved away silently in the darkness. In moments the townsmen began coming up into sight over the rocks. They gathered around Sheriff Masden and huddled close to one another, their frightened eyes darting back toward the edge of the hill line. "Help me get these men out of here, Iron Tree," Masden whispered in a bitter tone. "See to it they get back to town alive."

"What about you, Sheriff?" asked Iron Tree.

"I can't bring men out and get them shot up like this, then turn tail," said Masden. "I've got to go on after Creed and his men, just like I set out to do."

"They will kill you, Sheriff," Iron Tree said flatly.

"Then that's the way it'll have to be," said Masden.

"What about Dayton Clifford?" asked Iron Tree.

Looking off in the darkness in the direction Clifford and his guides had taken, Sheriff Masden replied, "May Dayton Clifford and his men rot in hell!"

The old Indian nodded silently and slipped quietly away toward the horses.

In the rocks below, almost a full hour passed before Barton Creed began to wonder if the posse had given up and left. Finally it was Mongo Barnes who asked, "What about me climbing up there and checking this out? I'll give you a nightbird call if it's all clear."

"Go ahead," said Creed. "We've got you covered."

In the darkness, Mongo climbed and crawled from brush to rock up the steep slope until he reached the upper edge and peeked over at the stretch of level land where Masden and his posse had been. Seeing only the flat, dark land before him, he let out a relieved breath, turned and gave a short nightbird call to Creed and the others.

Hearing Mongo's signal, Creed grinned at Denton the Blade and said, "That's what I like, men who give up quick and go running home first time we shoot a few bullets into them." He stood up and dusted his trousers. Raising his voice only slightly he said, "Get the horses. Let's circle up there and see what kind of damage we done."

When they had mounted and found a thin path that reached the top of the hill, Creed found Mongo waiting for them at the spot where the wounded men and their horses had been before Masden led them away. "Look at this, Creed!" Mongo said. "There's blood everywhere!" He sounded excited as he held up a bloody hand for all the men to see. "We must've shot the hell out of them!"

Creed stepped down and walked back and forth slowly, looking at the ground and running his boot across dark splotches of blood. "Damn! I'll say we did," he murmured, surprised at the amount of harm they'd dealt out. "For being the ones under attack, we sure as hell sent them away licking their wounds."

"I say we get right after them!" said Mongo, the sight of blood getting him more and more excited. "Kill every one of them sonsabitches!"

But looking down at the ground, studying the hoofprints that led across the stretch of flatland, Creed noted that three sets of prints moved off in a different direction from the others. "No, forget it," he said firmly. "We're going after these three." He pointed down at the separate sets of prints.

"But why?" said Mongo. "We've got the whole posse on the run, wounded. We can leave them strung out dead from here to Olla Sucia if we hurry!"

"I've got a strong feeling that these are the tracks of Clifford and his men," said Creed.

"Why would he split off from the others?" asked Mongo.

"I don't know *why* he would split off from the others," Creed said, getting testy. "It just strikes me as something he would do!" He looked around at his men. "I don't have to remind any of you what this bastard did to us—and I don't need to tell you how bad I want to skin him alive. Do I?"

The men shook their heads and murmured in unison.

"Ray! Can you ride?" he asked Hightower. "If you can't we're going to have to leave you behind."

"Damn right I can ride," Hightower rasped, the side of his neck swollen and caked with dried blood beneath the wadded-up shirt he held against it. "I ain't being left behind—not till I get my hands on Dayton Clifford."

Looking at Mongo, Creed asked flatly, "Any questions?"

Seeing an air of tension between Creed and Barnes,
Arnold Prather rode forward and said, "There ain't
no questions far as I'm concerned, except how tall a
stick do you want to put Clifford's head on."

"Yeah." Billy Drew grinned. "Let's quit yapping
and get to killing that snake!" He handed Mongo the
reins to his horse that he'd led up the hill for him.

With his eyes still black and swollen from the beating he'd taken from Billy Drew, Mongo accepted the
reins with an embarrassed look, saying, "Much
obliged." Swinging up into his saddle he raised his
hat and ran his fingers through his sweaty blond hair
and said to Creed, "No questions. Hell, let's ride."

For the next several hours they followed the three
sets of hoofprints until they reached a surface of flat
solid rock that stretched for more than three miles
along the rim of a broad land basin. Billy Drew and
Mongo rode off from the others to try to locate the
hoofprints again, but they soon returned in the darkness, having failed in their efforts. Creed looked all
around the dark, endless land and said, "It'll be daylight in a couple more hours. We might as well rest
these horses and pick up the tracks when the sun's
up."

"Hell, yes," said Billy Drew, dropping down from
his saddle. "I'll boil us up some coffee."

Creed started to swing down from his saddle as
well, but something on the far horizon caught his
attention and he froze for a second, staring at a distant glow of firelight. "Well, well," he chuckled, im-
mediately climbing back into his saddle. "It looks
like Dayton Clifford ain't as damn smart as he thinks
he is. He's gone and built himself a good cozy fire!"

The men all turned and looked out at the tiny glow

against the dark land. "Huh-uh," said Mongo. "This must be some kind of trap or something. Clifford ain't that stupid."

"Seeing is believing, Mongo," said Creed, gigging his horse forward, while the rest of the men summoned up their tired animals and fell in behind him.

When Millie Tristan and the twin first awakened to the sound of someone creeping through the pines surrounding their campsite, they piled their blankets over their saddlebags and slipped out of the clearing into the dark pines surrounding them. The campfire had burned down to a soft glow in the night, but it still cast a dim light on what appeared to be two unaware sleepers to Creed and the others as they came forward in a crouch.

Recognizing Creed as soon as he came into the glow of firelight, Millie whispered into the twin's ear, "It's Barton Creed."

The twin only nodded.

"There's Mongo Barnes," Millie whispered, seeing Mongo creep into the light behind Creed. "But you already know this, don't you?" she whispered suddenly, as if his answer might reveal something to her.

Looking into her eyes in the darkness, the twin said, "Maybe you'd better tell me who these others are too."

As the others came into sight circling the opposite side of the fire with their guns drawn, Millie named them in turn, except for Billy Drew, whom she'd never met.

"Now what do we do?" she asked. "These men will kill for horses and coffee. They won't give a damn that you're Blake's brother."

"I think when it comes to these men I'd better convince them that I *am* Blake Carly," the twin whispered.

"After spending all this time convincing everybody that you're not?" whispered Millie.

"Yep, if it'll keep us alive." Nodding at the double-barreled shotgun in Millie's hands, the twin said, "Cover me."

Creed and Mongo Barnes eased forward, stepping around the fire. Seeing a turned-over coffeepot lying beside the glowing embers, Mongo asked in a whisper, "Reckon we've spooked them away from here?"

Creed replied as he stared at the two piled blankets, "No, I think we've just caught *Mister* Clifford sound asleep."

Mongo nodded toward two horses standing just outside the firelight. "Where's the third—?"

But Creed raised a hand, silencing him. Then he gestured for the others to circle around the campfire and move in slowly as he and Mongo moved forward. At less than ten feet away from the two blanketed figures, Creed held his pistol forward at arm's length, cocked and aimed it. "On your feet, Clifford!" he shouted. Mongo waved the others around quickly. Having gotten no response, Creed jumped forward and shouted again as he kicked one of the blankets, "Damn it! Wake up, you son of a bitch!"

From the edge of the campsite came the sound of a woman's voice that startled the men and caused them to reel toward it with their guns aimed and ready to fire. "Why, Barton Creed, my goodness! Are you blind?" said Millie Tristan, a slight chuckle in her voice. "Can't you see the blankets are empty?" She jiggled the cocked double-barreled shotgun in her hands and added, "So would your belly be right now if I hadn't recognized you."

"Mil—Millie?" said Creed, looking her up and down in disbelief. "Is that you?"

"Yep, it's me," said Millie. "Now everybody quit squeezing the hardware so tight."

"My oh my!" said Creed. "I never expected to see you out here like this."

The other men stood staring, their guns lowering a little as their mouths dropped open. Millie grinned, keeping the shotgun leveled at Creed's belly from ten feet away. "Then this is going to be a day full of big surprises for you, Creed," she said. Looking at Mongo Barnes, she said, "Morning, Mongo." Her eyes moved from man to man as she addressed all of them except Billy Drew by name.

As Millie spoke, the men saw the Carly twin step forward from the shadowy pines into the clearing, his face obscured by his lowered hat brim. "Keep them covered, Millie," he said in a quiet voice.

"I knew you wouldn't be out here alone, Millie Tristan," said Mongo, turning his pistol toward the twin.

"Easy, Mongo," said Creed, hearing something familiar in the man's voice. Looking closely, Creed saw something familiar in the man's build and his bearing as well, but recognition had not caught up with him yet. "What kind of surprises are you talking about, Millie?"

Creed had hardly gotten the words out of his mouth when he gasped aloud. The twin lifted his hat and revealed his face. "Is this enough surprise for you?" the twin asked.

The rest of the men gasped as well. Their faces

turned white in fear and disbelief. Ray Hightower screamed, dropped his gun and bolted out of the clearing before catching himself and easing back in, his face red with shame. Yet the men didn't seem to notice Hightower's movement as they stood staring. It was as if they saw the dead walking among them.

Creed recovered quickly. Swallowing a knot in his throat, he managed to say in a raspy voice, "Blake Carly—the last time I saw you, you was deader than hell!"

"Ease your gun down, Creed," said the twin, "and I'll do the same."

Creed did as he was told, but his eyes stayed wide with disbelief, staring at the twin. Creed motioned for the others to lower their guns as well. Only Millie kept her gun cocked and ready. Yet no one seemed to notice as they all ventured in warily for a closer look at their recently deceased comrade.

"Blake," said Mongo, "I don't know what the hell you've done or how the hell you did it, but if that wasn't your blue corpse with a hole in its forehead we pulled out of El Río, I'll eat horseflies for breakfast!"

"He'd do that anyway," said Creed, trying to offer a friendly smile but knowing there was a fearful nervous twitch preventing it. "But he's right about us pulling your dead ass out of the river. What the hell is going on with you?"

"That man you saw was my twin brother, Abel Carly," said the twin.

Creed and his men looked suspicious and still a bit dumbstruck at the sight of him. "Twin *brother*?" said Creed. "I never heard you mention nothing about having a twin *brother*! How come you never mentioned it to any of us?" He cocked his head, giving the twin a dubious look.

"It was nobody's business," said the twin. "There's a lot more I might not have mentioned about myself." He looked around at the other men. Millie watched, wondering if he was trying to remember all the names she'd just told him, or if he'd known all their names to begin with. "Howdy, Raymond," he said to Hightower, who still held the wadded-up shirt against his wounded neck. "Howdy, Blade—Spivey, Prather." He stopped at Billy Drew.

"His name is Billy Drew," said Hightower in his rasping injured voice, "and he's one tough ole boy. He beat the shit out of Mongo here."

The twin started to comment, seeing Mongo's swollen eyes. But before he could speak, Creed, who had been staring closely at him, said bluntly, "Where the hell are all those damn gold coins? Or did you decide that was *nobody's business* either?"

The twin just stared at him.

"Don't even try to act like you ain't going to tell me, Blake," said Creed. "I know you got the truth out of Tarpin, and I know you left him dead on the ground."

"What if I told you Tarpin never gave it up about where the gold was hidden?" said the twin.

"I'd have to say you was lying," said Creed. "We've been pards a long time. But this kind of money has a way of turning men like us into fighting dogs." His hand halfway started to raise his pistol again.

"Take it easy, Creed," said the twin. "If anything happens to me, you'll never see all them pretty gold coins." He grinned, but even as he did, he raised his own pistol slightly, his hand tightening around it.

"I ain't seeing any of them right now," said Creed firmly.

"Take it easy, like he said, Creed," said Mongo. "You know Blake has to needle everybody a little. Hell, it wouldn't be him is he didn't." Mongo chuckled. "Right, Blake?"

Watching, her hands still clasped around the shotgun and ready to fire at any second, Millie breathed a short sigh of relief when she saw the twin give her a nod and lower his pistol again.

"Creed, you're wound tighter than a Tennessee fiddle. You ought to know everybody here is going to get what's coming to them if I have any say in it."

"I ain't sure how you mean that," said Creed, not giving in just yet. "We was suppose to have met up in Estación del Sol. We was there, but you wasn't."

"Oh, I was there all right," said the twin, lying. "You can ask Millie here. I heard you'd already been there and left. I figured I'd run into you along the way. I wasn't going to fool around too long and take a chance on somebody else getting there before I did. We might be pards, but damned if I was going take that kind of chance." He looked around at the men again. "Is there anybody who can blame me?" He looked straight at Mongo Barnes as he asked, "Is there anybody here who would have waited any *longer* before coming after the gold on his own?"

Millie watched, seeing the twin turn the attitudes of the men in his favor. "He's got a point there," said Billy Drew. "All this talking aside, why don't we just get on with it?" Ray Hightower nodded in agreement in spite of his neck wound. The others murmured and nodded with him.

"That's what I say," said the twin. "Anything we need to talk about we can talk about while we go after the gold."

Creed seemed to ease down a little. "So, you got the best of Tarpin, just like you said you would?"

"No problem at all," said the twin. "I've got all the directions, right up here." He tapped his forehead.

"Why didn't you draw it out on a map for us as soon as you got a chance?" said Creed. "That's what we all agreed you would do, in case something happened to you."

The twin didn't answer. Instead he stooped down and picked up the overturned coffeepot. "It'll soon be morning. What say we boil us up some coffee, then get on the trail?"

Chapter 15

During the night the ranger had heard the tail end of the gun battle between Creed and the posse from Olla Sucia. But the faintness of the gunfire had meant it was too far away for him to investigate. Had he not been following Carly and the woman, he might have broken away and gone to see what the shooting was about. But like as not he would have traveled half the night to find nothing but a chuck wagon and a band of drunken cowhands returning from a drive, their pockets full of money, their bellies full of whiskey, shooting at the moon.

As it turned out, sticking to the trail he was on, Sam discovered seven extra sets of hoofprints with the first morning light as he crossed a dry creek bed and headed up into the high hills. The two sets of prints left by Millie and the Carly twin showed him that their horses had been traveling at a good steady pace across this rough terrain. But these seven new sets of prints had come up onto the trail at a hard run. The length and depth of the prints showed that the seven riders continued at a run for a while, in places covering the twin's trail entirely. Yet in other places the riders had slowed to a walk and veered

away as if they had lost their trail and had to search
for it again in the darkness.

"Looks like I'm not the only one interested in your
comings and goings, Carly," Sam said down to the
hoofprints. He stopped Black Pot at the crest of a
jagged rise lined with mesquite brush long enough to
gaze off in the direction of last night's distant gunfire.
Whoever was trailing the twin and the woman, the
ranger concluded, had started following them sometime during the night, coming from the same direction where he'd heard the gunfire. At the rate these
seven horses traveled he was certain that by now
they had caught up to Carly and the woman.

"Friends of yours, Carly?" he murmured to himself, gazing off through a drift of dust across the arid
flatlands. "We'll see."

Nudging the big Appaloosa forward, he rode on,
not realizing that had he crossed that dry creek bed
fifty yards farther along, he would have seen another
set of tracks—those left by Dayton Clifford and his
two trail guides.

Ten miles later the ranger topped a ridge and saw
a dusty paint horse grazing on a nearby clump of
wild grass, its reins dangling to the ground, its saddle empty, a length of bedroll hanging loose behind
its saddle. On the ground he saw a crumpled hat.
Ten feet farther he saw a body stretched out in the
sand, facedown, partially obscured by a stand of brittle mesquite brush. He stepped down from his saddle
and walked toward the body, taking up the reins to
the grazing horse on his way.

Drawing nearer to the body, the ranger heard a
low groaning sound. When he stopped three feet
away, he saw a hand stretched out in the sand holding a cocked Colt. Seeing the man struggle to lift the

gun, the ranger clamped a boot down on the wrist, saying, "That'll be enough of that." He twisted the gun free and stood up, reaching for a canteen hanging from the horse's saddle horn.

"Go on—get it over with!" the man rasped. "You cutthroat son of a—"

"Whoa now," said the ranger, cutting him off as he uncapped the canteen and stooped down to the man. "I mean you no harm, mister. Here, let's get some water in you and start all over." He lifted the man over onto his back and cradled his head on his lap. It was then that he saw the sheriff's badge on his chest and said, "Roland Masden. I thought I recognized that paint horse."

"Ra—Ranger Burrack?" said Sheriff Masden in a dry, broken voice. Before the ranger could even answer, the sheriff's dry dusty lips found the canteen cap and took a spilling swig of tepid water.

"Yes, it's me, Sheriff," said Sam. "Have you got any holes in you, or anything broken?"

"Naw," the sheriff groaned. "My horse took a roll coming down that slope. Is he all right?"

"He's walking all right," said the ranger, giving the paint horse a quick look. "You'll want to check him closer soon as you get your bearings."

"Lucky we're not both dead, a fall like that," said Masden. He struggled to raise himself up.

"Here, let me help you," said the ranger. He assisted the sheriff into a sitting position.

"Obliged, Ranger," Masden groaned, rubbing the back of his head. He swigged again from the canteen, then capped it and tried to stand up. The ranger gave him a pull to his feet. "My goodness," the dazed sheriff said, struggling to get his footing. "I must've landed on a rock."

"Take it easy," said Sam, helping him steady himself by placing one of his hands on the horse's rump. "What are you doing out here, anyways?" As he asked, the ranger reached up, tucked the dangling blanket roll back into place behind the saddle and dusted it off with his hand.

Coming around, Sheriff Masden said, "What am *I* doing here? This is New Mexico Territory, Ranger. The question is what are *you* doing here?"

Looking around at the land, the ranger said, "This might be too close to call, Sheriff. I'm following a man and a woman out of Benton Wells. I brought the man in for a killing, but the judge turned him loose. What about you?"

Masden looked ashamed. "I got misled into coming out here by a crazy man hunter from Chicago named Dayton Clifford. We was supposed to bring down Barton Creed and his men together. But no sooner than we caught up to Creed, Clifford skinned out on me. Creed killed some of my townsfolk. Now I'm bound to go find him and make things right. If I run into Clifford along the way, I wouldn't mind shooting a couple of his toes off just for good measure."

Right away the ranger saw more than just coincidence between Barton Creed and the Carly twin. "Sheriff, the man I'm trailing is either Blake Carly or his twin brother."

Masden just looked at him for a second. Thinking he couldn't see what he was getting at, the ranger said, "Blake Carly always rode with Creed and his men."

"I know that," said Masden. "But it ain't Blake Carly you're trailing. I saw Blake Carly go onto the ground with my own two eyes. He had a big bullet hole in his head. This man hunter Dayton Clifford is the one who killed him, or so he claimed. He's the one who dropped his body on my doorstep anyway."

The ranger thought about it for a moment, trying to picture what had happened to the Carly twin's body after he and the other twin had left it adrift down the Rio Grande. Finally he shook his head, saying, "I can see this is all going to take some serious explaining, Sheriff. Are you able to ride now?"

"I can ride," said Masden. "Just let me stand here a minute longer, get my brain headed in the right direction. I'll check out this old paint horse and get back in the saddle.

After a few more sips of water, Masden checked his horse over thoroughly, then wet his bandanna, wiped his face with it and climbed up into his saddle. He said to the ranger, "I don't know if we're in your territory or mine, but I reckon it won't matter by the end of the day. We'll be crossing the corner of Colorado and heading into the Utah range anyway."

"Wherever their trail leads us, as far as I'm concerned," said the ranger.

"Me too," said Masden. "I'm sure glad to have somebody with me who knows a gun from a dinner fork."

The ranger nodded and nudged the Appaloosa forward. They rode on, talking as they went, each telling the other the particulars and circumstances that had brought them out into the wilds. At noon when they rested their horses in the shade of a rock draw, Masden considered everything the ranger had told him about the Carly twins and said with a look of contemplation, "No matter which one this man really is, he still has to live with knowing he killed his own brother."

"Yep," said the ranger, "and that just makes it all the harder to figure. Every time I think about it I come up with a different set of answers. But no matter which one this man is, he's shown me he's capable of killing."

"Yep," said Masden, "and whichever one this is, he still walked away from a hanging because he claims a man who looks just like him was going to kill him and take *his* identity."

Sam nodded. "It has a bad taste to it, doesn't it?"

"I'll say," Masden remarked.

"One thing I keep asking myself," said Sam, "is how can an ordinary cowhand like Abel is supposed to be get the best of a killer like Blake Carly is supposed to be? You'd think that Abel Carly might hesitate, being more affected by killing his own brother than some hard case like Blake."

"Maybe neither one was as good or as bad as they were made out to be," said Masden. "You know the old saying, 'There's some good in the worst of us and some bad in the best of us.' "

"That's interesting, Sheriff," said the ranger, thinking about it. "You're saying that maybe Blake was ruthless enough to want to kill his brother and take over his identity, but when it came down to it he wasn't *bad* enough to get it done. Maybe Abel, no matter how *good* he was, in the end wasn't so good that he would allow his life to be taken from him without putting up a fight, even killing his brother."

"Yeah, something like that," said Masden. He scratched his head, wincing as his finger ran across the knot left from his fall. "I sure don't envy you

this one, Ranger," he said. "But why are you fooling
with it anyway, now that the judge turned the man
loose?"

"That's something else I keep asking myself," Sam
replied. "I reckon I just can't let go of it. It bothers
me that something like this can happen."

"Me too," said Masden, "now that I know about
it." After a pause he asked, "What do you suppose
Dayton Clifford has to do with all this?"

"I don't know," said the ranger. "Since he was
paid to hunt down Blake Carly and now Blake Carly
is officially dead, I can't see him having any interest
here at all." He looked off into the distance. "There's
more to it than we know about. I'm hoping to find
out farther down the trail."

Creed and the Carly twin rode side by side, Millie
Tristan rode close behind the twin, and the other
riders rode single file behind her. They kept their
horses at a slow walk up a steep trail into a maze of
rock canyons where the land lay broken and up-
turned. Riding at the rear, Billy Drew ventured his
horse up beside Denton the Blade and asked him
quietly, "What's the deal on the woman?"

Denton the Blade turned and looked at him with
a bemused expression. "Best you don't let yourself
start thinking about her, Billy," he said.

Billy grinned, rubbing his dark beard stubble as he
gazed ahead at Millie Tristan, the sway of her body
with each step of her horse. "Hot damn, Blade, she's
a looker."

"She's a looker, all right," said the Blade. "But you
don't want to get Blake Carly down your shirt—her
neither, as far as that goes."

"Prather said she's a whore," Billy commented.

"Yep, she is a whore. But she got stuck up against Blake a couple of years back and I don't reckon she's got her fill of him yet." He nodded forward. "As you can see, she don't allow much space to get behind them."

"But if she's a whore . . ." Billy let his words trail off.

"You ain't listening to me, are you?" The Blade grinned.

"I reckon not," said Billy. "See, I don't think it's fair a whore won't give it up to whoever wants it and has the money to pay for it, do you?"

The Blade shrugged. "It's hers to do with as she pleases, I suppose. If you've got ideas about her, I'm telling you for your own good, she ain't worth it."

"I've got money, I'll *pay* her," said Billy, not about to be discouraged. "I just ain't going to be turned away because she's got something struck with Blake Carly." He spit and rubbed his hand across his lips. "Sometimes you have to slap a hardheaded whore around a little bit, just to loosen her up."

"You'll likely end up with a mouth full of buckshot if you get heavy-handed with Millie."

"I'll take my chances," said Billy. "That's what life is all about ain't it, taking chances?"

"Sure, now that I think of it," said Denton. He just looked at the young gunman for a moment, seeing all the makings of an entertaining afternoon. Finally he said, "And what about Blake Carly? Are you going to slap him around too?"

Billy shrugged. "If I have to. He doesn't impress me near as much as he does everybody else here." Billy puffed his chest out a bit. "I think I've proved to everybody that I can take care of myself."

"That's true enough," said the Blade, considering

it. After a moment of contemplation he said, "Well, then. Since you don't owe me any money, I say *have at it.* See how it all works out."

Billy Drew gave him a cold look. "I wasn't asking your permission, *Blade.*"

"I realize you weren't, Billy," said Denton. "I was just commenting on the matter." He nudged his horse forward, putting a few feet between himself and the young gunman.

They rode on throughout the day and stopped in the afternoon atop a broad rock shelf overlooking sparse pine lands hundreds of feet below. Across the deep canyon another land shelf stretched out flat for miles before reaching upward into a line of jagged purple hills. Stepping down from his saddle, the Carly twin gazed out across the canyon and said to Creed, beside him, "Past those hills is Dead Man's Canyon. That's where we're headed."

"Dead Man's Canyon ain't no small place," said Creed. "I think you ought to tell us right now where the coins are, in case something should happen to you along the way."

The twin smiled and stared out across the deep canyon. "Now what on earth could happen to me between here and there?"

"Anything could happen," said Creed. "You know that as well as I do. You could step too close to a rattler, or your horse could slip and take a tumble. In fact, step back away from that edge." He gave the twin's shirt a pull. "Hell, from this high up, it'd be Christmas before you landed!"

"I'll be careful," said the twin, taking a step back. "Much obliged for your concern."

"I ain't trying to be cagey," said Creed. "But damn it, I want that gold so bad I can taste it. You can't blame me for wanting to know right now, especially after thinking you was dead and all. Besides, I take offense that you don't want to trust me, as long as we've rode together, all the tight places we've been through!"

"We'll be there tomorrow night or the next morning," said the twin. "We can all wait that much longer. After that we'll be rich." He grinned and walked back to where Millie sat looking down at him from her saddle, the double-barreled shotgun lying across her lap.

"You sure have been looking and sounding too much like Blake Carly not to be him," she whispered, leaning down to him.

"So far, so good," said the twin. "If the coins are where my brother said they are, all we've got to do is get our share and get away. From there we'll go anywhere you like, Millie," he said secretively between them. As he spoke he laid a hand on her knee and squeezed slightly. "I never want to look at another lost calf or a branding iron again in my life."

Millie smiled. "Guess what I never want to look at the rest of my life—except you, of course."

As the men gathered their horses closer, seeing Millie and the twin together, Billy Drew said to Denton the Blade, "By God, they both know what seeing them act that way does to a man like me. She's asking for it."

Denton the Blade sighed quietly and watched Billy gig his horse forward a few more feet, then come to a halt and drop down from his saddle. "Damn fool," Denton murmured to himself.

"Huh? What's that you say?" said Arnold Prather.

"How's your wound, Arnold?" Denton asked.

"Better, much better," said Prather. He grinned. "I

started getting better as soon as I saw that we still had a chance at getting the gold."

"That's the spirit," said Denton. His voice lowered. "Let me ask you something. If it come down to a showdown between them two"—he nodded toward Billy Drew and the twin—"which one would you put your money on?"

"Right now I've got no money," said Prather. "But if I did have, I'd bet on the new man, Billy Drew."

"Is that a fact?" said Denton.

"Sure is," said Prather. "You saw how he handled Mongo. And how fast he is with a gun! Nothing against Blake Carly, but I'd bet on the new man." He cocked an eye at Denton. "Why, is there something brewing?"

"I think there just might be," said Denton. "If there is I'll cover your bet."

"I can't bet," said Prather. "I told you I ain't got no money."

"Neither do I," said Denton, "but we've got money coming, and a pretty good chunk of it at that. So, what do you say? Want to wager on a gunfight?"

Prather grinned, getting interested now that he realized he had plenty of money coming to him. "Well, hell, yes then!" he said, keeping his voice low. "I'll take the new man against Blake. For how much?"

Denton the Blade's expression lit up with greed as he stared at him. "All of it, of course."

Chapter 16

When Prather and Denton the Blade had made a campfire a few yards from the edge of the rock shelf, Denton whispered to Prather, "Arnold, watch this." Turning to Millie Tristan and the twin who sat against a rock ten yards away, he said, "Millie, you're the only woman here—how about boiling us up a big pot of coffee?"

"Denton," Millie said matter-of-factly, "kiss my ass." She didn't even look up as she said it, but continued to casually inspect her fingernails, her hands lying on the shotgun in her lap.

The men all laughed and hooted, taunting Denton. But Denton didn't seem to mind. He smiled and shook his head. Then, turning to Billy Drew, who sat ten feet away in the opposite direction, he shrugged and said, "See? Hardheaded as a mountain goat."

Billy Drew didn't smile. He looked at Denton for a moment, then turned his somber gaze to Millie Tristan.

"Here we go," Denton whispered to Prather, watching Billy Drew stand up slowly and walk across the campsite toward Millie. "I got him primed and smoking."

Stopping three feet from Millie and the twin, Billy Drew stared down, threw a silver half-dollar onto Millie's lap, and said, "There's my money. Come with me, whore."

The campsite fell silent.

"Fifty cents?" Millie looked up from the half-dollar and said calmly, "What is it you want to do, short stuff, *dance*?"

Beside her the Carly twin started to stand up. But Billy Drew had planned things out. He moved fast, kicking the shotgun off Millie's lap, sending it bouncing and sliding across the flat rock. His Colt streaked up and leveled in the twin's face, inches from his right eye. "Sit tight, Blake Carly!" he hissed. "I'm going to ride this whore like she ain't never been rode!" He reached down, grabbed Millie and jerked her to her feet. "Let's go, whore, else we'll do it right here in front of Blake and everybod—"

He stopped, cut short by Millie's knee coming up solidly into his groin, lifting him onto his toes. He jackknifed forward before she could grab his Colt from his hand. But the gun was useless to him anyway. He stood bowed deep at the waist, both hands, gun and all, pressed to his aching groin. He made a deep choking sound in his chest, staggered backward a step and sank to his knees.

"Jesus!" Prather whispered to Denton. "Looks like she just put a halt to everything!"

"Naw, your boy Billy is coming back up. He's too stupid to lay still."

A straight razor appeared in Millie's hand as if out of thin air. She stepped forward before the twin could stop her. "Now then, short stuff, get your hands out of the way. I'm going to lighten you up a little."

"She's a corker, ain't she?" Denton chuckled, whispering to Prather.

"All right, Millie! That's enough!" Creed shouted, he and Mongo both stepping in between them. The twin was also on his feet. He stepped around quickly and raised his hands in front of Millie, afraid to grab her, judging by the wild look in her eyes.

"Easy, Millie," the twin whispered. "It's over. Let it go."

"It's not over! He'll come back at us! I know his type! I'm going to cut his throat!" she hissed, taking a step forward, staring past the twin at Billy, who still hadn't straightened up. Her knuckles turned white around the razor handle.

"Not now, Millie," said the twin, blocking her. "You've got to cool down."

"Yeah, Millie," said Mongo, not minding too much what she'd done, after the way Billy Drew had beaten him in front of everybody. "If he comes back at you we'll all kill him. Right, boys?" He shot a glance around at the others. To his satisfaction they all nodded.

"Calm her down, Blake," said Creed, reaching down between Billy Drew's legs, wrenching the pistol from his hand and shoving it back into his holster. "Billy, you calm down too," he said, patting the bowed-over gunman on the back.

Billy groaned painfully.

Mongo stepped around beside Creed, and together they forced Billy Drew to stand upright. A string of saliva swung from the young gunman's lips. "Gawd . . . damn . . . you!" he gasped, staring at Millie through red and watery eyes.

"You want some more?" Millie shouted, holding the razor out, shaking it at him.

"Millie, stop it!" said the twin.

"You better get her under control, Blake!" said Creed.

"She's all right now. Ain't you, Millie?" said the twin.

"Yeah," Millie spat, glaring at Billy Drew. Mumbling under her breath, she added, "I'll nut that son of a bitch!"

"Millie shouldn't have been facing Billy anyway!" Denton the Blade shouted, seeing that things might die down if he didn't stoke them up a little. "Blake, why didn't you take care of him?"

"Stay out of this, Denton!" shouted Creed, not wanting to take a chance on anything happening to the twin before they found the gold.

"Sorry, boss," said Denton, tossing his hands up and pulling back, knowing he'd already said enough to keep things going without getting himself in trouble.

"That's right," said Prather. "Why *is* Blake Carly letting this woman fight his battles for him?"

Billy Drew's voice had started to come back to him. "That's what I'd like to know. All I've heard is how tough Blake Carly is—but all I've seen is him standing behind a whore, letting her protect him! Maybe this ain't Blake Carly. Maybe it's his chickenshit twin!"

"Billy, shut up," said Creed. "There ain't going to be no more fighting!"

But the Carly twin saw the look of doubt in Creed's eyes, and he said to Billy Drew, "This wasn't about Millie at all, was it, Billy?"

"Now you're starting to get the message, Carly!" said Billy Drew, his voice sounding stronger, his hand poised near the Colt on his hip. "I want to open you up and see if you really are Blake Carly inside." He gestured with his other hand. "I believe everybody here wonders if you are who you say you are."

The twin looked him up and down. Noticing that the others, even Creed, had fallen silent, he said, "Maybe you'll get your chance at me, Billy, once this is all over."

"Huh-uh," said Billy, shaking his head. "I ain't waiting to find out what you're made of. If you ain't Blake Carly, how do we know this whole trip ain't just you buying yourself some time until you can get away from us?"

Without answering, the Carly twin looked at the others, seeing the doubt beginning to register in their eyes. He knew he couldn't let that happen. "All right, Billy. You want it now—let's do it now." His hand poised near the double-action Thunderer in his belt.

"Whoa now! Wait a minute!" said Creed. "I can't take a chance on you getting killed here, Blake!"

"If he's Blake, you shouldn't have to worry about it!" Denton the Blade cut in.

"Keep it up, Denton," said Creed, "and I'm going to stick my boot down your throat!"

"He's right, Creed," said the twin, staring hard at Billy Drew. "This little punk ain't worth all the conversation he's causing."

Millie stared at the twin, hearing his bold talk. Yet she thought she saw something akin to fear in his eyes. She stepped farther back, out of the way, knowing that nothing Creed or she could say was going to stop this. Creed and Mongo also saw it was too late to stop anything. They knew that what Denton had said was right. If this was Blake Carly, they had nothing to worry about; if it wasn't Blake, they needed to know it now.

"Make your move, Billy," the twin said coldly.

Billy Drew tensed, his hand starting for his gun. But before his fingers closed on the handle a blast from Millie's shotgun slammed him backward across the flat rock surface until he stopped only a few feet from the edge.

"Damn, Millie!" shouted Denton the Blade, seeing a red mist hang in the air for a second before splattering across the rock. The rest of the men stood staring as Billy Drew rolled over onto what was left of his belly and pushed himself to his feet.

"You damn . . . whore!" he said in a voice that bore little human quality. He wobbled back and forth, smoke rolling out of him, his middle hanging in shreds. A few scattered beads of buckshot had sprinkled his face, some of them breaking his front teeth into sharp little stubs. Blood spewed from his lips. Still his hand fumbled for the gun on his hip. The shotgun roared again. The second blast lifted him off the land shelf altogether and sent him spiraling downward. His body bounced like a broken doll off the side of the rocky slope until the sound of his wet, solid landing resounded along the canyon floor.

The men stood in stunned silence for a moment, staring at the edge from which Billy Drew had taken flight. Red streaks lay strewn across the rock surface. Creed ventured closer to the edge, taking care not to slip in the blood. He looked down and shook his head slowly. Stepping back, he turned and said in a hushed tone, "By God, there went Billy."

At the end of a another silent pause Denton the

Blade looked up from the long streaks of blood across the rock surface and said, "That is one *shotgunning* whore!" Then he caught himself and raised his hand toward Millie, saying, "And I mean that in a most respectful way!"

Millie just stared at him, opened the double barrel, popped out the two spent loads and replaced them with two fresh loads she pulled out of her billowing white riding blouse. "I know you do, Denton," she said, clicking the shotgun closed. "I'm a whore, but I'm not going to be abused."

"We've seen that, Millie," said Creed. "Now why don't you give that two-eyed devil to Blake, let him hold it while you settle down some?"

She turned the shotgun around and handed it butt first to the twin.

"Looks like I win, Arnold," Denton the Blade whispered to Prather.

"How do you figure *you* win?" Prather remarked firmly. "The bet was Blake against Billy."

"Yeah, but Billy had a chance to kill him and he didn't," Denton said quietly.

"Like hell," said Prather. "Billy would've killed him, if she hadn't blown him in two!"

"Keep your voice down," said Denton. "We'll settle up once we get our gold."

"There ain't no *settling up*, far as I'm concerned," said Prather, not giving an inch. "They never fought. The whore stepped in and killed the bet."

"All right," said Denton the Blade, "if that's the kind of welching weaseling no good son of—"

"Shut up, both of yas!" said Mongo. Looking at the twin, he said, "Other than having these two ready to fight, you didn't prove a damn thing, did you?"

The twin said coolly, "I wasn't out to prove anything." His hand poised near the Colt Thunderer. "Do I *need* to prove anything to *you*, Mongo?"

"Hell, no, you don't!" Creed cut in. "Now let's stop this craziness!" He looked at the quarrelsome gunmen standing around scowling at one another. "We've all got ourselves a good chunk of money coming soon as we get to that gold! I hope we can stop killing each other long enough to get it done!"

"I didn't mean nothing against you, Blake," Mongo said grudgingly. "I'm glad that son of a bitch is dead, to tell you the truth. He was a new man. I couldn't see him getting a share of gold he had no part in."

"Oh?" said Creed, looking at him scornfully. "What part did you have in it?"

"I was riding with this bunch when we hatched the scheme," said Mongo. "That's what I'm getting at."

Ignoring him, Creed said to the others, "Let's get some coffee up and some grub cooked. We've got a long day tomorrow."

"Did you hear that?" Clifford asked the two guides when the first shotgun blast echoed across the canyon. "It's a shotgun," he said, answering himself.

Mazzel said as they stopped on the trail right before reaching the rocky summit, "No offense, Mister Clifford, but can you recognize a shotgun out in the wilds like this, being from a big city and all?"

Clifford gave him a flat stare. "Mazzel, I'm not from just *any* city," he said. "I'm from *Chicago*. If a person doesn't hear a shotgun now and then in Chicago he's not paying attention."

No sooner had Clifford finished his statement than the second blast sounded. Mazzel flinched and said, "Yep, it's a shotgun, all right."

"It's coming from across the canyon," said Clifford. "Come on. Let's get up there where we can take a look." He slapped the rump of Mazzel's horse, keeping the two ahead of him as he gigged his own horse up the steep trail.

At the top of the trail, they dismounted and took shelter in a high spill of rocks. Dayton Clifford hurriedly took his binoculars from a leather case and raised them to his eyes. He scanned the other edge of the canyon until he stopped suddenly with a slight gasp. Then he turned away from his binoculars with a strange look on his face. "Good God!" he said. "I must be suffering from too much sun!" Then he put his eyes back to the binoculars to reaffirm what he'd seen.

"What is it?" Mazzel asked, he and Lon Pence standing beside Clifford.

When Clifford turned his eyes away from the binoculars again, the strange look on his face was bemused, baffled. For a second he only stared at Mazzel as if in a trance state. Suddenly he shook his head as if to get his mind working again and said, "Here, you tell me what you see over there."

Mazzel gave Pence a look before taking the binoculars and raising them to his eyes. "Oh, my goodness," he said in a hushed tone. "It's Barton Creed and his men!"

"Keep looking," said Clifford, biding his time, watching Mazzel scan the far rock plateau.

"There's a woman, and a—*ayii*!" Mazzel shrieked as his eyes fell upon the twin. He dropped the binoculars as if they had turned red-hot.

"Watch it, Mazzel!" shouted Clifford, catching the binoculars before they tumbled onto the rocks. "These are not cheap instruments, you fool!"

"But—but he's dead!" Mazzel stammered.

"Hardly," said Clifford, raising the binoculars to his eyes again. "Dead men don't get around that good."

"What are you talking about?" asked Pence, seeing the look on both of their faces.

"It's Blake Carly—or else his ghost!" said Mazzel, his voice trembling.

"Please—" Clifford groaned disdainfully without lowering the binoculars from his eyes.

"His ghost?" said Pence, his eyes widening.

"Both of you shut up," said Clifford, "before you work one another into a frenzy."

"Then you explain it to us, Mister Clifford," said Mazzel, keeping himself from sounding too demanding.

"I *can't* explain it," said Clifford as he watched the twin and Millie Tristan talking to one another silently, as if they were only a few feet away. He smiled, easily recognizing the chemistry between the two. "But not being able to explain an occurrence doesn't right away mean it's something *supernatural*."

"It doesn't?" Pence asked Mazzel.

Mazzel gave him a look implying that Clifford didn't know what he was talking about.

"No, it doesn't," said Clifford, lowering the binoculars again, this time with a look of satisfaction on his face. He tried handing them to Mazzel, but Mazzel refused.

"Huh-uh," Mazzel said. "I've seen all I want to see!"

But Pence took the binoculars and raised them to his eyes warily. "Oh my God!" he said after a moment of searching the group across the canyon. "It really is a ghost!"

Clifford smiled as he fished out his pipe, filled it,

packed it, and held it in his mouth. "You can both be grateful to this ghost for making your jobs a lot easier for you."

Pence lowered the lens. The two looked at Clifford.

"You both said Dead Man's Canyon is too big to search for the gold?" He struck a match and lit his pipe. Shaking the match out, he said, "Here's the man who can take us right to it." He grinned smugly and blew out a long stream of smoke.

Mazzel and Pence looked worried. "He'd never do that, Mister Clifford. This man Blake is a hardened outlaw. Why would he lead us to that gold?"

"Because we have something he wants," said Clifford, reaching out for the binoculars as he spoke.

"We do?" Mazzel asked reluctantly, both he and Pence staring intently, hanging on Clifford's words with worried looks in their eyes.

"Oh yes, we do," Clifford grinned. "And it's something he wants so bad that he will do whatever we tell him to do, once he knows we've got it."

"What is it we've got?" Pence asked.

Raising the binoculars to his eyes, Clifford puffed on the pipe clamped between his teeth as he focused on the twin and the woman again. "Oh, we don't have it just now," he said, smiling slightly. "But I'm certain we'll have it very soon." Lowering the binoculars and looking around at Mazzel, he said, "We'll rest the animals for a few minutes, then we're on our way."

"On our way?" Mazzel and Pence looked stunned. "Mister Clifford, it'll be dark soon. We can't be traipsing around on the high trails after dark! Nobody in their right mind travels out here after dark!"

Tapping his fingertips on his bone-handled pistol butt, Dayton Clifford said, "You know—it occurs to me that we had this very same conversation recently, back when poor Rawhide Hale was still among the living."

Although he was frightened, Mazzel continued, hoping to get the man hunter to listen to reason. "Yes, we did, Mister Clifford," he said, "and I hope you won't shoot me as well. I ain't refusing to do what I'm told. But man-oh-man, we're lucky not to go off one of these trails during the daylight, let alone at night, in a quarter moon!"

Clifford tilted his head slightly. "Mazzel, I realize that you and I can't see in the darkness, but these horses see most proficiently in the moonlight. Now rest them out a while and get your sorry behinds ready to ride." He wagged a gloved finger, cautioning them. "Don't disappoint me."

Mazzel and Pence watched him turn and walk away, a curl of pipe smoke drifting back over his shoulder.

"The trouble with him," Pence said in a low voice, "is that nobody ever sat him down and told him what folks can and can't do out in this kind of country."

"Yeah," said Mazzel, "and because he doesn't know any better, he just plunges ahead and does it."

"We need to shove him off a cliff tonight," whispered Pence, "before he gets us both killed."

"Anytime you're ready, shove away," said Mazzel. "I'll be right behind you."

After a pause, Pence said, "Well, it would be good to get our hands on that gold first, wouldn't it?"

Mazzel just looked at him without answering, then turned and walked off toward the horses.

PART 3

PART 3

Chapter 17

As soon as the horses were rested, Clifford and the two trail guides traveled down and out across the canyon floor. When they reached a thin stream running along the bottom of the steep, rocky walls, they heard the low snarling of a pack of wolves and the soft padding sound of paws on rock as the animals scurried away from the body of Billy Drew. The dead outlaw lay draped over a boulder in the pale moonlight as if he'd been served up to creatures of the wild on their own dinner table.

"Good Lord," Mazzel whispered under his breath, gazing skyward to where the tall black wall of rock stopped beneath the thinly lit sky. "That's what awaits us up there if we don't watch our step."

Clifford chuckled and drew on his pipe. "Stop being such a pessimist. It wasn't losing his footing that got that man killed. I have a feeling those two shotgun blasts we heard played an important part in it." Raising the Colt from across his chest, he aimed it at the dead outlaw and said, "Bang! Bang!" Then, twirling the Colt, he looked at Mazzel and Pence, who sat staring at him, and said, "What's the holdup, men?" The Colt stopped twirling and came to rest pointed at Mazzel's chest, Clifford's thumb lying over the hammer.

"Not a thing!" said Mazzel. "We're on our way!" He gigged his horse forward, Pence doing the same right beside him, and the two hurried across the shallow stream and onto the upward winding trail.

It took them most of the night to get near the spot where they'd seen Creed's men and Millie and the twin. Once they caught sight of a small campfire just off the trail less than a hundred yards ahead, they stopped and quietly stepped down from their saddles. Walking over close to Mazzel and Pence, Clifford whispered, "From now on, none of us says a word. We're going to slip in closer. You two are going to stay back here with your horses ready while I lead my horse in closer and wait for an opportunity to grab the woman and bring her back with me. When I come riding back, be ready to go. Once we've got the woman with us, this man will do whatever we ask."

"But that woman will be fighting you like a wildcat," Mazzel whispered. "Won't they all hear her and come running?"

"I don't think so," said Clifford. "You let me worry about that. Just make sure I don't come back here and find that you two have taken leave. I would never be able to forgive you for something like that."

"We'll be here, won't we, Lon?" said Mazzel.

"You bet," said Pence. "You've got our word on it."

Clifford smiled and slipped away into the darkness, leading his horse behind him. No sooner was he out of sight than Pence whispered, "Here's our chance. Let's take it!"

"No," said Mazzel. "I'm not going anywhere until he gets back here."

"Are you crazy?" said Pence. "We've been looking for an opportunity like this!"

"I had a hard enough time getting up that trail with nobody hounding me," said Mazzel. "I ain't about to try going down it with Clifford on my tail wanting to kill me and the Creed gang right behind him! I'm sticking for now. If you want to go, here's your chance."

Pence looked him up and down, then said, "Oh, I get it now. You figure to let me go on my way, then you and Clifford won't have to split none of the gold with me." He gave a dark chuckle and said, "Well, you can just forget about it, Mazzel. I'm sticking too."

Along the last few yards of the trail, Clifford looked to the east and saw a thin silver wreath on the horizon. He knew that timing was important. He wanted to have enough daylight to get down the trail quickly if anyone awakened and caught on to what he was doing. Tying the reins to a short scrub cedar, he opened his saddlebags and took out a small green bottle and a wadded-up bandanna. Then he slipped closer to the glowing campfire on foot and eased in silently between rocks and brush until he could see the layout of the campsite.

On one side of the fire lay Creed and his men, the way Clifford judged it. On the other side lay two figures close together, the way only a man and a woman would lie. Perfect, he told himself, easing through the rocks until he stopped less then twenty feet from the two sleepers. Sinking into the cover of rock, he prepared himself for what could be a long wait. But to his surprise, less than ten minutes had gone by when the woman sat up and rubbed her eyes.

Before the woman had risen to her feet, Clifford had taken out the green bottle, uncorked it, and sprinkled a few drops of chloroform onto the bandanna. He watched her step into her trousers and boots, pick up the shotgun and walk into the darkness, then he hurried along in a crouch, capping the bottle and putting it away as he went.

A few feet into the darkness, Millie Tristan relieved herself and stood up buttoning her trousers. She thought she heard a cedar twig snap somewhere behind her. She paused, stooped down to pick up the shotgun and listened intently. But she heard no other sound. Looking around the dark terrain, she started to walk back toward the campsite when suddenly Clifford swooped out of the brush from behind and was upon her, knocking the shotgun from her hand.

She tried to shout, but his hand clamped over her lips, pressing the wadded-up bandanna half inside her mouth. She smelled the smothering odor of chloroform and struggled against Clifford's viselike grip.

"Shhh," the voice purred in her ear. "Don't fight it, relax with it. I'm not going to kill you. Breathe, breathe deep."

She tossed her head back and forth wildly, attempting to free herself of the hand and the smothering bandanna, but already the effects of the chloroform had begun to take hold. Clifford held her bent backward against his knee, keeping her off balance, unable to make any trick she knew work for her. In seconds she succumbed to the drug and swooned limply against him. Her fingers, which had been reaching back to claw at his face, ceased their attack, and her hands fell to her sides. "There, now, that wasn't so bad, was it?" Clifford whispered.

Reaching down with the woman lying unconscious in the crook of his arm, he laid the photograph of the dead Carly twin on the shotgun and quietly carried Millie back to where he'd tied his horse. In moments he brought the horse back to where the two guides stood waiting for him. Seeing the woman lying over the saddle, Pence said in a trembling voice, "Oh, Lord God, he's done it! Now we're in for it, sure enough!"

"Shut up, Lon!" Mazzel whispered, stepping forward as Clifford motioned to him. "Is she dead?" he asked Clifford.

"Don't talk stupid," said Clifford. "Of course she's not dead. I told you I was going to get her and hold her hostage, didn't I?"

"Yes, you did," said Mazzel. "I reckon I just wasn't prepared for it to really happen is all."

Clifford gave him a disgusted look. "I think you've spent too much of your life around cheap-talking fools." He gestured toward the woman and handed Mazzel his reins. "Hold this horse while I get her across my lap and tie her hands. I'm sure she's going to be a wildcat when she comes to."

"When she *comes to*?" Mazzel asked. "What did you knock her in the head with?"

Clifford didn't answer. Instead he swung himself up onto his horse behind the saddle long enough to raise Millie's limp figure and get her draped across his lap. "You two stay close in front of me and move fast," Clifford said quietly. "It won't be long before daylight. They'll know she's missing. Blake Carly will come riding hard once he spots our tracks."

Looking back in the darkness, Mazzel said, "Don't

worry. We'll move fast now, steep trail or not! I don't want to tangle with any of Creed's bunch, especially one that I know is already dead and gone to hell!"

Ray Hightower and Barton Creed were the first two men up from their blankets and huddled near the fire making coffee. But it was the Carly twin who awakened and noticed that Millie wasn't there. He pressed his hand to her blanket and found it cool to his touch. Standing up, he looked all around and saw her small bootprints heading out into the brush. "Creed!" he said with a degree of urgency, as if having already sensed that something was wrong. "How long ago did Millie leave camp?"

Creed looked around as if he had not noticed one way or the other. Realizing that they hadn't seen the woman, he and Hightower stood up together. "Hell, I didn't see her when I woke up," said Creed. "What about you, Ray?"

Hightower shrugged. "I didn't see her—not that I was looking for her."

"I better go look for her," said the twin, picking up the Colt Thunderer and sticking it into his belt.

As he hurried away, Creed said to Hightower, "Get that coffee boiling. I'll go keep an eye on him."

Rushing along in Millie's footprints the Carly twin came upon the shotgun and the photograph only seconds ahead of Creed. But he had picked up both the shotgun and the image of his dead brother when Creed arrived.

"What's this?" Creed asked warily, his hand on his gun butt as he scanned the rocky terrain. "Where's the whore?"

"Don't call her a whore. Her name's Millie," the

twin said absently, staring at the photograph, trying to make sense of what was obviously a message someone had left for him. He looked at the man's bootprints on the ground, seeing how they came up behind Millie's, then noting how Millie's had disappeared.

"Where the hell is *Millie*, then?" said Creed, giving her name a bit of sarcasm.

"He took her," said the twin. "He picked her up from behind and took her." As he spoke he turned, his eyes following the man's tracks out into the brush.

"He who?" asked Creed, looking at the photograph as the Carly twin held it out for him. Creed tried to take it, but the twin kept a grip on it. "Oh hell!" said Creed, looking closely. "What kind of crazy son of a bitch would want to leave something like this behind?"

"The same kind of crazy son of a bitch who would shoot a dead man," said the twin.

"What the hell?" said Creed, examining the photograph even closer. "Your brother didn't have any bullet holes in his chest when we found him!"

"That's what I was getting at," the twin murmured, still searching the endless land. "Now you tell *me* the only kind of person who would even want a dead man's picture, let alone do something like this."

It came to Creed in a flash. "A bounty hunter! Dayton Clifford! That bastard, that turd, that male-buggering rotten son of a bitch!" He clenched his fists in rage and gritted his teeth. Then he suddenly looked confused. "But *why*? Why would he do this—take the whore and leave this photograph?"

"He wants me to come looking for her," said the twin with quiet resolve, staring off across the rough land.

"Well, he didn't have to go to all this trouble to get us down his shirt, that bastard!" said Creed, once again seething with rage. "We'll be on his tail like flies on a bear! Come on, let's get the rest of the men up!"

"No," said the twin. "He wants me to come alone."

"Bull!" said Creed, giving the Carly twin a suspicious look, already starting to wonder if the twin and Millie might be up to something. "How do you know that's what he wants you to do?"

"Because he said so," the twin replied, moving his hand off the bottom of the photograph where Clifford had written with a lead pencil two words: "Come alone."

"Oh." Creed was taken aback at seeing the words, but only for a moment. "Well, to hell with him and what he wants! We're all going! We'll kill him!"

"No," said the twin. "He'll kill her if he sees all of us coming after him. That's the message he's giving me here, without him even having to say so." Carly paused, then said, "I have to go alone."

"I'll be damned if you will," said Creed. "For all I know you and the whore could have hatched up this whole thing just to cheat us out of the gold!"

"You know better than that, Creed," said the twin.

"No I don't," Creed insisted. "To tell you the truth, you ain't acting like the Blake Carly I know." He nodded at the photograph. "I'm getting doubts about who that picture is of in your hand and who it is I see standing in front of me!"

"I'm the same Blake Carly I've always been, Creed," said the twin.

"Oh yeah?" Creed said defiantly. "Well, the Blake Carly I know had no great love for that whore Millie Tristan that I can recall."

"Stop calling her a whore, Creed," the twin warned.

Pointing a finger, Creed said, "Aha—see? That's just what I mean! You never was so sensitive about her being called a whore before! I've heard you call her a whore yourself. As I recall, you avoided every town you thought she might be in for the past year! Now all of sudden you're afraid something is going to happen to her?"

"Maybe I've changed," said the twin, but his tone of voice didn't sound convincing. "Maybe I've come to realize how much Millie means to me."

"Huh-uh!" Creed shook his head. "You can't sell that syrup to me. I know better!" As he spoke his hand went to his pistol butt. "We're all riding with you, *whoever* you are."

Before his hand could get around his pistol he saw the Carly twin's thumb cock both hammers on the shotgun, the barrel pointed more deliberately at his face. "While you've got your hand there," said the twin, "raise that pistol with two fingers and drop it over this way."

"Damn it, wait a minute," said Creed, wanting to back things off a little. "This has gotten too far out of hand. All right, I believe you're Blake Carly, and I trust you to go after the woman alone! Let's stay friends here!"

"Whoever you think I am doesn't mean much to me one way or the other," said the twin, "but you better understand that it won't matter to you either once these hammers fall."

"Damn it to hell," Creed grumbled, lifting his pistol and pitching it near the twin's feet.

In the campsite, Ray Hightower had awakened the rest of the men when Creed went off following the Carly twin. Now that Creed hadn't returned, the men had strapped on their gun belts and stood adjusting their pistols in their holsters as Mongo asked Hightower, "And you've seen no sign of the whore at all this morning?"

"Not at all," said Hightower, drawing his gun, checking it and holding on to it without holstering it. He had started to say something more of the matter, but the sight of Barton Creed walking in slowly with the twin holding the tip of the shotgun barrel under his chin made him stop cold, gasp and say, "Holy Moses! Look who's coming here."

"All right, men," said Creed, his head tipped up at an awkward angle, his eyes wide, "don't nobody do anything stupid! You know Blake here is a worse killer than all the rest of yas put together!"

"What the hell is this?" said Mongo, his hand closing around his gun butt.

"Damn it, Mongo!" said Creed. "Do whatever he tells you! The man ain't playing around! Somebody stole the whor—I mean the *woman*," he said, changing his word quickly. "Blake here is going after her without us! That's what we're all agreeing to, you hear me?"

Mongo and the men just stared for a moment, letting it all sink in. Then Mongo said, "Somebody snatched the whore, right out from under our noses?"

"Don't call Millie a whore, Mongo," said Creed,

his eyes widening even more. "She's as good as the rest of us!"

"I never said she wasn't," said Mongo, bemused and not understanding. "Who snatched her?"

As Creed spoke, the twin guided him around the fire toward the horses. "We're thinking that bastard Dayton Clifford did it," said Creed, "unless anybody can come up with a better guess."

"Blake! What the hell are you doing with that shotgun to Creed's chin?" asked Hightower, not seeing the reasoning behind it. "You're one of us! Start acting like yourself again!" He started to walk toward them. "Quit all this craziness before somebody gets—"

"No! No! *Please!*" Creed shouted. Holding the shotgun under Creed's chin with one hand, the twin held the Colt Thunderer in his left hand, his arm around Creed's waist. A shot exploded from the pistol and kicked up dirt an inch from Hightower's toes. He jumped back.

"Is that acting like *myself*?" the twin asked. "Is that some Blake Carly shooting? If it's not good enough for you, take another step and I'll clip you into a steer!"

"Whoa! Hold it, Blake!" said Hightower. His hands flew up into the air. "Tell us whatever you want. We'll do it! Just take it easy!"

"That's smart thinking on your part, Ray," said the twin. "Raise the gun with two fingers and drop it."

"There you are," said Hightower, doing as he was told.

"Get over there and saddle me a horse," said the twin. Looking at the others, he said, "All of you now, use two fingers. You know what I want. Let me hear some hardware hit the ground."

The twin held Creed close to him and stepped closer to the horses to keep a better eye on Hightower as he untied Carly's horse from the others. "Give me Millie's horse too," said the twin. "Then turn the rest of them loose and shoo them out of here."

"Do what?" said Hightower.

"You heard him, Ray, damn it to hell!" Creed shouted. "Can't you see what a tight spot I'm in here?"

The twin watched tensely until the horses had been run off into the brush. For good measure, he fired two rounds from the Thunderer, spooking them on their way.

"We'll be half the day chasing them horses down," said Mongo.

"That's the idea, Barnes," said Carly, taking the reins to Millie's horse.

"It ain't right, you leaving us on foot this way," Mongo said.

"The horses won't go far," said the twin. "And I'm not taking your guns. I'm doing my best to try to get out of here without killing any of you."

"It still ain't right," Mongo said, spitting at the ground.

"Shut up, Mongo!" Creed raged.

The Carly twin eased away from Creed and stepped into the saddle, keeping the shotgun aimed down in Creed's face. "I know you'll be following me, and I know you'll be wanting to fight. But I'm going after Millie. If we meet again, I'll still take you to the gold. You've got my word on that."

Creed and the men, standing unarmed, just stared at him, watching him back the horses out of sight into the brush and turn them toward the thin trail.

When they heard the hoofbeats riding away, Creed bellowed at the men, "What are you waiting for? Get the damn horses! This is the second time the whole bunch of us has been put afoot by *one* man! What the blue blazing hell are we doing wrong?"

Chapter 18

The ranger and Sheriff Masden had heard the sound of a single gunshot moments earlier when the Carly twin had fired at Hightower's feet. They had followed it to the stream where the remains of Billy Drew had been strewn about during the night and now lay glistening in the sunlight. "Lord God!" Masden said in a hushed tone. "Looks like the wolves and coyotes are doing all right for themselves. What do you suppose happened here?"

The ranger brushed a hand back and forth, shooing flies away from him. "Not much happened here," Sam replied. He looked upward, judging the height from which the body had fallen. "It looks like it all came from up there. This is just where it ended."

As they both looked up, they heard two more pistol shots—the shots the Carly twin fired to spook the horses away. "Sounds like something's *still* going on up there," said Masden, the two of them already gigging their horses toward the steep trail leading up into the rocks.

The two lawmen did not see Clifford and his guides hurrying down another trail seventy yards to the left at a dangerous pace, their horses struggling and at times sliding on loose dirt and rocks. But farther up, near the top of the jagged hillside, the ranger and the sheriff did look back and across the rough terrain in time to see the twin leading Millie Tristan's horse down that same trail. Before the twin went out of sight behind a large boulder, Sam said, "I didn't have time to recognize the rider, but that looked a lot like Carly's and the woman's horses."

"Then where's the woman?" said Masden, looking away from the spot where they'd seen the twin and up along the cliffs above them.

Nodding toward a narrow path that cut toward the other trail, Sam said, "Let's see if we can't ride over there and find out. He was riding like a man with dogs nipping at his tail."

They cut across on the winding path until they reached the trail the twin had ridden down. But rather than following the twin right away, the lawmen rode up the trail to see what the shooting had been about earlier. After less than half a mile they stopped at the sound of hooves running toward them. In seconds a bareback horse came trotting by at an easy gait. Masden gigged his horse alongside it, snatched its dangling reins and brought the animal to a halt. Not far behind the fleeing animal came a cursing voice, shouting, "Come back here, you lousy, flea-bitten son of a bitch, you!"

The lawmen pulled their horses to the side of the trail and wrapped the bareback animal's reins around Masden's saddle horn, then stepped down from their saddles and stood waiting in silence until the man came trotting around the turn in the trail and slid to a halt to keep from running into them. He awkwardly started to reach for his gun, but then stopped cold as the ranger cocked his big Colt and leveled it in his face.

"Raise them over your head!" the ranger said in a calm, firm voice.

The gunman knew what the ranger meant. Muttering a curse under his breath, he raised his hands high and let out a long breath. "All right, Ranger. I ain't breaking no law up here. Now what?"

Sam asked Masden, "Is this one of Creed's men?"

"Yep," said Masden. "This is the one they all call 'the Blade' or some such nonsense."

Denton the Blade looked offended. "My name is Denton Ermy. Only my *friends* call me the Blade." His gaze narrowed toward the ranger. "You lawdogs ain't my friends."

"I'm glad to hear that, Mister Blade," said the ranger, lifting Denton's pistol from his holster and shoving it into his belt. "Now I won't feel so bad cracking your head for lying to us when I ask you a question."

"What question?" Denton said with a sneer.

"First of all, where's your knife and your hideout gun?" the ranger asked.

Denton the Blade said haughtily, "I'm not carrying either a knife or a—"

His words cut short as the ranger's gun barrel made a quick swipe against the side of his head. "Any man called 'the Blade' is bound to have a knife and pistol hidden *somewhere*."

"Lord, Ranger!" said Sheriff Masden in stunned protest.

But as the outlaw sank to his knees, the ranger jerked the small sleeve gun from his still raised hand and pitched it to Masden. "There—just in time," said the ranger. "Another second he would've been taking a shot at one of us."

The sheriff looked at the little pistol and said no more on the matter. Sam reached up under the wobbling outlaw's riding coat and pulled out a long, slim dagger. Shaking his head, he pitched the dagger to Masden, then pulled Denton up onto his feet.

"Now then, Mister Blade," said the ranger, "before I hit you on the other side of your head, why don't you tell me what you're doing up here."

"Chasing down our damned horses," said Denton bitterly. "Seems like that's about all we do these days."

The ranger drew his pistol barrel back threateningly. Denton the Blade took on a frightened expression. "No, really, Ranger, it's the truth! Blake Carly scattered all our horses and took off on us! We're gathering them up now so we can get on his trail!"

"Blake Carly, huh?" Sam asked, giving Masden a glance. Then he asked Denton the Blade, "How do you know he's Blake Carly, not his twin brother, Abel?"

Denton shrugged. "Hell, I guess nobody can say for sure. But he sure enough acted like Blake—except when it came to that whore. He seems to have gone awfully sweet on her all of a sudden."

"Where is she?" Sam asked.

"Dayton Clifford took her. Blake's gone alone to get her back."

Masden and Sam looked at one another. "Dayton Clifford," said Masden. "That figures."

"How far ahead are Clifford and the woman?" Sam asked.

"I don't know for sure," said Denton. "A good ways, I reckon. They was already gone when I woke up. Creed and Mongo are about ready to kill Blake if they get their hands on him." Denton paused, as if thinking it over. Then he said, "Naw, I reckon that ain't so. They won't kill him. Not just yet anyway." He caught himself and stopped talking.

"Why not?" the ranger asked.

But Denton had shut up on the matter and just stared straight ahead, saying, "I've said too much already."

"Lower your hands," said the ranger, realizing that the outlaw had nothing more to tell him. Taking a pair of handcuffs from behind his back, Sam pulled the outlaw's wrists close together and clicked the cuffs around them. Then, he gave him a slight push and said, "Let's go round up your pals."

They mounted and rode their horses upward at a quiet walk until they heard the sound of men and horses gathered a few yards ahead of them beyond a large pile of boulders. Once again the lawmen stepped down from their saddles and moved forward on foot. This time they carried their rifles with them, first handcuffing Denton the Blade to a tall scrub cedar and stuffing his bandanna into his mouth. "Are we going to try and take them all down?" Sheriff Masden asked in a whisper, as the two of them checked their pistols and rifles.

Sam looked at him closely. "We're not going to *try* and take them down, Sheriff. We're going to do it. If there's any doubt about it, let's talk it over and get it straight in our minds before we go a step farther."

Masden shook his head. "No, I'm fine. It was just a figure of speech. I'm ready when you are."

"All right," Sam nodded, clicking his Colt shut. Gesturing toward the sound of the voices beyond the boulders, he said, "Let's spread out going up to the boulder. Keep about fifteen or more feet between us if we can."

"Any shooting order?" Masden asked, trying to keep his voice from sounding shaky. "I mean, should we try to kill Creed first?"

"There's no shooting order as far as I'm concerned," said the ranger. "Creed's the leader, but they're all hard cases. We'll take them as they come. Are you all right?" Again he looked the sheriff up and down.

"Hell, yes, I'm all right," said Masden in a sharp voice. "I can handle myself, Ranger. Make no mistake about that."

"Good," said Sam. "Let's get it done."

On the other side of the boulder, Barton Creed wiped his forehead with a damp bandanna and finished saddling his horse roughly, letting his anger at the Carly twin show. "I get my hands on that son of a bitch, he'll wish it was him that died first instead of his brother!"

"Where's the Blade?" asked Mongo Barnes, looking around as the rest of the men saddled their recaptured horses and readied them for the trail.

"I don't know," said Dick Spivey, still looking drawn and weak from his wound. "I saw him a while ago, chasing his horse down the trail."

"Where's Hightower?" asked Mongo.

"I'm over here," answered Ray Hightower. He and Arnold Prather had found their horses together, grazing in the sparse clumps of wild grass.

"Then everybody's here except Denton," said Mongo. "I suppose we'll catch up to him down the trail somewhere."

Creed started to say something, but before he got his words out, the ranger's voice called from atop the boulder behind them. "Barton Creed! You and your men are under arrest! We've got you covered! Throw down your guns and put your hands in the air!"

Creed and the others turned slowly, looking up, then back and forth, getting an idea of how many lawmen were standing above them. Seeing only the ranger and Sheriff Masden, Mongo said to Creed in a low voice, "It's only that sheriff from Olla Sucia and some damned ranger is all."

"That ain't just some damned ranger," Dick Spivey whispered from a few feet away. "That's the ranger that took down Junior Lake and his whole gang. They say he learned a lot about shooting from the gunslinger Lawrence Shaw."

"Yeah?" said Barton Creed, dropping the reins to his horse. "Well, he's going to learn a hell of a lot *more* about shooting from *us* today!" His hand streaked down for the pistol on his hip. "Kill them!" he shouted. Yet, after drawing his pistol and firing one shot, he ducked behind Mongo Barnes, then down under his horse as gunshots filled the air.

The ranger's first shot hit Mongo high in his shoulder and drove him backward against his horse. Mongo fired repeatedly as he sank to the ground shouting, "Damn you, Creed!"

Sheriff Masden took a graze on his right arm as he shot Dick Spivey dead, a spray of blood rising in the air amid the thick gunsmoke. In seconds the smoke was so thick it provided cover for the outlaws but not for the lawmen. The ranger turned his rifle fire toward Arnold Prather. Two shots lifted Prather off of his feet and sent him rolling backward, firing wildly as he came to rest against the side of a tall boulder.

Ray Hightower managed to get several shots off,

one of them slamming Sheriff Masden in his shoulder, before a shot from the ranger hurled Hightower over a short rock and left him lying dead. "Don't shoot!" Creed pleaded from beneath his horse. "I'm not shooting, see?" He stuck his empty hands out so the lawmen could see him drop his gun.

Squinting to see through the smoke, the ranger kept his rifle aimed and said, "Step out of the smoke so we can see you."

"Creed, you dirty bastard!" shouted Mongo Barnes, his voice thick with blood. "You ain't giving us up!"

"The hell I ain't," said Creed. "This whole show has been jinxed from the start! We can't even keep horses under ourselves!"

"I'll kill you myself!" shouted Mongo, staggering toward Creed as Creed stepped forward with his hands raised high above his head. Mongo fired, the shot grazing the side of Creed's head but not even knocking him off his feet. Before Mongo could fire again, one shot from Sheriff Masden knocked him to the ground, dead.

Creed winced, holding a hand to his bloody head. He looked at Mongo Barnes lying facedown in the dirt in a pool of blood and said, "He never did know when to call it quits, Ranger, but I do!" He wiggled his raised hand. "See, no gun here! I give up, plain and simple! Don't shoot me! I'm already bleeding to death!"

"You're going to be all right, Creed. Stay right there where you are. We're coming down," the ranger called out. Cautiously, he and Sheriff Masden stepped sideways, circling the boulder to a point where they could jump down while keeping an eye on Creed through the heavy, drifting smoke.

Shaking his bloody head, Creed said as they walked over to him, "I don't know what the hell got into these boys, doing what they did in Olla Sucia. I tried to stop them, but they just quit listening to me. It was like they lost their minds!"

"Shut up, Creed!" Sheriff Masden said in disgust. "You're the one who did the killing in my town. And you're the one who's going to swing for it!"

"Huh-uh!" said Creed. "You've got it all wrong, Sheriff! It wasn't me who did it. It was these ole boys!"

Taking out his handcuffs, Masden lowered the outlaw's hands and cuffed them roughly. "You're lying, Creed," he said. "Remember what you told those townsmen before you rode out? You said, 'Tell your sheriff to come looking for us if he's tired of living.' Well, here I am, Creed." He gave Creed a shove backward toward a rock.

"Take it easy, Sheriff! You can see I need some medical attention," said Creed, watching blood from his bullet graze drip to the ground around his boots.

"What's the story on the woman and the Carly twin?" the ranger asked, leading Creed's horse over by its reins. He tossed Creed a rag.

Creed shook his head and pressed the rag to the graze. "That damn Blake. He caused every bit of this, him and that whore of his."

"Denton the Blade told us everything already, Creed," said the ranger, "so save your breath."

"He did?" said Creed, looking surprised. "You've got Denton Ermy somewhere?" He looked all around as if he might see him. Then he said, "He told you everything? About the gold coins and all?"

"Every bit of it," said the ranger, giving Masden

a look. "But I'd like to hear your version, just to compare it, see which one of you is lying to us."

"Hell, I'll tell you whatever you ask me, Ranger. I'm not going to lie about nothing." He grinned. "I can hire me an attorney to do that for me."

Ignoring Creed's remark, Sam asked, "Are you sure this is Blake Carly, not his twin brother, Abel?"

Creed cocked his head slightly, and said, "You know, that has had me stumped ever since we met up the other night. See, I never even knew Blake Carly had a twin brother. We found a body in the Rio Grande, thought for sure it was Blake—then this one shows up, swears he's Blake Carly. All I knew to do was watch and listen."

"And?" the ranger asked.

"If he's not Blake Carly he sure fooled all of us. Said he knew where the gold coins were hidden— over there in Dead Man's Canyon." He nodded his head toward the other side of the rocky hills. "Hell, maybe he was the other one, though. Maybe he was just stringing us along, waiting for a chance for him and the whore to get away. Maybe I just wanted to believe he was Blake because of the gold."

Masden said to the ranger, "If he's telling everybody that he is Blake Carly, does that help you raise a case against him?"

"No," said the ranger. "Not if it's like Creed says, if he was just saying it to protect himself and the woman."

Creed looked back and forth between the two lawmen and chuckled grimly. "Sounds like whoever this is, he's got you chased up a stump, Ranger."

Sam only stared at him.

"I'll tell you this, though," said Creed. "I never

knew Blake to care so much for that whore like this man does all of a sudden."

"Is that so?" said the ranger.

"Sure as hell is," said Creed. "That's what all this trouble is about. He put us afoot so he could go after that whore alone. Blake Carly never acted that stupid in all the while I've known him."

"What about the gold coins?" the ranger asked flatly, wanting to hurry things along and get on the twin's trail.

"It's holdup gold, set up by some banker and a crooked sheriff named Tarpin over in Benton Wells. They had it hidden in Dead Man's Canyon. Blake was supposed to find out exactly where in the canyon, then come meet up with us and go get it. It was a sweet setup, but somewhere it all went to hell on us."

"Sheriff Ed Tarpin was crooked?" Masden asked, looking disappointed.

"That comes as no surprise to me," said the ranger. He turned back to Creed and said, "Come on, get on your feet. We've got to get some rocks over these bodies and get moving."

"Are you going to kill ole Blake, Ranger?" asked Creed, standing up.

"That's an interesting question," Sam replied. "If he really *is* Blake Carly there's still nothing I can do to prove it. If he's Abel Carly out to save that woman's life, then it's my duty to do everything in my power to help him."

Chapter 19

Except for watering the horses and checking on their unconscious hostage, Dayton Clifford and his guides didn't stop until the sun had dropped low in the western sky. When they finally did come to a halt on a stretch of flatlands, Millie Tristan jumped to the ground and staggered slightly in place. Then she began cursing Clifford, the same as she had earlier when he had allowed the chloroform to wear off for a few minutes before giving her another dose. A few miles ahead of them the flatlands fell into a deepening valley, then farther along into a narrow passage between two towering rocks.

Millie rubbed her forehead with her tied hands and said to Clifford in a groggy voice, "I bet this is the only way you've ever gotten a woman in your life! You snake-eyed, pasty-faced son of a bitch!"

"Always quite the lady, though, aren't you?" Clifford replied, drawing calmly on his pipe. As Millie continued to curse at him, he gestured for the guides to come closer, both of them staring at Millie as if in fear. "Mazzel, Pence," he said, "throw a rope around our guest and let her walk for a while. I'm tired of listening to her snoring."

Mazzel reluctantly took a rope from his saddle horn and uncoiled it. "I'll rip your heart out!" Millie spit at him, pointing a finger. "When Blake Carly gets through with you two, there won't be enough left to—"

"Shut up, woman!" shouted Clifford, cutting her off. Looking at Mazzel in disgust, he said, "Never mind the rope! We'll keep an eye on her." Looking back down at Millie, he said, "Any time you can stop foulmouthing me, I'll take you back on my lap."

"I'd rather die!" Millie rasped.

"Suit yourself," said Clifford, motioning her forward with the sweep of a hand, "but do keep up."

"You're the main one Blake is going to gut when he catches up to us," said Millie. But she stomped forward onto the trail, wobbling slightly, her boots raising a low wake of dust.

Looking ahead into the distant passage between the rocks, Clifford said to Mazzel and Pence, "I take it that is Dead Man's Canyon?"

"That's it, all right," said Mazzel. "We should be there in two, three hours at the most."

"Good," said Clifford. "I'm certain that by now Blake Carly is on his way. We'll trade him the woman for the location of the gold, and everybody will be on their way."

Overhearing them, Millie said over her shoulder, "If you think Blake Carly will give up that gold for me, or anything else, you're out of your mind!"

"Oh, I don't think so," said Clifford. "I watched through my binoculars. The way I saw him looking at you, I'd say he is dumbfounded by you."

"Yeah, no kidding?" Millie said over her shoulder, giving him a coy look in spite of the situation. "Well, I like to think I have gone to great lengths to show him some *special* attention, if you know what I mean."

"Indeed," said Clifford, getting involved with her in conversation. "Let's hope it has worked. If for some reason he decides not to come for you, I'm afraid I'll have to kill you." He smiled, looking her up and down with rapt attention. "That would be such a pity."

"And this is all about the gold coins?" Millie asked, putting a little extra sway into her walk as her balance came back to her and her head became more clear. Walking along, she felt his eyes on her. She knew the walk, the movements, the way to keep him coming closer with every word, every expression.

"Yes," said Clifford. "The sooner I can put my hands on the gold, the sooner I'll take my hands off of you, so to speak."

Thinking about it for a moment, Millie said, "I hate to say this, but I'm not certain the twin knows where the gold is hidden."

"The twin?" Clifford drew his horse to a stop. Behind him the guides did the same. "What do you mean, *the twin*?"

"Oh, haven't you heard?" said Millie tauntingly. "There's a fifty-fifty chance that Blake Carly isn't Blake Carly at all. In fact, the law even let this fellow walk away from a murder charge where there were *eyewitnesses*, who identified him." She looked back and managed a smile. "Because he said he's Blake Carly's twin brother, Abel." Seeing that Clifford was staring at her as if unsure what to say or do, she motioned for him and the other two to follow her. "Come on, boys. I'll tell you all about it sometime."

"Hold it!" said Clifford, stepping down from his

saddle with a cold look in his eyes. "You'll tell me all about it right now!"

"Huh-uh," said Millie. "I'm not talking about anything until I get some hot coffee to clear my head and a meal in my belly."

"I can make you talk," Clifford warned.

Millie shrugged. "Sure you can, but can you make me tell you the truth? All the truth? So help me, Hannah?" She smiled and hiked a hand on her hip in defiance.

Clifford grumbled under his breath, "Damn whores. They're the same wherever you find them." Then he shook his head and said aloud to the guides, "All right, Mazzel, Pence—we're making a camp here."

Looking at the flat stretch of land, then at one another questioningly, the two stepped down, took down their saddlebags and tossed them on the ground. Millie smiled to herself, watching them. She looked back across the rugged land they had crossed, knowing the twin would be following them. He was somewhere right now watching them, she thought, waiting for the best opportunity to make his move.

She'd done her part, Millie reminded herself. She had stopped Clifford in his tracks, right here in the open at the best possible place. If there were any lingering doubts about whether it was Blake or Abel Carly she'd been with, this would settle it. Blake Carly would know that she was busily setting things up for him. With Blake Carly it would go without saying that come nightfall she would distract Dayton Clifford by any means necessary. She smiled, feeling the first cooling breeze of night blow in across the hot flatlands.

"Now what about this twin situation?" Clifford

asked, trying to ignore the way the breeze pressed her riding blouse against her bosom, outlining every curve of her body.

Millie smiled, lifting her face to the breeze. "In a minute, Clifford," she said softly. "First, I'd like a pan of water, some soap, and a towel, if it's not too much trouble." She smiled suggestively. "A lady likes to *freshen up* between rides."

"Mazzel!" Clifford shouted over his shoulder without taking his eyes off Millie. "Get the lady a pan, some water, whatever else she requires."

"Yes, sir, Mister Clifford," said Mazzel.

"I hope you realize that I am expecting nothing but cooperation from you," Clifford said to Millie, stepping closer to her.

"Of course, silly," she said coyly, taking a half step back from him, in a way that very subtly held him at arm's length without laying a hand on him. "Where there is gold involved, I'm always cooperative, especially when there's a chance I might get myself a share of it." Staring at him, she let her eyes gaze past his shoulder and search the distant hills behind them, along the trail that had brought them here. Although she saw no sign of anyone following them, she knew the Carly twin was there.

And so he was.

At the far edge of the flatlands Blake Carly rode back and forth restlessly behind the cover of a low rise and watched the two guides set up camp, the men appearing as little more than tiny dots moving along the side of the open trail. In the west the sun grew dimmer, the evening cooler. It would soon be night, and there could be no better place than this for the twin to make a move and get Millie away from Dayton Clifford. Yet he'd seen the dust of the horses behind him throughout the day, and he knew they were too close to ignore. It had to be Creed and his men, he thought.

But regardless of who it was, whatever move he planned to make tonight, these riders behind him had to be considered. "Damn it," he cursed quietly to himself, looking back along the trail. He hadn't seen the dust for the past couple of miles, but that brought him no hope that he was no longer being followed. On the contrary, it more than likely meant that his followers had drawn close enough to slow their horses to a walk, or perhaps had begun flanking him, slowly and up close in such a way as to raise no dust. Whatever the case, they were still back there, still dogging him.

"Sorry, Millie," he murmured, after thinking things over. Turning his horse off the trail, he led the spare horse out across the land and proceeded ahead, circling wide of the camp but still headed toward Dead Man's Canyon.

She awakened in the middle of the night, carefully lifted Dayton Clifford's arm from across her and sat up naked on the blanket. She saw Mazzel staring wide-eyed at her in the flickering glow of the campfire, the guide still sitting diligently where Clifford had told him to with a rifle across his lap. She sighed, not caring one way or the other that Mazzel and Pence had witnessed her and Clifford in the act. What she did care about was the fact that in spite of her setting everything up for the Carly twin, he hadn't shown up. She picked up her riding blouse and slipped it on without buttoning it, then stood up quietly and tiptoed across the dirt to the campfire. "Is there any coffee left?" she whispered.

"Ye-yes, ma'am!" Mazzel whispered in reply. He started to rise and pour her a cup, but she stopped him with a raised hand.

"I'll get it," she whispered. "You've been busy all day and night." She stepped over, picked up a cup, and poured a slim stream of the remaining coffee into it. "You liked watching, didn't you?"

"Ma'am I— That is, *no*! No *ma'am*!" Mazzel stammered nervously, worried but still unable to turn away from looking at Millie's nearly naked body in the glow of firelight. "I was told to keep guard, so I had to!"

"Don't worry," Millie whispered soothingly. "It was all right with me." She shrugged a shoulder, knowing his eyes were on her naked breasts. "Sometimes a lady finds it fun to have her work admired."

"Lord God," Mazzel murmured under his breath.

Before sitting down near Mazzel she looked out through the darkness and wondered for a second if maybe she'd been wrong. Perhaps the twin wasn't Blake Carly after all. Blake would have known, she told herself. He would have known and he would've been here. He would not have let her put herself out that way, not for free, not to some low-life man hunter, in front of a couple of flunkies like these.

No, she told herself, it was Blake Carly, of course it was. But he wasn't about to take a chance on getting her caught in a crossfire should things suddenly go wrong in the dark of night, especially if he hadn't been able to shake Creed off his trail and come along, the way Clifford's message had told him. She sipped her coffee, giving Mazzel a soft, seductive gaze. Blake Carly was no fool. For whatever reason, he hadn't been able to work in concert with the way she had set things up for him. But he *would* come. She was sure of it. Blake wouldn't let her down and go get the gold for himself—*would he*?

"So, Mister Mazzel," Millie asked in a whisper, putting such a thought out of her mind, "what's a couple of big strong men like you and Mister Pence doing working for a bully like Dayton Clifford?" She smiled and placed a hand on his thigh, near his rifle stock, adding. "It's clear he mistreats you both."

Mazzel uncomfortably moved his thigh away from her hand, and with it his rifle. "Mistreats us? Oh, *no, ma'am!*" Mazzel said, his voice sounding shaky as he tried to keep it lowered. He shot a frightened glance toward where Clifford lay sleeping. "Mister Clifford has been more than fair to us all along! He paid us the last time we worked for him! I expect he'll be more than generous with us this time too—once our job is done!"

Millie sipped her coffee and leaned in closer to Mazzel, giving up on the rifle for the time being but pressing her bare breasts against the side of his arm, saying, "Who are you kidding? There's not even a shallow grave waiting for you and your friend once the gold is found. He'll leave you staring straight up with buzzards picking out your eyeballs."

Who was he kidding? Mazzel repeated the question to himself and swallowed hard, thinking about Kenny and Rawhide, and realizing that in spite of how hard he and Pence tried to convince themselves otherwise, Millie was right. "Ma'am, if we get some of the gold, that's good. But if we don't get nothing but the satisfaction of a job well done, then that's all right too." He shot another frightened glance toward Clifford.

"Hey, big fellow," Millie whispered, "you don't have to worry about him hearing you. He's not the first man I've rode into the ground. He'll be lucky if he can stand up without falling come morning." As she spoke, her hand crawled across his thigh and squeezed firmly. "But then, I don't have to tell you— you saw the whole thing."

"Yes, ma'am," said Mazzel, drawing his thigh farther away from her. "But like I said, me and Lon never meant to watch, we was just doing our jobs!"

"And quite an admirable job you've done," blared Dayton Clifford's voice out of the stillness of night. Startled, Mazzel almost dropped his rifle. Lon Pence sat bolt upright on his blanket, his eyes darting back and forth.

"Mister Clifford!" said Mazzel. "I was just explaining to the young lady here how happy me and Lon are to be doing a good job!"

"I heard it all, Mazzel," said Clifford, standing up from his blanket and stepping into his trousers. He picked up his pistol from beneath the blanket, then turned to Millie and said, "Why don't you give yourself a rest, Millie? It appears your boyfriend has decided not to come calling on us tonight. Too bad. I realize how much you were looking forward to his visit."

Seeing that Clifford hadn't been fooled by her, Millie said in a haughty tone, "But he will be here, Clifford, and when he does get here, I'm going to enjoy watching him shoot you apart, one piece at a time!"

"Careful now," said Clifford, walking closer. "At our little dinner talk you convinced me that this might not *even* be Blake Carly I'm waiting for. In which case, he might have no idea where the coins are." He wagged a finger. "Now that fact alone makes you less appealing to me. Couple that with the fact that you're really not all that interesting on a blanket, and I might have to just go ahead and shoot you and search for the gold by myself." He smiled. "How does that make you feel about yourself?"

"Not interesting on a blanket?" Millie raged. "Why, you dirty son of a bitch, I'll show you how it makes me feel!" She lunged into Mazzel, knocking him sideways as she tore the rifle from his hands.

Clifford stood frozen in place as she cocked the rifle hammer and pointed it at his chest. "Now, Millie, would you really be heartless enough to shoot me, after all we've just been through together?"

"Ha!" said Millie. "Say hello to the devil for me!" She pulled the trigger. Nothing. Looking stunned at the rifle in her hands, she worked the lever, but no cartridge came out of it. "Empty!" she shrieked wildly, pulling the trigger again. "I should've known a bastard like you would have some trick up your sleeve!"

"How could you take me for such a fool as to trust these idiots to stand guard around you with a loaded rifle?" said Clifford. "I knew you would get your *whore* hands on it sooner or later." He chuckled, walking closer, the pistol hanging loosely in his hand. "This must be a new experience for you, being on the *receiving* end."

Millie frantically levered the rifle again. "Stay away from me, you bastard!" she screamed. Again she pulled the trigger; again nothing happened. Seeing the look of evil intent in Clifford's eyes, she drew the rifle back and swung it at him like a club.

But he caught the barrel in his hand and yanked it away from her. "I might just keep you around, Millie!" he said, stepping forward slowly and deliberately, watching her cringe and shrink back from him. "Given enough time I bet I could train you as well as I've trained these two buffoons! Eh, Mazzel?" he said over his shoulder.

"Right, Mister Clifford," Mazzel said in a dejected tone.

"All you'll ever get me to do is cut your stinking throat in your sleep, you pig!" Millie spit in his face.

"You disgusting little trollop!" Clifford said, his usual cool demeanor coming apart on him. Without warning, he swiped her jaw with the barrel of his bone-handled Colt. The blow knocked her sideways and to her knees. In her addled state, barely hanging onto consciousness, she tried raising her face defiantly to Clifford, to spit at him once more. Seeing her toughness, Clifford put more force behind the next blow from his pistol barrel, this time swiping it across her other cheek and sending her to the ground, where she lay limp and still. The two guides looked at her, then at one another, wondering if she was alive.

Wiping spit from his face, Clifford chuckled and said, "Don't worry, boys—you can't kill one of these *things*." Rolling her over with the toe of his boot, he looked at the fresh swelling gashes on her cheeks. "Throw some water on her," he said over his shoulder, picking up the rifle and walking away.

Mazzel ran to Millie, stooped down and cradled her on his lap. "Hurry, Lon, get some water!" he said, yanking his bandanna from around his neck and shaking it out. Millie managed to moan faintly. "Don't you worry, ma'am, you just take it easy. Me and Lon are going to look after you."

A moment later as Lon poured water onto Mazzel's wadded-up bandanna and Mazzel touched it gently to Millie's battered cheek, Millie opened her eyes partway and looked up at the two guides. "There now, ma'am," Mazzel said in a guarded tone to keep Clifford from hearing him. "Everything's going to be all right."

"Ki—kill him," Millie managed to whisper before closing her eyes and drifting away again.

The two guides just looked at one another without saying a word.

Chapter 20

At daylight when the ranger and the sheriff pushed on with their prisoners toward Dead Man's Canyon, Denton the Blade said, "This man is in sore need of medical attention here, Ranger." Riding close beside his wounded pal Creed, Denton reached over and adjusted Creed's head bandage for him.

Watching them from behind, the ranger said, "That sure sounds like something Creed would have you say for him, Denton."

"It's no joking matter, Ranger," Creed cut in. "I've lost a lot of blood from this head wound. I could die from it!"

"It's a graze, Creed," said the ranger. "It's not a head wound." Giving Sheriff Masden a knowing look, the ranger said to Creed, "Are you saying I should get off of the Carly twin's trail and take you somewhere to a doctor? We'll never see him or the gold coins again if we do that."

The ranger's words stumped Creed for a second. Looking at Denton Ermy, he said, "You couldn't keep your damn mouth shut about it, could you?"

Denton's eyes widened. "About what? The gold?"

He pulled his horse farther away from Creed's to keep Creed from grabbing him.

Creed growled, "Hell yes about the gold! What else could I be talking about?"

Denton looked dumbfounded as Creed jerked his horse around and rode back beside the ranger. "All right, Ranger, here's the deal!" he said, talking quickly and sternly, his bloody head no longer seeming to be a problem. "We all saw where Blake's tracks split off the trail yesterday evening. He's circled around Clifford and the woman. It's plain to see that he's gone off after those gold coins instead of saving the whore. All the four of us has to do is join sides and take him down as soon as he gets his hands on it!"

Stringing him along, the ranger said, "I'm not sure he even knows where it is, Creed. If this really is Blake Carly there might be a slim chance that he found out from Ed Tarpin before he killed him. But what if this is Abel Carly? How would he know where it's at? Is Blake the kind of man who'd tell his brother something like that?"

"He *might* if it was his kin he was telling," said Creed.

The ranger smiled thinly. "From all I've ever seen, gold has a way of cutting all family ties."

"All right, that's true," said Creed. "But damn it, this is Blake Carly, Ranger! I can safely swear to it on a stack of Bibles."

"Then you're the first person I've found who can swear to it," said Sam. "Even this Millie Tristan didn't seem too sure about it from what I saw of her."

"She's a stupid whore, Ranger. Besides, Millie wasn't about to admit it to you. She couldn't bear to see ole Blake take those long last steps up the gallows stairs." Creed scrunched his shoulders up. *"Brrr!* It makes me shiver just thinking about it."

"Maybe you better think about it, Creed," Masden cut in. "It's coming your way, soon as we get you two back to Olla Sucia."

Ignoring the sheriff, Creed kept working on the ranger. "Come on, Ranger Burrack! For God sakes!" he said. "Don't tell me you really fell for all that *other twin* bullshit! This is Blake Carly we're talking about. I've known that rascal too long to be taken in by him. Hell, if there was any way of knowing it, him and his twin have probably fooled folks that way their whole life. That's the way twins do, you know."

"Is that a fact?" Sam asked, staring straight ahead toward the towering rocks in the distance.

"Sure it is. I've heard of it," said Creed. "They trick women into going first with one then the other. They stand in for one another all the time, take advantage of folks. Hell, we even had a president who had a twin—nobody ever knew about it. His twin would be conducting affairs of state whilst the real president was off fishing or hunting buffalo somewhere!"

Sam and Sheriff Masden both gave him a dubious look until Creed backed down and said, "All right, that ain't exactly true. But the rest of it is, especially when it comes to a scoundrel like Blake Carly. All I'm saying is, we can get that gold ourselves and split it four ways. We all ride off our own ways and who'll ever be any the wiser for it?"

"You're a murderer, Creed," said Masden. "Do you think you can deal your way out of something like this?"

"Yes, I do," said Creed flatly. "I believe you two

are smart enough to take the gold and let me and Denton just ease off into the sunset." He grinned and looked the two dusty lawmen up and down. "Come on now, you know you want to. What do you say?"

The ranger stared straight ahead, saying, "We're going to find Dayton Clifford and get the woman from him. If we come upon any gold and it's reported stolen from anywhere, we're going to take it in and see to it that it gets to its rightful owners."

"But that's the damn government!" said Creed. "Who cares about government gold? Even the government don't care after a while—they just go out and get some more!"

"If we find it, it's going back, Creed," said the ranger.

Gigging his horse ahead of the ranger, Masden said, "Creed, it's still early morning and I've already heard enough of you to last me all day."

"God! How I hate people like you!" Creed bellowed, watching Masden ride forward. "I've wasted my whole damn life trying to get my hands on this kind of fortune—never gave a damn who it belonged to. Then somebody like you comes along and acts like it don't mean a damn thing to you!"

"That ought to tell you something about yourself, Creed," said Sheriff Masden over his shoulder.

"Yeah, what?" the outlaw asked. "That I was born smart enough not to pass up a good thing if it comes my way?"

Beside Creed the ranger shook his head and said, "We're going after the woman. If we come upon any stolen gold, it's going back with us. That's the whole of it. Now get up there with Denton. You two can better understand one another."

No sooner had he sent Creed on his way than Sam

saw Sheriff Masden look down at the ground, slowing his circling horse. "Ranger, take a look at this,"
he said.

"I see it," said the ranger, gigging his Appaloosa
forward to the blackened ground where Dayton Clifford's party had made camp the night before. Stepping down from his saddle, he took off his glove and
pressed his palm to the remaining ashes.

"Did they get an early start?" Masden asked.

"Not too early," the ranger replied.

"Clifford is a big-city man," said Creed. "Doesn't
want to get up before there's enough daylight to look
down and see between his toes." He scowled. "I'd
like to get my hand around his throat before I go
back to Olla Sucia and hang."

"Both of us," said Denton the Blade.

"Be quiet, both of yas," said Masden.

Sam looked carefully at the footprints, scrapings
and markings in the dirt. "Looks like one of them
gave Millie a hard time."

"Ha!" said Creed. "I saw how far Billy Drew got
trying to give that whore a *hard time!*" The two outlaws laughed, their cuffed hands resting on their saddle horns.

Sam gazed off first in the direction they'd seen the
twin's single set of tracks go the evening before. Then
he gazed toward Dead Man's Canyon with a concerned look in his eyes. Noting the ranger's expression, Sheriff Masden said quietly, "I know what
you're thinking, Ranger."

Sam looked at him. "Do you?"

"Yep," said Masden. "You're thinking we'd do
better if we split up, one of us go after the Carly
twin, the other go after the woman."

The ranger motioned Masden to the side, out of

hearing of the two outlaws. "It might be better for
Millie's sake," Sam said. "The quicker we get to her,
the better her odds of staying alive. Just letting Clifford know that a lawman is on his tail might get
Millie some better treatment."

"So, which one do you want to go after?" Masden
asked. "Just let me know. I'll go along with your call
on it."

"Obliged," said the ranger. "Our problem is those
two." He nodded toward Creed and Denton Ermy.
"Once we split up, they're bound to try to make a
break for it."

With a trace of resentment in his voice, Masden
said, "Ranger, I'm a lawman. I can *handle* prisoners."

"I know you can, Sheriff," said Sam. "But it's
going to be rough trailing the twin with these two
slowing you down. The twin is going to be traveling
hard and fast. I think you ought to dog Clifford while
I ride Black Pot around and try to get to Carly, let
him know we're on his side as far as getting Millie
set free. I might have a chance of talking to him once
he sees it's me following him. I'm afraid if he sees
you, all he'll think is that there's a lawman after
him."

Masden said, "Then you really do think this is
Blake Carly, don't you?"

"I've thought about it ever since I first caught up
to him that day, Sheriff," the ranger said. "I still can't
say for certain who he is. Whoever he is, I hope I
can talk enough sense into him to get Millie freed
without any bloodshed."

Masden considered the matter, looking ahead at
the trail leading toward Clifford and the woman,
then off at the thin trail Carly had taken to circle
around them. "What you're saying makes sense,

Ranger," he said at length. "Go on after the twin. I'll dog Clifford. I'll keep him so busy he won't have time to think about hurting the woman."

"I figure Clifford is going to have the twin meet him somewhere inside the canyon," Sam said, taking the key to the handcuffs from his vest pocket and handing it to Masden without the two prisoners seeing him do it. "Once I get around in front of Clifford we'll have him closed in between us."

Masden slipped the key into his trouser pocket and said, "Good luck, Ranger."

Watching from their saddles, Creed and Denton Ermy exchanged a glance when the ranger stepped up into his saddle and turned the Appaloosa off of the main trail and out across the flatlands. "Look like the ranger is leaving us without even saying good-bye." Creed grinned.

"Yeah, can you imagine that?" Denton murmured as the ranger nudged the Appaloosa into a trot, kicking up the dust.

"Pay attention, Blade," said Creed. "We're about to get ourselves *pardoned* and *released*, the hard way."

Sheriff Masden turned his horse around and rode back to where the two sat waiting. When he got a few feet from them, he stopped and backed his horse enough to let the prisoners past him. "Come on, boys, after you," he said, gesturing them ahead with the rifle he carried in his right hand.

But the two only sat staring at him.

"Let's go. Move it," Masden said, not yet realizing that the two were deliberately stalling him.

"Huh-uh," said Creed. "We're not going anywhere till we know why the ranger just rode off and left us."

"Don't concern yourself with *why*," said the sheriff,

catching on quickly to what the pair was up to. "You're prisoners. Now get moving!"

"We're prisoners," said Creed, "but we've still got a right to know what's going on around us, especially when it involves our well-being."

"You've got no rights, Creed!" said Masden. He levered a round into his rifle chamber. "Either move out, or the next sound you hear will be the *last* sound you hear."

Reluctantly, Creed nudged his horse forward, Denton the Blade doing the same a step behind him. But they moved slowly, keeping their horses at a slack walk. "This is about the best we can do, Sheriff," said Creed, "what with me wounded and these horses plumb tuckered out already."

Masden's rifle shot kicked up dirt at Creed's horse's hooves, causing the horse to buck once and bolt forward, almost throwing Creed from the saddle before he could get the animal under control. Denton Ermy's horse veered away, but Denton reined it back onto the trail and kept it from bolting across the flatlands. "Jesus, Sheriff!" Creed shouted, moving his horse at a quicker pace. "We were doing like you told us! There's no cause for you doing something like that!"

"You'd be well advised not to try testing me again, Creed!" said Masden.

Already a good distance out on the flatlands, the ranger turned his head slightly toward the sound of Masden's single rifle shot. Looking back, he saw the sheriff riding along a few feet behind the prisoners, all three of them advancing at a good steady pace. "Keep them worried, Sheriff," he said to himself. Smiling slightly, Sam nudged the big Appaloosa into a faster trot and continued on his way.

*   *   *

Along the trail toward Dead Man's Canyon, Masden kept the outlaws moving along until the noon heat became intense and the animals were frothed and winded. Near the mouth of the canyon where a thin stream of water ran out of a steep rock wall, Masden kept his rifle aimed at the two prisoners as they watered their horses a few feet from him. Denton Ermy looked over at the sheriff and said, "Sheriff, I sure hope that ranger left you the key to these cuffs, in case some emergency arises."

"Don't worry yourself, Denton," said the sheriff. "We'll be meeting up with the ranger soon enough."

Denton and Creed gave one another a look. "So you do have the key?"

Masden just stared at him without answering.

Creed dropped down beside his horse and drank from the stream, then swished his face back and forth, pushed himself up with his cuffed hands and stood up slinging water from his hair. "What I was trying to tell that ranger before about the gold coins would have been a damn good idea. I don't know why he just dismissed it out of hand!" He shrugged and took a step toward the sheriff.

Masden raised the rifle, pointed it toward Creed, and slipped his thumb across the hammer.

"Whoa, easy now, Sheriff!" said Creed, chuckling under his breath. "I've already seen you don't mind pulling the trigger. I'm just making some noontime conversation here."

"We've got nothing to talk about, Creed," said Masden, "unless you want to discuss how long the drop is from the trapdoor to hell."

"That's *cruel*, Sheriff," said Creed, shaking a finger at Masden but not daring to take another step toward

him. "Let me ask you this. I heard what the ranger
had to say about the gold coins, but I never heard
you say how you felt. Have you ever seen that much
government gold in one place, up close, to where
you could dig your fingers down in them sparkling
coins, raise them up and let them just jingle down?"

"Shut up, Creed," said Masden. "I have no interest
in breaking the law." Noting that his horse had finished drinking, he looked away from the outlaws
long enough to jerk the reins and lift the animal's
head.

Creed grinned. "Aha! That's the pretty part of
these gold coins!" he said. "You ain't breaking the
law! The law was already broke. All we're doing is
getting the coins from whoever it was broke the
law." As he spoke he eased forward a step and
stopped. Denton saw him get away with it and did
the same thing.

"You sure can twist things around, Creed," said
Masden, his rifle dipping a bit as he seemed to think
about what the outlaw had said.

"I didn't twist things around, Sheriff," said Creed.
"I'm just calling things the way they are. If they look
twisted, then I reckon that's the way I found them.
Still, we're talking about an awful lot of shiny gold
coins. Too much to just ignore." He rubbed his
thumb and finger together in the universal sign of
greed. He took another step forward, this time not
as slyly. And this time he raised his cuffed hands
slightly and said, "Do you mind, Sheriff? I hate talking this far away. We are cuffed, after all. It ain't like
we're going to pull out a gun and start blasting away
at you."

Masden didn't answer, nor did he stop the pair
from taking another step toward him. "I never heard

exactly how much all these gold coins amounted to," he said.

"Well, now, let me think," said Creed, scratching his head, coming closer yet. "It's a hell of a lot, that much I'm sure of." Looking back over his shoulder, he said, "Ain't that right, Denton?"

"Oh, yes!" said Denton, having picked up a fist-size rock from the stream and keeping it well covered in his cuffed hands. "It's one hell of a lot of money, even cutting it up *three* ways!"

Chapter 21

When the ranger heard a shot from a rifle, followed by three rapid blasts of pistol fire, coming from the direction of the trail that Sheriff Masden and the prisoners were riding, he stopped short. But he realized that whatever had happened, there was little he could do about it. He'd ridden hard and passed between the two rock towers into the canyon nearly half an hour ago. Before he'd made it into the narrowing downward depth of the canyon he'd spotted the Carly twin almost a full mile ahead of him, riding hard across a long spill of piled-up boulders, the spare horse right behind him. Whatever trouble Sheriff Masden was having with the prisoners, Sam hoped the sheriff would be able to handle it on his own.

"Let's go, Black Pot," he said, nudging the Appaloosa forward, following the Carly twin, certain that the twin had spotted him coming through the pass into the canyon.

The Carly twin had also stopped at the sound of gunfire in the distance. He looked back from the shelter of rocks on his way up a steep path to a higher, better-concealed trail along the canyon walls. His first concern was that the gunfire might have come from Dayton Clifford's group. He knew that Millie was headstrong and hot-tempered. He also knew she would take whatever opportunity to escape that presented itself to her. But with the ranger on his tail there was nothing he could do but push on to the old mining town. That was where Clifford was headed. That was the common meeting spot, the place Dayton Clifford was referring to when he said to meet him in Dead Man's Canyon.

"Damn it!" the twin cursed under his breath as he gazed back toward the gunfire and saw the ranger coming up onto the stretch of spilled boulders. If he had to, he'd lie in wait for the ranger somewhere along the ridges ahead. Without a rifle, ambushing a man like Sam Burrack wouldn't be an easy feat. When it was him and his brother being followed, he'd seen firsthand how good the ranger was at trailing a man. But if it had to be that way, he could do it, he reminded himself, pushing his horse upward, pulling the other horse along.

The ranger and the Carly twin weren't the only ones who heard the gunshots. Having arrived at the abandoned mining town, Dayton Clifford had pitched Millie Tristan to the ground and stepped down from his saddle beside her when the distant shots resounded up from the canyon.

Millie rolled over onto her back and looked at Clifford through swollen eyes. "I'd start worrying if I was you, you lousy son of a bitch," she said through split and bruised lips. "When Blake sees what you've done to me he'll kill you so slow, you'll feel every second of it."

"Shut up, whore!" Clifford idly drew back his boot and kicked her in the ribs. She yelped in pain, then lay silent, knowing the two guides had been watching, the same way she'd made sure they were watching every time Clifford had hit her throughout the day.

With terrified looks on their faces, Mazzel and Pence ventured forward. "Mister Clifford," said Mazzel, a slight tremor in his voice, "you shouldn't ought to be kicking her that way."

"Oh really?" said Clifford, opening and closing his puffy right fist. "Well, I can't keep hitting her. She's wearing my fists out!" He laughed. "I'm lucky I can still draw my gun and shoot it if I need to."

"Mister Clifford," said Pence, "we can't stand by and watch a woman be treated this way. She's beat all to hell."

"Oh, I see," said Clifford. "This is another one of those *'We don't do things this way out here,'* isn't it?"

"Yes, it is, Mister Clifford," said Mazzel. "The fact is, if you keep this up, that poor woman is going to die on us!"

"Please!" said Clifford, gigging Millie with the toe of his boot. "Look at her. She's nothing but a smelly washed-out common street whore! I'd be doing her and Carly both a favor if I shot her right now."

"Then shoot me," Millie said, pain showing in her swollen, trembling face.

"Not until I get the gold, Millie dear," Clifford said in a mocking voice. He shrugged. "Then, who knows, perhaps I'll shoot you and Carly both." He gave Mazzel and Pence a wink. "It would sure mean a larger cut of the gold for us, eh, boys?"

Mazzel and Pence didn't answer. Instead they stepped in between him and Millie and scooped her up. "You've got to stop aggravating him, ma'am,"

Mazzel whispered. "You don't want him to keep on hitting you, do you?"

"Sure she does," Clifford cut in, overhearing Mazzel. "This is her way of hoping the two of you will become so outraged that you'll turn against me and defend this poor helpless woman. Isn't that right, Millie?"

Millie stood slumped, half conscious, holding a hand to her battered jaw.

"But what you don't realize, Millie," said Clifford, "is what a splendid job I've done of *training* these two." He grinned smugly. "These men are *mine* now. They've become like obedient trail hounds to me." He looked at Mazzel and Pence. "They have learned to fetch and heel. They both fear and respect me." He raised a finger for emphasis. "More importantly, they do my bidding." He gave a proud grin. "They wouldn't betray me—they wouldn't dare! But I suppose these are things far too sophisticated for a stupid whore like yourself to comprehend!"

"Go to hell, Clifford," she rasped in a sudden surge of energy. "You're full of yourself worse than any *boy-woman* I've ever seen. You're only one step away from wearing a red dress and carrying a parasol, you white-blooded—!"

"Whoa, easy now, Millie!" Mazzel said, trying to talk over her and keep Clifford from hearing what she'd said.

"Why, you filthy little trollop!" Clifford had heard her anyway, and he drew back his bruised right hand to punch her in the face.

But Mazzel quickly pulled her away, saying, "Come on, Lon, let's tend to her, get her cleaned up some."

Chuckling, Clifford took out his pipe and clamped it between his teeth. "You do that, Mazzel. You and Lon tend to the whore and get her cleaned up real good. I'm tired of getting my hand dirty every time I hit her." He gazed at the sun-bleached buildings and fading business signs of the abandoned mining town. "I've heard of places like this," he said as the two guides carefully led Millie to a boardwalk and sat her down, "but I never thought I'd see one!"

"Kill him!" Millie hissed, grabbing Mazzel by his shirt and pulling him close to her. "Look what he's doing to me."

"Please, ma'am, hush! For all our sakes!" Mazzel whispered, his voice trembling.

"What's the name of this place, Mazzel?" Clifford asked, striking a match and lighting his pipe, not hearing Mazzel's conversation with Millie.

"It used to be called Dead Man's Ridge," Mazzel said. "But as you can see it ain't been a town for many years now."

"Dead Man's Ridge," said Clifford, shaking his head and flipping the burnt match away as he blew out a stream of smoke. "We've got Dead Man's *Ridge* located in Dead Man's *Canyon*." Chuckling, he pointed along the boardwalk at all of the buildings, some boarded up, others standing wide open to the elements. "Everything here must belong to dead men!" He nodded toward a creek snaking through the hillside below them. "I suppose that must be Dead Man's *Creek*?"

"Well, now that you mention it," said Mazzel.

"No! You're kidding!" Clifford laughed aloud. "It really *is* called Dead Man's Creek? That's wonderful! Simply wonderful!"

"Go get some water for her, Lon," Mazzel said just

between himself and Lon Pence. Giving Pence a stoic, guarded look he added, "Bring back anything *else* you think we might need."

Lon Pence walked to the horses while Mazzel comforted Millie, holding her hand and brushing her hair back from her eyes. Seeing Clifford wander off a few yards, looking the town over with interest, Mazzel told Millie in a low voice, "Don't worry, ma'am, me and Lon ain't allowing him to beat you any more."

"Much obliged," Millie moaned, her swollen eyes studying Mazzel's. "Are you two going to be able to do it?"

"I don't know," said Mazzel, "but we ain't taking no more abuse. We might not be no more than a couple of *trained dogs* to him. But even trained dogs will bite if you force them into a corner."

Looking toward the horses, Millie saw Pence returning with the canteen in one hand and the rifle in the other. "Make sure that rifle is loaded this time," Millie said, starting to perk up and take charge. "Don't give him a chance to get his hand on his Colt. Shoot him while he's not looking."

"Oh, the rifle is loaded, ma'am," said Mazzel. "We checked it out along the trail. As far as when we'll shoot him, we ain't going to start no trouble, but if he tries to lay another hand on you, we're going to make him sorry."

"Make him *sorry*?" Millie gave him a skeptical look. "We are talking about the same thing here, aren't we? You are going to kill him?"

"Well—yes, ma'am," said Mazzel. "That is, if he starts beating on you again."

"You don't seem very sure of yourself, big fellow," Millie said, her hand instinctively coming out and stroking Mazzel's chest as she spoke.

"Ma'am, me and Lon ain't what you call *man kill-ers*," said Mazzel. "True, we make a living guiding folks to hunt large game. Lots of times it's folks who just need to be led into killing something as big as a buffalo or a bear. But we will kill Clifford, just like I said we will, if he forces us into it."

Millie watched the big man stand up and turn to meet Lon Pence and take the canteen from him. "Well, shit!" she said to herself in disappointment. But her eyes went to Clifford, who had turned and was walking toward them. Taking the canteen from Mazzel as he stooped beside her, she took a sip, swished it around and spit it out. "You know how sometimes you and you partner had to lead people into being able to kill?" Without waiting for an an-swer, she said, "Let's look at this as sort of the same thing, all right?" She patted his broad shoulder and began pushing herself to her feet.

"Huh?" said Mazzel, helping her up without knowing why.

Walking closer, Clifford said, "That's enough at-tention to the whore, boys. Let's get settled in here and get ready for Blake Carly's arrival." He pointed toward a boarded-up saloon. "Mazzel, take her in there and tie her to the bar rail. Lon, get the horses out of sight. As soon as we settle with Blake Carly, we'll want to be on our way quickly."

"Clifford, you rotten bastard," said Millie, stag-gering in place as she tried to steady herself for what she knew was coming. "I'm going to enjoy watching Blake turn you into a steer right in front of Mazzel and Lon!"

"You again?" Clifford said, sounding almost bored with her. He reached into his coat pocket and took

out the bottle of chloroform. "I suppose it must be
time to close your eyes for the evening."

"No!" Millie shouted, seeing her plan about to fall
apart. "If you come near me with that stuff I'll rip
your eyes out! You *tiny-peckered* son of a bitch!" She
stared coldly at him, thinking that ought to do it. She
was right.

Clifford's face reddened. His fist tightened. "Have
it your way, whore!" He jammed the bottle of chloroform into his pocket and balled his fist. "I think I'd
enjoy seeing you spit your teeth into the dirt." He
took a step toward her. She stood her ground, even
jutting her chin slightly.

"Hold it right there, Clifford!" Mazzel said, stepping between Clifford and the woman.

Clifford looked surprised, but only for a second.
"Oh? *Clifford*, is it?" he said, noting the difference
that had come over Mazzel. "And what happened to
Mister Clifford all of a sudden?" His right hand went
up to his bone-handled Colt. "Have you forgotten
your manners?" But he didn't attempt to tap his sore
fingers on the pistol butt the way he always had
before.

Mazzel ignored Clifford's question, saying, "You
ain't going to hit her again, Clifford." He stood firm,
his big boots planted shoulder width apart.

Looking Mazzel up and down, Clifford cut a
glance toward Lon Pence just in time to hear him
cock the rifle in his hands. "You boys do realize how
fast I am, don't you? I mean, fast enough to shoot
you both before that rifle can get a shot off?"

"That makes no difference, Clifford," said Mazzel,
standing his ground. "We ain't watching you beat
this woman no more."

"Go on. Kill him, Lon!" Millie said beside Mazzel.

"Hold it, Lon!" said Mazzel, on the chance that Lon Pence might follow Millie's command. "We ain't going to kill nobody if we can keep from it."

"But you said he killed your friends!" said Millie, trying to work the two into a killing state of mind. "This is your chance to avenge them! Go on, kill him!"

Staring at Clifford, Mazzel said, "We ain't out for revenge. But there'll be no more beatings for the woman."

"Well, hell," said Millie, reaching out her tied hands for the Colt in Mazzel's holster. "I'll kill him myself!"

"Huh-uh!" said Mazzel, catching Millie's hands before she could lift the pistol. "I said no killing, and I meant it." He gently pushed Millie and held her at arm's length.

"Mazzel, you're making a big mistake," said Millie. "Kill him and I'll see to it Blake splits the gold with you and Lon. You have my word on it!"

"Ha!" said Clifford. "The word of a whore! Don't make me laugh!"

"Listen to yourself, Clifford!" said Millie. "You even sound like a woman! No wonder you could just barely—"

"That's it, she's dead!" Clifford raged, cutting her off. As if his anger had caused him to forget that a rifle stood poised to shoot him, his injured gun hand came up with the Colt and fired it at Millie from less than ten feet away. But his hand wasn't at its fastest in its sore and swollen state.

Mazzel saw what was coming and had a split second to jerk Millie out of the line of fire and take the bullet himself, high in his left shoulder as he put

Millie behind him. "Oh God!" Mazzel said, throwing his free hand to the wound, having felt the bullet slice through him.

Lon Pence hesitated, but only for a second. Then, seeing the blood fly from Mazzel's exit wound, he fired. His shot lifted Clifford off his feet and landed him onto the boardwalk. But Clifford wasn't out of the game. He rolled over onto his back, half sitting, and hammered a shot into Pence's chest. Pence staggered backward, dropped the rifle and fell to the ground. Mazzel backed away from Clifford's cocked Colt pointing at him.

"Damn it to hell!" Millie shouted. She made a dive for the rifle in the dirt, but Clifford fired a shot that slammed into the ground only an inch from her fingers, kicking dirt into her face.

"Don't make me kill you, whore!" Clifford shouted, standing, his hand pressed to the bleeding wound in his side.

Millie froze in place, knowing she'd taken things as far as she could. "You won't get the gold if I'm dead, Clifford!" she shouted, reminding him.

"I want the gold, but I will put a bullet in your scheming head!" Clifford replied, taking a halting step along the boardwalk.

"All right, hold it!" Millie said, drawing her hands back from the rifle and coming quickly to her feet with her tied hands above her head. "I'm done! All right? See?" She wiggled her fingers. Then she looked at Mazzel standing with blood running down his chest from his shoulder and at Lon Pence lying dead on the ground. "You can't blame a lady for trying, can you?"

Clifford managed a dark chuckle under his breath. "My, my, what a bloody bunch of sinners we are."

Then he turned his pistol toward the remaining trail guide, saying quietly, "Mazzel, in spite of all the work I put into you and this other fool, you've still disappointed me."

"Wait, Mister Clifford!" said Mazzel, holding a hand to his bleeding shoulder wound.

"Oh, now it's *Mister* Clifford, is it?" Said Clifford with a cruel grin. The Colt bucked once in his hand and sent Mazzel backward onto the ground. Mazzel moaned and tried to crawl away, but two more shots silenced him and left him lying facedown in the dirt.

Millie shook her head and said in disgust, "I told both of those fools to kill you while you weren't looking. But no, they said they couldn't kill a man that way." She spit on the ground and ran her hand across her swollen lips.

"You really are a cold-blooded, heartless slut, aren't you?" he said to Millie, looking bemused at his discovery, as if just realizing that what he'd been saying about her all along was true.

"I'm alive," Millie said. "That's more than I can say for you once Blake—"

She stopped short at the sound of hoofbeats coming from the direction of the hills less than a hundred yards away. Clifford also heard the hoofbeats and turned his pistol in that direction. He saw the spare horse the Carly twin had been leading come running toward them, leaving a trail of dust behind it. "Millie! Get up here, quick!" Clifford demanded.

Millie hesitated, turning her gaze back at the approaching horse with saddlebags flapping on its sides.

"Don't test me, whore. I'm warning you," said Clifford.

Millie relented and walked over to the boardwalk

and stepped up beside him, still gazing at the horse until it ran into the main street, saw them and circled around and stopped in the middle of the street. It stood scraping a hoof restlessly, its eyes taking in the two bodies lying in the dirt.

From the hills came the twin's voice calling out, "Clifford. I'm up here. I've brought the gold. Look in the saddlebags. Then let's get down to business."

"Yep, that's Blake Carly, all right." Millie smiled in spite of her split and swollen lips. "He went straight for the gold. But he didn't forget about me."

"Shut up!" Clifford shouted. Spooked by the sound of Carly's voice, he grabbed Millie and held her against him for cover as he looked back and forth between the horse and the hillside. "That's what I say, Blake Carly," Clifford shouted. "Let's get down to business." Using Millie as a shield he stepped out from the cover of the boardwalk and down into the street.

Chapter 22

Using the spare horse for cover and still holding Millie against his chest, Clifford eased his hand down into the saddlebags, pulled out a handful of gold coins and let them spill from his fingers back into the bag. Hanging on to one coin, he called up toward the hills, feeling confident, "This is a good start, Blake Carly, but it'll take a whole lot more gold than this to get me to turn this whore loose!"

"That's just a few thousand dollars' worth, to show you I have it, Clifford," the twin called out. "Now if you want a full share of it, send Millie up here unharmed."

"*Full share?*" Clifford laughed at his proposition. "What do you take me for, Carly, one of these burnt-faced *frontier* idiots?" As he spoke he felt blood run down from the wound in his side. "I don't turn the whore loose until I get *all* the coins." He looked at the bodies of Mazzel and Lon Pence lying dead on the ground. "I'm talking about *all* the coins, not a *share*." Easing back to the boardwalk, he said, "Bring down the rest of the coins and I'll hand you the whore. That's the only way this is going to work."

"All right. I'm coming down," said the twin.

"Like hell you are!" Millie shouted. "You stay there until this bastard turns me loose. Don't take his word for anything. You can't trust a word he says!"

Clifford thumped her on the head with his pistol butt, just hard enough to remind her of what he could do if he decided to get tough. "You're like every whore I've ever seen. You just have to try to take control, don't you?" He shook her roughly. "Keep your mouth shut, or I promise you won't live to see the end of this!"

Millie fell silent.

In his cover on the hillside, the Carly twin had been so busy keeping an eye and his rifle sights on Dayton Clifford that he had failed to see Creed and Denton the Blade come riding into town hidden from sight along a narrow alleyway behind a weathered, boarded-up mercantile store. They had heard the shooting and rode toward it, as if certain that the sound of gunfire would lead them to the gold. Stepping down from their horses and quickly tying their reins around a telegraph pole, the two moved along behind the deserted buildings in a crouch. They had used the rifle butt to break the connecting links of their handcuffs, and the short links of shiny chain still dangled from their wrists. After hearing the last of the conversation shouted back and forth between the Carly twin and Dayton Clifford, Denton Ermy asked Creed, "Think we ought to let Blake know we're here? That we're on his side?"

Creed gave him a stern look. "After the way he done us? I ain't on his side. Are you?"

"I'm just thinking it might be easier, the three of us," said Denton.

"No," said Creed. "We're taking this gold ourselves. As far as I'm concerned, it's just you and me against both of them. Blake had his chance—to hell with him now. Him and his whore too." Looking at Sheriff Masden's rifle in Denton's hands, Creed said, "You get up on the roofs where you can do us some good with that rifle. As soon as it looks like one of them has gotten their hands on the gold and thinks it's all over, we'll step in and take it away from them." He grinned. "Gold is no different than that whore, I reckon. It jumps from one man's hands to the next, free as a wild bird."

Levering a round quietly into the rifle chamber, Denton smiled and said, "Yeah, but this time it ends up in ours!"

Creed watched him climb a brittle-looking set of stairs up the back of the mercantile building. "Yeah, that's what they *all* say," he murmured to himself.

Fifty yards behind the two escaped outlaws, the ranger had seen them slip into town along the back trail and followed them. He concluded right away that Sheriff Masden had been left lying dead somewhere out on the flatlands. But rather than raise a fight with the outlaws right then and have his gunfire tell Dayton Clifford and the Carly twin that he was coming, he held back and waited. He wasn't here to cause the twin any harm, but he wasn't sure the twin would understand it that way. If the twin was *Blake* Carly, Sam wasn't sure it would matter to him one way or another why he was there. Blake Carly was still a killer. So were Creed and Denton Ermy, and so was Dayton Clifford.

There were too many guns in the mix and too much gold at stake to trust anybody here, Sam reminded himself, stepping down from the saddle, drawing his rifle from his saddle boot and nudging the big Appaloosa aside. In the alleyway ahead of him he saw Denton Ermy hurry up the stairs and slip into the second floor of the empty building. Headed for the roofs, Sam told himself. He leaned against the rear of a building out of sight and checked both his rifle and his Colt. Then he eased forward, watching Creed take a position behind a pile of empty wooden crates at the alley's edge.

The twin moved his horse easily along the thin, steep path to the stretch of land that supported the abandoned mining town. He asked himself if this was the way his brother would have done things. But then he gave a faint, tired smile as the irony came to him. "Which brother?" he asked himself under his breath, as if in the course of things he had lost sight of himself. *Whoever you are, you'll have to live with what you've done,* he heard a voice say inside him. The voice brought a weariness that ran to the depth of his bones, knowing that that same voice would speak to him the rest of his life. "I'm sorry, Brother," he said aloud. Then he said to himself, *Is this how you would have played it, Abel? Would you have come here, allowed yourself to be drawn to these circumstances? If not for me would you be risking your life for the very things that a good man knows will destroy him?*

But instead of Abel Carly answering him, he heard inside himself another voice ask, *Is this how you would have played it, Blake? Would you be riding down here now to save a whore you once left behind because you were tired of her? Has killing me made you look at the world through different eyes? Are there things that now matter more to you than yourself?*

"I guess today will tell us both who we are,

Brother," he said to himself, giving his horse a nudge and hearing the muffled sound of gold coins jingling softly in his saddlebags.

"Here he comes," said Dayton Clifford, seeing the twin appear over a low rise near the edge of the hills. He pulled Millie to his chest and whispered near her ear, "Now is the time. Which would you rather do, watch me kill Blake Carly and ride out of here with me, richer than your wildest dreams? Or watch him die and take a bullet in the back yourself as soon as he drops the gold on the ground?" He chuckled. "Answer quickly now! Every second counts!"

Millie said without hesitation, "Don't take it personal, you pasty-faced turd. But I'd rather die crawling through the dirt to Blake Carly than ride in a silver-trimmed carriage with the likes of you."

Clifford's expression turned dark and mean as he raised an old, tarnished pistol and cocked it against the side of Millie's head. "Once a stupid whore always a stupid whore, I suppose," he whispered softly. In the back of his trousers rested the bone-handled Colt—his ace in the hole. Looking out at Carly, he raised his voice and said, "That's close enough! Turn your saddlebags up and empty the gold into the street. Let me see it!" As he spoke, he moved sideways off the boardwalk and out into the street, Millie pressed firmly against his chest.

The twin turned slightly in the saddle, having to take his hand away from the butt of the Colt Thunderer shoved down in his belt. He untied the saddlebags, lifted them with much effort and swung them around onto his lap. He raised one flap and tipped it enough to let some of the gold coins spill out in the dirt.

"Whoa, that's enough!" said Clifford, not wanting to have to deal with reloading the saddlebags.

"Jesus!" Barton Creed whispered, unseen behind the wooden crates. Sunlight sparkled on the coins, but only for an instant as they rained down onto the ground. Above the street, Denton Ermy had crawled up through a trapdoor from inside the mercantile and made his way along the rooftops until he'd gotten close enough to suit himself, then he'd eased forward and looked down on the street. His breath caught in his throat at the sight of gold pouring like glittering liquid from the saddlebags.

Millie gasped at the sight, too, but then collected herself and said to the twin, "Damn it, Blake! You shouldn't have done that! He means to kill us both! Can't you see that? Are you really Blake Carly? Blake would never have—"

"Shut up, whore!" Clifford cut her off, shaking her roughly with the gun held to her head.

"Don't call her that," the twin said, staring coldly at Clifford.

Dayton Clifford batted his eyes as if in disbelief, a bemused smile on his face. "Oh—well, then, please pardon me, *Missus Millie!*" he said in a mocking voice. Then to the twin he said, "There! Is that better?"

The twin just stared at him. "You've got the gold. Turn her loose."

"No, Blake!" said Millie. "Make him toss his gun down! Don't trust him! Please don't!"

"Enough of you!" said Clifford. He gave her a solid crack on the head, enough to addle her momentarily. Seeing the twin's hand start to reach for the Thunderer, Clifford said, "Huh-uh!" and pressed the gun barrel to Millie's bowed head. "You can have her with a knot on her head or her brains blown out. You decide!"

The twin just stared, helpless.

"That's what I thought," said Clifford. "Now ride in closer, scoop those coins back into the saddlebags, and tie the saddlebags onto my horse, the one on the end there."

The twin did as he was told, riding past the spare horse that stood in the middle of the street. When the saddlebags were secured, he backed his horse up a step and said, "Now toss your gun away and let her go."

Clifford thought about it for a second as if seeing if there was anything he'd forgotten. Finally he said, "Sure, why not? But first raise your hands." Watching the twin raise both hands chest high, Clifford chuckled at how easy this was going to be and tossed the tarnished pistol to the dirt. He gave Millie a slight shove and watched her stagger drunkenly until the twin nudged his horse forward, leaned down and lifted her onto his lap.

"No tricks while we ride out of here, Clifford," the twin warned him.

"Absolutely not!" said Clifford, as if appalled at such an implication. "I have the gold! You have the whor—that is, the *woman*," he corrected himself. "Everybody's happy!"

The twin backed his horse a few feet until he passed the small pile of coins lying in the dirt. On his lap, her face against his chest Millie Tristan moaned, "Oh, Blake, please don't . . ." But her words trailed off.

The twin whispered to her as he turned his horse in the street. "I had no choice. I love you, Millie."

"You love me, Blake? Really? In spite of what I am?" she said, as if she hadn't heard him correctly.

"I love you, Millie," he murmured. "I've loved you since the minute I saw you."

She gave him a questioning look, wondering just when it had been that he first saw her? Was it that day in the relay station? Was that the day this man had first seen her? "You're not him, are you?" she whispered.

"Shhh," he said, running a gloved hand along her bruised cheek. "Just rest for now. Let's get out of here."

Clifford stood staring with a flat expression, his pipe appearing in his mouth as if out of thin air. "That was too damn easy," he said to himself, raising the bone-handled Colt from behind his back, cocking it on the upswing. "Hell, what kind of rootin-tootin shootout was that?" he growled.

"Blake, look out!" Barton Creed shouted, at the last minute not able to stand by and watch his former pal take a bullet in the back. He sprang from behind the crates and fired at Dayton Clifford, but not quickly enough to keep Clifford from doing what he'd set out to do. Clifford fired a shot into the Carly twin's back, sending him slumping forward, Millie clinging to his chest, the bullet having buried itself in her heart. The sound of gunfire sent the spare horse bolting away, out of town, its saddlebags flapping and jingling.

Farther back in the alley, the ranger realized what was happening and hurried forward. He saw Creed crouched in the street, firing at Clifford, who had begun moving toward the cover of the abandoned saloon. But before the ranger could do anything, Denton Ermy shouted from the rooftop, "Creed! Behind you!"

Creed turned and fired at the ranger while Clifford

disappeared into the saloon. A rifle shot from the rooftop grazed the back of the ranger's gun hand deeply and sent his Colt flying to the dirt. But even as he felt the bullet hit him, Sam fired his rifle, knowing the shot had to count. Once the rifle fired he would have a hard time levering a new round into the chamber. But the shot did its job. It lifted Creed onto his tiptoes and sent him staggering backward, his hands going to his bleeding belly.

"You got me, Ranger!" Creed hissed, the pain in his belly gripping him tight. "But you're . . . dead too!" His eyes went to the rooftop, where Denton Ermy stood and aimed the rifle down at the ranger. "It was us who . . . killed Ranger Sam Burrack!" Creed said, his words halting.

Sam's eye fixed on Denton Ermy as he tried hard to lever a round into his rifle, the wound in his gun hand not that bad, yet bad enough to make his hand numb and useless for the time being. Denton the Blade had him, had him cold, the ranger thought.

"Wrong again, Creed!" The voice of Sheriff Masden boomed from the other side of the street at the same time a shot exploded from the raised pistol in his blood-caked hand. Atop the roof, Denton Ermy staggered as the bullet struck him in the throat. The rifle fell from his hands. He toppled over the edge of the low facade and fell choking onto the long metal pole that had once held a business sign. As he rolled off of the pole the cuff on his right hand snagged on one of the steel hooks that had held the sign in place, and Denton hung there wiggling and gasping, a long stream of blood pumping wildly from his throat. The ranger cut a surprised look at Sheriff Masden, who took careful aim and put Denton out of his misery.

"You sonsabitching lawdogs!" Creed gasped, sinking to his knees while above the street Denton the Blade hung limp, swinging by his arm.

"Yoo-hoo, Ranger," said Dayton Clifford, stepping back out into the open, seeing that the ranger's gun hand was wounded and that the sheriff was staggering, half dead on his feet, perhaps too weak to raise his pistol for another shot. "You haven't counted me out, have you?"

"Clifford, I'm not counting a coward like you one way or the other," said the ranger, already seeing the look in the man hunter's eyes. He knew he needed to stall him for as long as he could. As Sam spoke he opened and closed his grazed gun hand, trying to bring back the feeling in it. "I've seen you're nothing but a back-shooter. What is it you want?"

"Now my feelings are hurt," said Clifford, his pipe still in his mouth, lit now, smoke curling up from its bowl. "I think you know what I want, though. I want what I've wanted all along. The gold, Ranger!" he said dramatically.

"Then shoot me, and it's all yours," Sam said. "You can go back to Chicago and make up any bold story you want to about how you came by this." The ranger offered a thin, flat smile. "Of course you'll always know the truth, that you're nothing but a coward who can't face a man straight up."

"The way it's done out here, you mean?" said Clifford sarcastically.

"There's a lot to say about the way it's done," Sam replied, still buying precious seconds as he worked his gun hand, feeling some of the numbness dissipate. "It leaves a man knowing who he is when he holds a loaded gun and faces another man carrying one. There's an honesty in it that a coward like you will never know." Taunting him, the ranger could feel his hand coming around, getting its strength back. "You can kill me right now, Clifford, and leave here with all that gold, but remember my face every time you spend it—remember me telling you that on this day you have the chance to become the kind of brave man hunter you've always claimed to be. Remember that every time you lie to yourself and the rest of the world."

Clifford half turned to glance at the saddlebags full of gold. Then he gazed off to where the Carly twin lay slumped forward over Millie Tristan, riding back into the hills. Then, turning back to the ranger with resolve, he let out a long stream of smoke and said, nodding at the ranger's Colt lying in the dirt, "Pick it up, Ranger. Pick it up and holster it. We'll have a draw contest!"

Without another word Sam stepped over to his Colt, stooped down, picked it up and shook the dust from it, noting that it was still cocked, the bullet having hit it, leaving a deep indentation along the cylinder. He looked at Clifford holding his bone-handled Colt at arm's length, aimed at him. "I need to check it first, Clifford," Sam said, still stalling, still clenching and unclenching his gun hand. "I think it's jammed."

"I've given you all I'm going to, Ranger," Clifford said, grinning. "Let's do it the way *it's done out here*." His grin widened, as he realized he could now face a man with a loaded gun with the odds still tipped in his favor. He slipped his Colt into his belly holster and poised his hand near the butt. "Holster it, Ranger!"

Sam raised his big Colt with deliberation, making

no move toward holstering it, not sure if it would fire or not.

"Oh, no!" said Clifford, his eyes widening now in terror.

The gun bucked once in the ranger's hand, the shot sending Dayton Clifford backward and down, his own Colt still in his holster. Sam looked at the Colt in his half-numb hand, a bit surprised that the hand or the gun, either, one had worked.

"You—you cheated!" Clifford said, struggling to his knees, looking shocked and outraged, his bone-handled Colt still in his hand. "It—it—it simply isn't *right*," he said haltingly, watching the ranger walk forward slowly, examining his damaged gun and the bloody graze on his hand.

From a few yards away Sheriff Masden called out in a weak voice, "Shoot him once for me, Ranger!"

"This is . . . terrible!" Clifford whined, glancing at his pipe lying in the dirt. "The way . . . you set me up! And with my hand hurt, too!" His lip trembled like a child's. "Is this the way *it's done* out here?"

"I don't know about here," said Sam, looking around the high, rugged terrain and the abandoned mining town. "I'm from Arizona."

"Oh, that is *so* cruel! This is . . . *so unfair!*" Clifford said, struggling to raise the Colt for a shot. "So viciously, brutally unfair!"

"Tell it to the devil," Sam said. His Colt bucked again and Dayton Clifford fell backward, staring blankly up at a calm, clear sky.

Sam reached down, picked up the bone-handled Colt, shoved it into his belt and walked over to Sheriff Masden, who had taken a canteen from his saddle horn and plopped down on the edge of the boardwalk, dirty, bloody and exhausted. "Are you going to be all right, Sheriff?"

"I did a foolish thing, Ranger," he said. "I let their talk about gold tempt me enough to let my guard down."

"If you did," said Sam, "you've more than made up for it." He gestured toward the body of Denton the Blade hanging by his handcuff from the sign pole like an advertisement for some macabre stage show. "You saved my life."

Sheriff Masden shook his head. "I didn't do nothing. Go on after Carly and Millie Tristan. I'll rest here a spell and then follow you."

The ranger glanced at Clifford's horse standing at the hitch rail with its saddlebags stuffed with gold coins. Seeing him look at the horse, the saddlebags full of gold on the ground, Masden said, "Don't worry, Ranger. I'm over it."

Chapter 23

Sheriff Masden sat watching as Sam swung up into the saddle and within a moment disappeared into the hills, the dust of the Carly twin still standing in the air above the thin trail. Looking back, Sam saw Masden get up, walk stiffly to Clifford's horse and lead it away from the hitch rail. Without a second look, the ranger rode on, climbing the trail until it became an even thinner path, then only a set of hoofprints up onto a high level of upthrust rock and loose dirt covered sparsely with low brush.

When Sam saw the twin's horse standing beside an overhanging cliff with its saddle empty and its reins hanging loose, he reined the Appaloosa to a halt and called out, "Carly! It's me, Sam Burrack. I'm not here to bring you harm! I know you and the woman are both hit! I came to help you!"

"You can't help us, Ranger," Carly called out, his voice strained. "Go on away."

"I can't do it, Carly," said Sam. "Not until I see you're both all right."

"It's your job, huh, Ranger?" Carly said.

"Yep, it is my job," said the ranger. "I'd appreciate it if you'd let me do it."

"You're not even in your territory, Ranger," said Carly. "So don't you owe nobody a thing here."

"You're dying, aren't you?" Sam asked bluntly.

After a silence, the twin said, "Yes, I believe I am."

"And Millie?" Sam asked. "She's already dead, isn't she?"

"Yes," the twin said softly. "Millie's gone."

"I'm sorry to hear that, Carly," said Sam, lowering the tone of his voice. "I'm coming in there—don't shoot me."

"Come on, then, Ranger," Carly said. "I'm past shooting anybody."

The ranger walked up over a rocky rise and under the cliff overhang where the twin lay stretched out on the dirt, holding Millie Tristan against him, stroking her hair back from her battered face and staring longingly at her. "She's about the prettiest thing I've ever seen, Ranger, don't you think so?" he said, knowing Sam was there without looking away from Millie's closed eyes.

"Yes, Carly, she's a fine-looking young woman," the ranger said softly.

"We'd talked about taking the gold and going to Mexico. I wish we could have pulled it off," he said. "God, I just wish we could have."

"I'm sorry, Carly," Sam said, raising his dusty sombrero from his head and letting it hang from his hand. "What about you? Can I do anything for you?"

"Some water, maybe?" said the twin.

"I'll get some," said Sam.

He went quickly to where he'd left the Appaloosa and came back twisting the cap off his canteen. Stooping down, he saw the blood on the twin's lips and realized the bullet had shattered a lung. On the twin's chest he saw where he'd stuck a tip of his

andanna into the wound to help him breathe. "I
vish I could do something for you," the ranger said,
helping the twin lift his head and take a sip of the
tepid water.

The twin swallowed, but the water came back up,
mixed red with blood. He coughed and shoved the
canteen away from his lips. "I just wanted enough
to wet my mouth." He stared at the ranger and said,
"If you could leave us alone here for a few minutes,
I'd sure be obliged."

The ranger stood up and nodded. But turning to
go, he stopped and looked back at the twin. "You
can tell me now, Carly."

"Tell you what?" the twin said, sounding tired and
running out of breath.

Sam just looked at him.

"Oh, that," the twin said. "I expect you deserve to
know, after all the trouble you've gone through."

"I'd appreciate it," said Sam.

"I'm not Blake," said the twin. "It's like I told you
all along. I'm Abel, the good twin," he added in a
ironic tone.

"I see," said the ranger, still uncertain.

Catching the look on Sam's face, the twin said,
"Believe me, if I was Blake I wouldn't deny it this
late in the game." He coughed and sliced a breath
in pain.

"I saw some strange behavior that had me wondering," said Sam. "There were times I thought you
must be Blake wanting to live out Abel's more quiet
life. Other times I saw you as Abel wanting to be
Blake Carly the outlaw."

"I wanted to be him, after killing him," said the
twin. "I must have thought that becoming him
would take away some of the guilt I felt." He looked

at the woman's face. "And I have to admit, there was
something about being Blake Carly that appealed to
me—there always was."

"Every man envies the outlaw," said Sam, "until
they live the outlaw's life for a while. You got a taste
of it, Abel. How did it feel to you?"

The twin smiled, a trickle of blood running down
from his lips. "That's the first time you've called me
by my name, Ranger." He coughed, then said, reflecting, "How did it feel? Well, it felt like being
somebody, Ranger. If I had got the gold, and Millie
and me had made it to Mexico, I might have been
Blake Carly for the rest of my life." He stroked the
dead woman's forehead. "No matter what Blake
Carly was, he was never looked at as a *nobody*, like
I was."

"You've been a good man all your life, Abel," said
the ranger. "I'd think that at a time like this that
would mean something to you."

"It does," the twin replied. "But having tasted that
life for a while, I have some regrets." He brushed his
hand across Millie's hair. "See, I never had a woman
like Millie Tristan in my life, not without paying for
her, not for more than ten minutes at a time." He
smiled gently at Millie's face. "She was an outlaw
woman, no two ways about it. But my God, Ranger,
imagine having a woman like that loving you . . .
wanting to do everything for you . . . treating you
like you're something special."

The ranger saw a tear glisten in the corner of the
twin's eye and looked away, hearing the hooves of
two horses coming up the hillside toward them. "I
reckon that truly was something, Abel," he said.

"Oh, yes—it was," the twin whispered. "It's the
only thing I've ever seen worth dying for." He re-

laxed down onto the dirt face-to-face with Millie Tristan while Sam turned and walked out to meet Sheriff Masden, who was leading Clifford's horse behind him.

"Are they dead?" Masden asked quietly, gazing into the darkness beneath the cliff overhang.

Sam shook his head and sat down on a rock, his sombrero still dangling from his hand. "Millie's dead. It looks like Abel ain't far behind her."

Masden stepped down from his horse and walked over to Sam. "Abel, huh?" he said, keeping his voice low. "So that's who you've finally decided he is?"

Sam thought about it and said, "Indians believe there's times when a man takes on the spirit of the one he kills. Do you believe that?"

"I've heard it," Masden said. "I expect there are times when I can believe it."

"Me too," said Sam. "This is one of those times. I believe the Carly twin *is* who he said he is . . . and he said he's Abel."

"You appear to still have some doubt," said Masden.

"Maybe," said Sam. "But whoever he is, he's one man who had two bodies. I reckon that has to be a lot to deal with, all in one lifetime." He stood up and put on his sombrero and carried his canteen back to the Appaloosa. "We're going to bury them here, side by side," he said, looking out across the endless, desolate canyon. "This is where their lives together led them to." He stopped and considered it for a second, then said quietly, "I suppose they both could have done worse."

Ralph Cotton

JACKPOT RIDGE   21002-6

Jack Bell is a good gambler—so good that Early Philpot wants him
dead. But up in the mountains, Jack can outlast any lowlife posse Early
can rustle up. And he's willing to put them all to the test.

JUSTICE   19496-

A powerful land baron uses his political influence to persuade local
lawmen to release his son from a simple assault charge. The young man
however, is actually the leader of the notorious Half Moon Gang—a
mad pack of killers with nothing to lose!

BORDER DOGS   19815-8

The legendary Arizona Ranger Sam Burrack is forced to make the most
difficult decision of his life when his partner is captured by ex-
Confederate renegades—The Border Dogs. His only ally is a wanted
outlaw with blood on his hands...and a deadly debt to repay the Dogs.

BLOOD MONEY   20676-2

Bounty hunters have millions of reasons to catch J.T. Priest—but Marshal
Hart needs only one. And he's sworn to bring the killer down...mano-a-
mano.

DEVIL'S DUE   20394-1

The second book in Cotton's "Dead or Alive" series. *Los Pistoleros*
were the most vicious gang of outlaws around—but Hart and Roth
thought they had them under control...Until the jailbreak.

Available wherever books are sold or at
www.penguin.com

More adventure from

JASON MANNING
featuring Gordon Hawkes

Mountain Vengeance   0-451-20277-5

After years on the move, hiding from those who branded him an outlaw, Grodon Hawkes and his kin at last find a real home in the secluded Colorado Rockies. But it comes with a price—flesh and blood.

Mountain Honor   0-451-20480-8

When trouble arises between the U.S. Army and the Cheyenne Nation, Gordon Hawkes agrees to play peacemaker—until he realizes that his Indian friends are being led to the slaughter...

Mountain Renegade   0-451-20583-9

As the aggression in hostile Cheyenne country escalates, Gordon Hawkes must choose his side once and for all—and fight for the one thing he has left...his family.

Available wherever books are sold or at
www.penguin.com